"Look at me, Anne,"

Simon whispered hoarsely.

At first she resisted, but finally, Anne raised her eyes to meet his. She saw no mockery in their blue depths... only warmth and tenderness and desire. Unmistakable desire.

"I've missed you," he said gruffly. "I've missed everything about you, from the way you nibble on your lip when you're in deep thought, to the way you used to sing along with the radio when you were happy. And I've missed holding you in my arms, missed kissing you and making love to you. Why, time was, on a rainy afternoon like this, making love was the first thing we'd do."

Anne's voice went soft. "I've missed you, too, Simon. More than I can say."

"Have you?" Now his eyes were teasing. "In that case, let's see about making up for lost time."

Dear Reader,

Welcome to Silhouette **Special Edition** . . . welcome to romance. Each month, Silhouette **Special Edition** publishes six novels with you in mind—stories of love and life, tales that you can identify with—romance with that little "something special" added in.

This month, Silhouette **Special Edition** is full of special treats for you. We're hosting Nora Roberts's third book in her exciting THE CALHOUN WOMEN series—*For the Love of Lilah*. Each line at Silhouette Books has published one book of the series. Next month look for *Suzanna's Surrender* in the Silhouette Intimate Moments line!

Silhouette **Special Edition** readers are also looking forward to the second book in the compelling SONNY'S GIRLS series, *Don't Look Back* by Celeste Hamilton. These poignant tales are sure to be keepers! Don't miss the third installment next month, *Longer Than . . .* by Erica Spindler.

Rounding out August are warm, wonderful stories by veteran authors Sondra Stanford, Karen Keast and Victoria Pade, as well as Kim Cates's wonderful debut book, *The Wishing Tree*.

In each Silhouette **Special Edition**, we're dedicated to bringing you the romances that you dream about—the type of stories that delight as well as bring a tear to the eye. And that's what Silhouette **Special Edition** is all about—special books by special authors for special readers!

I hope you enjoy this book and all of the stories to come.

Sincerely,

Tara Gavin
Senior Editor

SONDRA STANFORD
Secret Marriage

Silhouette Special Edition

Published by Silhouette Books New York

America's Publisher of Contemporary Romance

With affection for my cousins,
Frances Roper Taylor and Harriet Roper Olmos

SILHOUETTE BOOKS
300 East 42nd St., New York, N.Y. 10017

Books by Sondra Stanford

Silhouette Romance

Golden Tide #6
Shadow of Love #25
Storm's End #35
No Trespassing #46
Long Winter's Night #58
And Then Came Dawn #88
Yesterday's Shadow #100
Whisper Wind #112
Tarnished Vows #131
Stolen Trust #530
Heart of Gold #586
Proud Beloved #646

Silhouette Special Edition

Silver Mist #7
Magnolia Moon #37
Sun Lover #55
Love's Gentle Chains #91
The Heart Knows Best #161
For All Time #187
A Corner of Heaven #210
Cupid's Task #248
Bird in Flight #292
Equal Shares #326
Through All Eternity #445
A Man with Secrets #560
Secret Marriage #686

SONDRA STANFORD

A fourth-generation native Texan, Sondra Stanford sets many of her novels in her beloved home state, although she enjoys traveling elsewhere in search of fresh locales for her books. Sondra believes that love *is* life, and she tries to reflect that philosophy in her work.

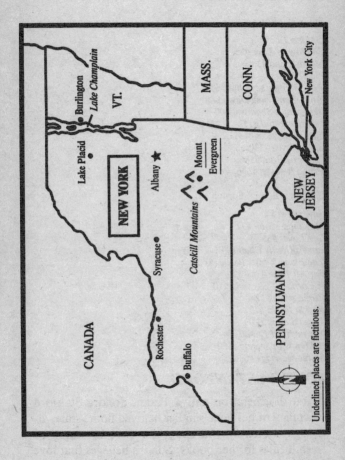

Underlined places are fictitious.

Prologue

The three children pushed their way through the under-brush as they headed toward the stream. The morning was fresh with the scent of clover and damp earth; dewdrops clung to grasses and leaves, sparkling beneath the sun-light. Although it was spring, the air was crisp and cool, sharp enough to require sweaters. It was a day made for being out-of-doors, a day made for the innocent joys of childhood.

The two boys, one blond-haired, one with hair as black as midnight, wore jeans and sneakers; baseball caps sat at jaunty angles on their heads. Each carried fishing gear. They were ten years old, carefree and happy, and whether they caught any trout today was purely incidental to the pleasure of their outing. They had been best friends from the day they'd started school together in the first grade, and nothing pleased them more than to spend a fine Saturday in each other's company.

The little girl was an uninvited tagalong. She was nine years old, a young fresh-faced promise of the beautiful woman she would one day become. A year before, Lorraine had suffered a great loss when both her parents had been killed in a train accident in Virginia. Afterward, she had been sent to live with her widowed grandmother in the Catskill Mountains. Her favorite new friends in the small town where she now lived were the two boys she was trailing.

"Wait for me!" she cried out in sudden distress as her simple dress and cardigan sweater snagged on a low-hanging tree branch. "Bucky! Cotton! Help me! I'm stuck!"

The blond-haired boy cast his friend a long-suffering look. "We never asked her to come along. Should we go back for her?"

The boy with raven-black hair shrugged his shoulders. "Guess so. She'll just yell 'n' cry if we don't. Who wants to listen to that while they're fishing?"

Cotton nodded. "Yeah. Besides, my mother told me to be nice to her on account of her not having any parents."

Bucky's dark eyes became serious. "That must make her feel real bad inside," he said somberly. "Okay, we'll be nice to her. Maybe I'll even let her fish awhile with my pole if she wants to."

The boys turned back to rescue the girl, and when she was freed, Lorrie favored her heroes with a beaming smile. An appealing dimple danced in her cheek. "Thanks! I was really stuck tight! When we grow up, I'm going to marry one of you," she declared.

Bucky flushed and grinned self-consciously while his friend doubled over with laughter. "Yeah?" Cotton challenged. "Which one of us do you intend to marry?"

Lorrie shrugged and tugged at a lock of her long dark brown hair. "I don't know yet. I like you both the same. I'll make up my mind before we're all grown-up."

"Maybe neither one of *us* will want to marry *you*," Bucky taunted as his courage returned.

"Oh, you will," Lorrie replied. "I know you will. And then we'll move to New York City and have lots and lots of fun."

"That's silly," Cotton retorted. "I'm never getting married."

"Me neither," Bucky agreed. "Anyway, Cotton and me got plans. We're gonna be business partners. We'll be too busy to marry any old girl, least of all you."

"Yeah," Cotton seconded his buddy's words. "And anyway, we're gonna stay right here in Mount Evergreen forever. We don't want to go live in the city, do we, Bucky?"

"Heck, no. My dad told me they don't even have one measly little fishin' stream in New York, so why would we wanna live there?"

"Yeah," Cotton said, settling the matter once and for all. "Neither of us ever wants to live there, so you'll just have to find somebody else to marry."

Bucky nodded vigorously. "Yeah! So there!"

Chapter One

Mount Evergreen's sole attorney, an elderly gentleman well past retirement age, rose to his feet and shuffled around his desk to greet the two visitors who had just been shown into his office by his secretary. His name was Benjamin Haydel, and he shook hands cordially with the sixtyish, silver-haired man and then bent toward the man's daughter and kissed her cheek.

"I hope you'll forgive the liberty, my dear." Mr. Haydel's eyes twinkled. "It isn't every day a beautiful lady visits my office. Besides, I can remember when you and Caroline Tarrant were skinny little imps who used to climb over my fence to swipe apples from my trees."

Anne Lancaster was surprised into laughter. The sound was husky and low, possessing a natural, seductive quality. She was twenty-seven years old and had blossomed into a rich, mature beauty that had only scarcely been hinted at in her earlier years. Thick and black as midnight, her hair tumbled in lush rippling waves around her neck and shoulders. Her eyes were a dark coffee-brown, and they flashed with intelligence and humor. In dramatic contrast to her hair and eyes, her skin was a pale creamy white; combined with her reed-slender body, it lent her a delicate appearance that was utterly deceiving. Now the dimple in her left cheek deepened and her eyes took on a sparkle of the old childhood mischievousness.

"Your liberty was my pleasure, Mr. Haydel," she replied as she gave the attorney's shoulder a friendly pat. "But how is it you knew about the apples? We were convinced nobody ever saw us."

Haydel chuckled. "You girls did no harm except to enjoy a few ill-gotten apples. We would have offered them to you, but Mrs. Haydel and I didn't want to spoil your fun." He waved a hand toward two chairs and invited the pair to be seated. "How have you been, Robert?" he asked as he rounded the desk and took his own chair. "It's been years since I last saw you, too. Are you still in the publishing field in the city?"

Robert Lancaster nodded. He had a handsome face with a strong forehead and heavy gray eyebrows above keen hazel eyes. His daughter bore little resemblance to him.

"Yes. I'm running the WJL Publishing Group of magazines."

"The W and the J partners having long since vanished from the scene?"

Robert nodded again. "Yes. Warren and Jackson were partners with my father, but Warren sold out to the others and when Mr. Jackson died a few years ago we bought his stock from his heirs. It's a wholly Lancaster-owned enterprise now, but there seemed no need to change the name."

"And you, Anne? Do you work in your father's company?"

Anne crossed long shapely legs beneath her dark gray tailored skirt. Shoulder-length hair swirled around the collar of her matching suit jacket as she leaned forward. The only relief to her somber attire was a wine-colored silk blouse.

"Only on occasion," she answered. "I'm a free-lance photographer. I work for a number of different magazines and do quite a bit of advertising photography, as well."

"She's an excellent photographer and much in demand," Robert bragged proudly. "I've been trying to bag her for WJL exclusively, but she refuses to be tied down, even though she'll inherit the business someday."

"You enjoy your independence, do you?" Mr. Haydel asked Anne.

Anne nodded. "I like knowing I can make it on my own."

"What about marriage?" Mr. Haydel probed. "Are there no eligible young men in all of New York City, or is it just that you won't let any of them get close enough to tie you down?"

"You just put your finger on it," Robert responded before Anne had a chance to speak. "I'm always introducing her to nice, eligible bachelors, but nothing ever comes of it. I'm beginning to fear Anne would rather be married to her career than to a man."

Anne grinned, calmly accepting her father's playful, half-serious jabs. "Well, a career doesn't litter my apartment with dirty socks or demand dinner on time," she said lightly.

The two older men chuckled at her droll outlook on what some people called marital bliss. They spent a few minutes longer exchanging pleasantries. Then Mr. Haydel said, "Before we get down to business, let me express my personal regrets concerning the death of your aunt. My wife and I were always quite fond of Miss Rebecca."

"Thanks," Robert replied huskily. "She was a fine lady."

"Indeed. How old was she, anyway?"

"Ninety-two last December."

The attorney shook his head with awe. "And she was active right up to the end. Only last month I saw her at our community fund-raiser for a new volunteer fire department building. Well," he added briskly as he perched his reading glasses upon his nose and picked up some legal-sized papers, "you must know I asked you here for the reading of her will."

Both Robert and Anne nodded and Mr. Haydel spoke again. "In a moment we'll get down to all the particulars, but in a nutshell, here it is—Anne gets the house, its contents, the car, Miss Lancaster's jewelry and a sizable sum of cash. Robert, you will receive the investment properties and the stocks and bonds. There are some charity disbursements we'll go over in a moment, but basically, the two of you inherit practically everything."

Anne's eyes widened in astonishment. "I don't understand. Why didn't Aunt Rebecca just leave everything to Dad? After all, he's her next of kin."

Mr. Haydel shook his head. "I have no idea, Anne. I suppose she just wanted to split the estate up between you as equally as she could."

"But..." Anne turned her gaze on her father. "Dad, what on earth will I do with that old house?"

Robert Lancaster replied promptly. "Put it up for sale, what else?"

"I suppose you're right," Anne mused. Her lips pursed as she considered the notion.

Anne tuned out most of the remaining discussion of the will. She supposed she should be grateful to her great-aunt for having been so generous with her in her will. She *was* grateful. Anne had adored her aunt, and she was pleased

Aunt Rebecca had cared enough about her great-niece to provide for her future. The problem was that Lancaster House was in Mount Evergreen.

Simon's town.

Anne swallowed hard and did her best to pay attention to what her father and the attorney were saying.

When they departed Mr. Haydel's office an hour later, Anne carried a box of jewelry that had belonged to Rebecca Lancaster, and Robert carried a large envelope containing stock and bond certificates. Following Miss Lancaster's written instructions, Mr. Haydel had taken the items from a safety deposit box at the bank.

Anne was lost in thought as her father drove slowly through the small hamlet at the foothills of the Catskill Mountains toward the house where their spinster aunt had lived out most of her ninety-two years. Memorial services had been conducted the previous day and afterward the house had been filled with guests coming by to pay their respects. So many people had come that it had seemed to Anne that "Miss Rebecca" had been known and loved by the entire population of five counties.

But the one man Anne had both dreaded and hoped would come to the house had not done so. If Simon had been at the memorial services, she had not seen him. And she would not have missed seeing him had he visited the house, despite all the people who had been there.

Anne gazed forlornly out the car window as her father drove through the small business section of Main Street. When the car passed the *Sentinel's* office, Mount Evergreen's only weekly newspaper, a lump swelled in her throat. Simon might be there now. The thought of being so near him made her hands tremble.

The car turned off Main Street and traveled along quiet residential streets studded with huge lawns and maple and spruce trees. Anne forced her mind away from its preoccupation with the man of her past. Robert turned the car into the driveway at Lancaster House, parking near the front porch.

Built at the turn of the century, Lancaster House was a large white wooden structure. Steep gables overhung the second-story windows, which were framed by black shutters. The house had been added onto haphazardly and often, so that the total effect was ungainly and without any distinguishable style, like an awkward, long-limbed child who had outgrown the clothes he was wearing.

The front lawn was lovely, however, with large shade trees and neat shrubs. Aunt Rebecca's favorite lilac bush spilled forth at one side of the house and beyond it was the garage. The backyard could not be glimpsed from the front, but it stretched for a full city block. Hidden amidst trees and shrubs at the far back of the yard was Aunt Rebecca's playhouse, a small replica of the original house before all the additions had been made. Like her great-aunt, Anne had adored the playhouse when she'd been a little girl; she and her friends had enjoyed many happy hours there.

Anne and Robert got out of the car. The early September air was fresh and pleasant. It was that wonderful time of year that hovered just between the heat of summer and the chill of autumn. The leaves on the trees were still green, but Anne knew it wouldn't be long before the colors would begin to turn to gloriously rich flaming crimsons, thrilling golds and soft browns.

When they entered the house, the spacious entrance hall greeted them with heavy silence. It was as though the light and soul of the house itself had been extinguished with Aunt Rebecca's passing.

The parlor was large, old-fashioned and eclectic. A blue brocade sofa faced the fireplace that dominated one wall.

On the mantel was a clock, two silver candlestick holders and a lovely rose-colored Favrile Glass vase made by Tiffany. A Sheraton chair stood next to the door, and a Victorian whatnot shelf, crammed with porcelain and crystal figurines, filled a corner of the room. On the walls were framed watercolor renderings of some of Aunt Rebecca's favorite flowers—tulips, roses, crocuses—all of which she had painted herself.

"I could go for some coffee before heading back to the city," Robert said as they entered the parlor. He dropped his packet of papers onto the low table in front of the sofa and shed his jacket.

"I'll put some on," Anne said, too weary to make her usual futile protests about the amount of caffeine her father consumed daily. While the coffee brewed, she made herself a cup of herbal tea.

When the drinks were ready, she carried the tray into the parlor and sat down beside her father on the sofa. Robert was shuffling through the certificates he'd brought from the attorney's office, so Anne picked up the box of jewelry she'd left on the coffee table and opened it.

The jewels were obviously valuable, but of a style that had been popular during the twenties and thirties. One by one Anne took out the pieces, brooches and necklaces and earrings, studied each for a moment, and then returned them to the box.

"What are you going to do with all that stuff?" Robert asked idly as he slid the certificates back into the manila envelope. "They're hopelessly outdated."

Anne shrugged. "I might have some of the stones remounted in new settings. Say, look at this, Dad. It's a plain gold wedding band. Whose could it be?"

"I can't imagine," Robert answered, puzzled.

"Maybe it was Great-grandmother Lancaster's? Aunt Rebecca's mother?"

Robert shook his head. "Can't be. Aunt Rebecca gave that away as a keepsake to a cousin who was particularly close to Grandmother."

Anne held the ring at an angle so that the light fell on the inside of the band. She hoped to find some initials that might indicate the owner of the ring, but there was nothing. She sighed with disappointment and murmured, "How odd."

Her father had already lost interest in the mystery of the ring. He lifted his coffee cup and said, "I guess I'd better be thinking about getting on the road. Are you going to ride back to the city with me today?"

"I'd like to," Anne replied, grimacing. "But I guess I'd better stay a few more days and figure out what to do with all Aunt Rebecca's possessions. I don't have any assignments scheduled until next Wednesday, so that gives me a full week to make some headway here. I suppose I'd better make the best of what free time I have."

Robert nodded. "It's going to take some doing, sorting through this old place."

"I'll say. Not only are there Aunt Rebecca's things, but your grandparents' belongings as well."

"Aunt Rebecca never threw out anything, so you'll probably even find some items of my father's and maybe some of my childhood possessions, as well."

"If I run across anything of yours that's really interesting, I'll let you know. Maybe I'll get lucky and find your old school report cards."

Robert grinned. "I told you, sweetheart. I was a model A-plus student at all times."

"Hmm. That's funny, Dad, because that's not what Aunt Rebecca told me."

"And whose word are you going to accept...that of your trusty old father, or Aunt Rebecca's wild tales?"

They both laughed. No one had ever been more ruthlessly honest than Aunt Rebecca. It had been a longstanding joke among all who knew her that one should never ask Rebecca Lancaster's opinion or testimony concerning any subject whatsoever unless one wanted the complete, unvarnished truth.

When her father went upstairs to get his bags, Anne kicked off her high heels and leaned back against the sofa cushions. This was the first really quiet moment she'd had since the day the news of Aunt Rebecca's death had come.

Smoky, the aging charcoal-gray tabby, came to rub against Anne's leg. He mewed plaintively. His whole world had been thoroughly disrupted in the past few days. He was so distraught he was off his food and simply wandered through the house like a lost soul.

Anne lifted him up to her lap and began stroking his fur. She supposed when she returned to the city, she would have to uproot Smoky and take him along. She had a deep affection for the cat. It was she who had found the abandoned kitten cowering fearfully in some bushes years ago. Anne had carried him home to Aunt Rebecca, and Smoky had reigned over Lancaster House ever since.

Robert came down the stairs again, carrying his bags. "Sure you won't change your mind and come back with me?" he asked.

"I'd love to," Anne replied, sighing as she moved Smoky to the sofa and stood up. "But it would only be delaying the inevitable. Now that the house is mine, I've got to do something about it."

Her father nodded. "Your best bet is to call Darryl Miller and list it with his agency."

"What about the furnishings? Is there anything here that you want, Dad? I'll probably sell or give away most of the stuff."

Robert shook his head, though his eyes were wistful as he took a long gaze around the room. "No," he said slowly. "There's nothing here I really want. I have my memories and that's enough."

After her father drove away, Anne went upstairs to the bedroom that since childhood had been hers to use whenever she visited. She changed out of her suit into jeans, a lightweight sweater and a pair of sneakers.

The house seemed more oppressively silent than ever now that her father was gone, and Anne suddenly could not bear it. She ran down the stairs with Smoky following at her heels.

Anne strode across the back lawn toward the clump of shrubbery that almost completely concealed the playhouse. She took a shortcut between the bushes, and pushed her way through. A moment later she was in the clearing in front of the whitewashed one-room building with its steep roof and black window shutters.

She found the key on its hook on the back of the nearest shutter, right where it had always hung. Anne unlocked the door and stepped inside. It had been five years since she had set foot inside the playhouse, but instantly she was transported back in time. So many of her special and important memories were here. Memories of Caroline Tarrant and other girls when they were young, giggling as they spilled out their hopes and dreams and secrets to each other on drowsy summer afternoons; memories of teenage parties here, hosted by Aunt Rebecca.

Memories of Simon.

It was here in the playhouse that Simon had first told her that he loved her. It was here, too, where they had had their last bitter quarrel.

But it was better not to think about Simon.

Anne stood near the door, looking at her surroundings. There was a gold tweed sofa beneath two windows. Next to it were lamp tables. Against the adjacent wall were built-in bookcases and cupboards. The shelves were crammed to overflowing with books; Aunt Rebecca had been a great reader. On the wall to Anne's left was a kitchenette counter with a sink, a refrigerator and a hot plate. Beneath the counter were more cupboards that in the past had contained the makings for coffee and tea and perhaps a box or two of cookies or crackers.

Today the room had a musty odor, as though it had not been used or aired out in quite some time. Her great-aunt had visited the playhouse frequently throughout her life, but, Anne supposed sadly, in the past few years, Aunt Rebecca had grown increasingly old and frail and had ceased to visit this special place. As well as enjoying it during her own girlhood, and allowing Anne and her friends to use it when Anne was growing up, Aunt Rebecca had continued using the playhouse herself as long as Anne had been coming here. It had always been her aunt's hideaway from the rest of the world and the concerns of daily living. She would come here almost every day and spend an hour or two reading, writing letters or working on one of her numerous watercolor paintings. But now dust lay everywhere and the odor of neglect was suffocating.

Anne sneezed. The involuntary act was the catalyst she needed to set to work. She threw open the windows, found a broom and a cloth to dust with, and began cleaning the playhouse.

The vigorous physical activity was exactly what she needed. There'd been far too much solemn sitting around the past few days. An hour later the room had taken on a clean sheen and the fresh air flowing through the windows had driven out the stale smell.

Ready for a break, Anne searched the cupboards, but there was nothing on the shelves except some very old, strong-smelling coffee. She resolved to bring a supply of herbal tea, instant hot chocolate, and coffee the next time she came.

In the meantime she settled for a glass of tepid water and then turned her attention toward the bookcases. Clearly it would take some time to sort through all the books.

Anne had never known what the cupboards below the bookcases contained. They had always been firmly locked and when questioned, Aunt Rebecca had said simply that the cupboards contained her "private things." Now Anne took the ring of keys and tried several in the lock before she found the one that fit. Feeling a little guilty, she opened the cupboards.

She found some dried-up tubes of watercolor paint, brushes, a supply of watercolor paper and a long row of ledgers, some so old and tattered that the leather bindings were cracked and brown. Curious, Anne pulled out the first one on the left and opened it.

It was not a ledger, after all, but a diary or a journal. The one she held must have been Aunt Rebecca's very first diary, written when she was about twelve years old. The handwriting and spelling were definitely those of a child.

Delight overcame the slightly sinful feeling of being a Peeping Tom. Anne carried the book with her to the sofa and began to flip through it. There were accounts of happenings at school, of long walks in the woods with her nature-loving father, of her painful attempts to learn embroidery, which it seemed Rebecca's mother despaired of her ever mastering.

Anne turned a few more pages and read an account of a picnic which included Rebecca's family and that of one of her friends. Rebecca wrote shyly about a boy name Douglas.

He's two years older than me, and very nice-looking. His smile makes my heart beat so fast! He is kind to me, but I wonder if he would even notice me at all if our fathers weren't partners and our mothers such good friends. Oh, how I want him to like me just for myself!

Anne smiled with compassionate amusement at the youthful Rebecca's crush on the boy named Douglas. She closed the journal and picked out two more from the cupboard to carry back to the house. She hoped that if Aunt Rebecca could see her, she would understand that Anne wasn't prying; she only wanted a deeper understanding of the aunt she had always adored.

Walking slowly back toward the house, Anne couldn't help but wonder why Aunt Rebecca had remained unmarried all her long life. As the passage Anne had just read proved, the young Rebecca had been as interested in handsome young boys as any other girl on the edge of womanhood.

Simon Tarrant walked out of the *Sentinel's* office and stood at the curb beside his parked car for a long moment. His blond hair riffled in the slight breeze as he inhaled the cool air. He squinted his blue eyes against the bright late-afternoon sunlight and idly watched a few cars pass along the street. What he was doing was killing time, stalling, and well he knew it. But all the same he continued to stand there like a lifeless mannequin.

It had been a long busy day and he was tired. He'd spent most of the day unsnarling an inventory mess at the Tarrant Inn Resort Hotel twenty-five miles away. When he'd returned to the newspaper office in Mount Evergreen, he'd become submerged beneath a hundred matters concerned with getting the paper out tomorrow. All he really wanted to do now was go to his apartment, put his feet up on the coffee table, order a pizza, and watch a little mindless television before going to bed. He was tired of thinking, tired of moving, and the last thing on earth he wanted at this moment was a confrontation with Anne.

Anne!

Just the thought of her tensed the muscles in his back and neck. Even his jaw clenched. Common decency demanded that he visit her to offer his condolences concerning her great-aunt's death, but he'd never dreaded anything more in his life. Their parting had been full of anguish and pain, like the severing of a nerve. There was no way of knowing what her attitude toward him would be after all this time. Would she be glad that he had come, or would she lash out at him with long-held rancor and resentment? All he knew for sure was that the meeting was bound to be difficult, even if it were a cordial one.

Simon had deliberately gone nowhere near Anne the past few days, although he had been acutely aware that she was in town. Skipping the funeral services for Miss Rebecca had made him feel somewhat guilty because she'd been a sweet old lady and an important person in the community. A write-up about her life would appear in tomorrow's paper on the front page, and Simon himself had written it. But he'd sent a young reporter to cover the services. Such an occasion, with so many other people around, was no time to thrust his presence upon Anne. It would have been the first time they'd seen each other in five years, and it would have been an utterly impossible situation for them both.

But now the time of reckoning was at hand, like it or not. Of course, it was entirely possible that she'd returned to New York today. All the same, Simon knew he had to try to see Anne this very evening. He felt he simply had no choice in the matter.

A part of him ached desperately to see her, but another part of him resisted vehemently. What could he say after all this time? What would she say? And how would both of them feel?

Forcing himself to move, Simon stepped off the curb and got into his white sports car. His actions were automatic as he started the motor and pulled the car into the street. All his thoughts were upon Anne.

He had always known her. Anne's mother died when she was only a toddler, and shortly thereafter Anne and her father had moved to New York City. But they had often returned to visit Robert Lancaster's aunt, Miss Rebecca Lancaster. Simon could remember Anne being a permanent fixture in Mount Evergreen during the summers from the time she was about five or six. She'd been here for most holidays, as well.

Simon's younger sister, Caroline, and Anne were about ten years old when they became good friends, and the girls were practically inseparable whenever Anne was in town. Many times Caroline spent the night with Anne at Lancaster House, or Anne spent the night at Caroline's. Simon had teased and pestered the girls whenever he could, but most of the time he'd paid them no attention whatsoever.

They were teenagers when he'd suddenly seen Anne through different eyes, and the nature of their casual relationship changed.

Just as the sun began to vanish behind the mountains to the west of town, Simon turned his car into the driveway at Lancaster House. His limbs felt unaccountably stiff as he got out of the car and walked toward the house, and the inside of his mouth was dry.

It was entirely possible that Anne might slam the door in his face.

But now that he had committed himself to being here, Simon did not waste any time. He took the porch steps two at a time. All the same, after pressing the doorbell, he found himself holding his breath while he waited for a response to the ringing he heard echoing within the house.

It was a full two minutes before the door was opened. By then, Simon had all but concluded that no one was here, and that both Anne and her father must have already returned to the city.

But suddenly there stood Anne. Her jet-black hair tumbled riotously around her shoulders. Her face, always of a pale creamy tone, turned completely white at the sight of him. Her deep brown eyes, fringed thickly with black lashes, flickered and widened with surprise.

"Simon!" she gasped softly.

Simon's gaze swept over her. She was wearing faded jeans that hugged her long slender legs and narrow hips. A lightweight blue sweater outlined her alluring breasts. Simon groaned inwardly. He'd never forgotten how exquisitely Anne was built, but had she always been quite so abundantly feminine? She stole his breath away!

"Hello, Anne," he said at last.

Anne shivered, yet strangely, she felt hot and tingly all over. Simon had matured wonderfully during the past five years. His squarish face was stronger, more compelling now, and his body had filled out to match. He was still trim and athletic-looking, but somehow he was also more solid and sturdy. His blond hair was slightly mussed, as though the wind had teased it, and his eyes were still as blue as a cold mountain stream. Inexorably her gaze was drawn to his lips...those fascinating, well-defined, chiseled lips that could soften so unbelievably in a tender moment. But to dwell on his lips, and inevitably to recall the feel of his kisses, was dangerous. She forced her attention away from his face and her gaze swiftly took in the rest of him. He was dressed in dark slacks and a pin-striped shirt with the collar open. Over the shirt, he wore a casual tan jacket that looked magnificent across his broad shoulders and chest.

A lump grew in Anne's throat while they gazed at each other. It was as though neither of them could get enough. Anne's heart hammered excitedly, and she couldn't have spoken just then if her life had depended on it.

Simon finally asked, "Mind if I come in?"

Bemused, Anne stepped aside. Simon came inside the hallway and shut the door behind him, and Anne said in a shaky voice, "Come into the living room...or rather, Aunt Rebecca's parlor. Can I get you something to drink?" She asked the last over her shoulder as she turned to lead the way.

"Thanks, no. I won't stay long. Have I interrupted you?" he asked when he saw the papers that littered the marble coffee table.

Anne shrugged. "I was looking through some of Aunt Rebecca's important papers." She sighed. "I hardly know where to start. Have a seat, Simon."

Cautiously, like wary adversaries, they both avoided the sofa and took chairs on opposite sides of the cluttered table. Their eyes met across the intervening space and clung for a long moment. It was as though time and distance had never separated them ... and yet, it also seemed as though they had spent a lifetime, a terrible endless lifetime, apart from each other.

Simon drank in the vision of Anne. How many nights had he dreamed of her, of seeing that beautiful canopy of dark hair swirling around her head, of kitten-soft skin and wide, generous rosy lips? How many times had he remembered the exact way she tucked her legs up beneath her when she was relaxing? Not that she was relaxed now. This evening Anne sat straight upright in her chair, feet firmly planted on the floor, while her hands fidgeted nervously in her lap. She was obviously as uneasy about this encounter as he was. He saw her pink tongue dart out nervously to moisten her lips.

Anne was glad she was sitting so far away from Simon. Her heart was still drumming madly beneath her breast. It was so wonderful, yet so agonizing to see him. Her gaze kept returning again and again to his lips as though she was mesmerized by the sight of them. It had been so long since those lips had touched hers, so long since those strong masculine hands had stroked her body.

It had been forever since the last time Simon had made love to her.

Abruptly she jerked her thoughts away from where they were leading. Somebody had to break the awkward silence that had fallen between them. Once more Anne licked her lips, and clasping her hands firmly together as though that would strengthen her, she said, "This is . . . a surprise."

"I came to offer my condolences," Simon answered softly. "I know how much you loved Miss Rebecca." Anne nodded but didn't speak, so after a moment, Simon continued. "I just wanted you to know how I felt. I didn't go to the memorial services or come to the house because I thought it might make things harder for you."

"Yes," Anne acknowledged. "It probably would have."

They were both silent for a while, and then Simon asked gently, "How have you been, Anne? You look wonderful."

She shrugged. "I'm doing all right. And you?"

"I'm fine, too."

"Caroline?"

Simon relaxed slightly. Caroline was a safe subject. "She lives in England now. She and Neal have two sons."

Anne nodded. "Bryan and Byron," she said with a soft smile. "I know. Caroline and I keep in touch from time to time. She wrote me that your mother died two years ago. I was sorry about that."

"Thanks," Simon said huskily. "It was a shock losing her. After his stroke, it was Dad we were so concerned about."

"Yes," Anne murmured.

Yes. Of course she knew that, Simon thought, grimly annoyed with himself. His father's precarious state of health had been the catalyst that had driven them apart.

Anne inhaled deeply, then asked politely, "And how is your father?"

"He's doing very well, considering," Simon answered. "He'll never be the same as he was before his stroke. He gets around and is fairly independent, although we have a housekeeper to take care of him and run his errands. How is your father? I thought he might also be here this evening."

"Dad's fine. He left late this afternoon to return home. I have a few days before my next assignment, so I stayed behind to sort through things."

"I suppose you'll put the house up for sale?" Simon asked.

"Most likely. But it's going to take me a while to clean the place out and get it into shape."

Another silence fell, but it didn't last long. "I've seen some of your photographic work in magazines, Anne. You're very, very talented. I'm glad you've made such a success of your career."

"Thanks. I suppose you're still fully occupied running the hotel and the newspaper?"

"That's right."

"Nothing's changed," Anne said, sighing softly.

Simon rose to his feet. "I'd better go. I only wanted to stop by and pay my respects. I know you must be tired."

"Yes," Anne agreed as she, too, rose to her feet. "I guess I am, at that. The last few days have been exhausting."

"It was good to see you again," Simon said in a low voice as he came to her and clasped her hand.

"You, too," Anne replied. She hoped her trembling wasn't detectable as he held her hand in his.

"If you're going to be here for a few days, I'll stop by again, if it's all right with you," Simon told her. "We need to talk . . . to try to resolve our 'situation.'"

Anne felt as though Simon had just slapped her in the face, although the expression in his eyes was gentle and kind. Stiffly she answered, "You're right. It should have been settled long ago."

When Simon was gone, Anne slumped against the front door as tears sprang to her eyes.

It had been the summer she'd been twelve and Simon had been fourteen that Anne had first taken real notice of him. He'd been around before that, of course, but she'd never really paid any attention to him, nor he to her. To Anne, he had simply been Caroline's older brother. But that summer had been different. Simon had teased her a lot, had seemed to enjoy hanging around her and Caroline. There had been swimming and picnics and horseback riding and movies, and somehow Simon was always there, and Anne had thoroughly enjoyed his easygoing friendliness.

She could have had no way of knowing at the time, of course, that someday she would make the terrible mistake of falling in love with Simon and marrying him.

Chapter Two

Anne spent an agonizingly long and restless night in her upstairs bedroom. She dozed only intermittently, and during wakeful periods listened to every creak or groan the old house made. She heard the rising wind sough through the trees outside her window and was annoyed by the sound of a loose, flapping shutter on one of the dining-room windows downstairs.

Mostly she thought about Simon. Seeing him brought everything back again—good times and bad, ecstasy and anger, with either emotional extreme being equally intense. Oh, how she had loved him and hated him!

She wished he had not come to see her. It had been hard enough being in Mount Evergreen, just knowing he was here, knowing that she might accidentally bump into him or simply see him from a distance. Yet it wasn't realistic to expect that he not approach her while she was in town. As he had pointed out, they had business to discuss—a problem that must be ironed out. Like putting a last dot to the *i* of their once earthshaking desire for each other, or crossing the *t* of their now long-dead relationship, which had at one time brimmed over with energy and vibrant joy, this discussion would place a final period at the end of their timeworn, empty shell of a marriage.

But Anne didn't want to think about that. Not tonight. Not yet. She was melancholy enough as it was, what with Aunt Rebecca's death. Seeing Simon again and remembering the way things used to be during happier days only intensified her sadness.

By daybreak, she gave up the unsuccessful attempt to sleep. It had begun to rain softly and to Anne it seemed the sky itself was weeping in sympathy for the tears permanently lodged in her heart. For years Anne had assured herself that she was finally, truly over Simon. She had convinced herself that if or when they should meet again she would feel nothing for him, that all feelings he had ever stirred within her had vanished as completely as steam evaporates in air.

What a laugh! With one glance at Simon as she'd opened the door and found him standing there last night, all the steadfast assurances she'd ever made to herself turned out to be just so many empty words. She'd been shaken to the core. She'd gone prickly hot, then icy cold, and had become completely flustered. Her first instinct had been to hurtle fresh accusations at him, to vent her pent-up hurt and anger and then slam the door in his face.

Then her heart had lurched into reverse and she'd ached to throw herself into his arms, to feel his large hands roaming her back and his breath warm against her cheek. And yes—might as well face it—she'd wanted badly to taste those firm yet endearingly tender lips again and to feel the heat emanating from his powerful thighs as they pressed against hers.

That thought sent a fire of shame and self-condemnation into her face. How could she still have such forbidden desires for Simon after all these years? *Where's your pride, girl?* she berated herself scathingly. *The man walked out on you!*

Nestled beneath the warm covers of a bed was definitely not the place to be thinking about Simon. With a burst of determined energy, Anne tossed back the covers and swung her bare legs over the side of the bed. Cringing at the shock she knew would come, she lowered her bare feet to the ice-cold plank floor.

Anne wasted no time pulling on jeans, sneakers and a much-washed gray sweatshirt with the peeling emblem I ♥ New York. Next, she gave her hair a swift, vigorous brushing and then ran downstairs to the kitchen to put on the kettle.

While she waited for the water for her coffee to boil, she went to the refrigerator. When she opened it, her heart sank. The light was out and there were beads of perspiration on the jars and containers. She touched the milk carton and it was clammy and cool, but by no means as cold as it should be.

She sighed. Big trouble, and it wasn't even seven a.m. yet!

The kettle whistled. Anne closed the refrigerator and went to pour scalding water into her mug over a teaspoon of instant coffee. She carried it to the table and, grabbing the telephone directory from the end of the counter, began searching the Yellow Pages for appliance repair shops even though it was still far too early to call anyone.

When the repairman arrived at mid-morning, Anne was sweeping the front porch clear of the damp leaves that had blown onto it during the rain and wind last night. The man who got out of the van and walked toward her was a little plumper than she remembered, but otherwise Charlie Davis hadn't changed much at all since the last time Anne had seen him. He was dressed in a blue jumpsuit with a name label sewn across the breast pocket. He had the same shambling walk and jolly grin Anne recalled from their youth.

Recognizing her, too, Charlie grinned and spread open his arms. Anne laughed, propped her broom against the porch railing and ran down the steps to meet him. Charlie gave her a hearty hug that almost squeezed the breath out of her. "Hiya, Annie. How're you doin'?"

"Fine. Just fine. It's great to see you, Charlie, though I have to confess I didn't know when I called that you were Davis Appliance and Electrical Repair Service."

"Yup," Charlie replied with a touch of pride. "It was my uncle's business, you know. I went to work for him after I got out of high school. When he decided to retire a couple of years ago, I bought him out." As they turned and walked toward the house, he added, "I was sorry to hear about Miss Rebecca's death. She was a wonderful influence on Mount Evergreen. There are a lot of things this town would probably still be without, like the public library and the community hall, if it hadn't been for her prodding the rest of us into action."

"Thanks," Anne said huskily, grateful for the tribute to her aunt. Then she changed the subject. "I hope you can get the refrigerator to work again without it costing too much. Until I decide what to do about the house, I want to avoid spending a lot on maintenance and repairs."

"That makes sense," Charlie answered. "But if it's the condenser, my advice is to go ahead and buy a new one. It wouldn't be worth replacing it on a thirty-five-year-old refrigerator."

"How do you know it's that old?" Anne asked, curious.

"Miss Rebecca told me when I came to repair the stove a few months ago. She was proud of the fact that all her appliances could be dated in two-digit numbers."

Anne laughed. "That sounds like her, all right...going on about how they used to make things to last."

"And how they don't anymore." Charlie grinned and nodded. "My mother says the same thing, so I guess it's true. Still, nothing lasts forever."

Fortunately for Anne's bank balance, it was not the condenser, and Charlie was able to repair the refrigerator with a minimum of fuss or expense.

While Anne sat at the kitchen table writing him a check, he asked, "Remember when our old gang used to have picnics on summer evenings?"

"How could I forget?" Anne retorted. "You guys were always trying to sweet-talk us girls into going skinny-dipping in the stream!"

Charlie chuckled heartily. "We never did succeed, though. More's the pity."

Anne laughed as she tore the check from the checkbook, stood up and handed it to Charlie. "How's Jody, by the way?" Caroline had written her several years ago that Charlie had married his high school sweetheart.

"She's fine. We've got two children now—a two-and-a-half-year-old son and a four-month-old baby girl."

"How nice! I suppose they keep your life from getting boring."

"Whew! Do they ever! But what about you?" Charlie asked. He took Anne's left hand into his and squinted at the bare ring finger. "You don't have a husband stashed somewhere back in the city?"

Anne's throat tightened and she pulled her hand away. "No," she replied, honest about the city part, at least. "I don't have a husband stashed back in the city."

"When we were in high school, we all thought for sure you and Simon would end up marrying each other." He shrugged. "Just shows you can't always tell, can you?"

"No," Anne answered hollowly. "I guess you can't."

Charlie picked up his toolbox and headed toward the front hall. "I know Jody would love to see you, Anne. How long are you staying in town?"

Anne shrugged. "I'm not really sure. At least through this week. And I'd love to see Jody, too...and your family."

"Jody'll call you. We'll have you to dinner one evening."

Anne smiled. "That would be very nice, Charlie."

"And speaking of Simon," Charlie added casually, as though they were still speaking of Simon, "we'll invite him, too. He's not married, either, and I bet he'd be thrilled to see you again. We can rehash old times and catch up on the past few years."

Anne's mouth went dry. "No, Charlie," she managed to get out in a firm, no-kidding voice. "I can't accept your invitation if you ask Simon, too."

"Why not? I tell you he'd love to—"

Anne shook her head again. "No," she said implacably. "Simon and I were over years ago. It's best to leave it that way."

"I never did know what happened to split up you two," Charlie said. "By then you were both away at college and I was here working at my uncle's shop. But you always seemed like the perfect couple, you know? What broke you up in the end?"

Anne shrugged dismissively. "It's ancient history, Charlie, and I'd rather not dredge it up again. But take my word for it, everyone would be uncomfortable if Simon and I were forced to break bread at the same dinner table."

"Okay," Charlie agreed pleasantly. "No Simon to dinner. Jody'll get back to you with the particulars."

After Charlie left, Anne felt more melancholy than ever. Charlie had opened a door she'd tried for years to keep closed, and now memory after memory of those idyllic summers she had spent in Mount Evergreen came rushing over her.

Every spring while she was in high school, Anne could scarcely wait until school was out for the term so that she could leave the stifling city heat for the cool green hills of the countryside; there she could roam in freedom and enjoy being with her friends. And by the time she was sixteen, she had one particular reason for being eager to return to Mount Evergreen every chance she got.

Simon.

Besides Charlie and Jody, their tight-knit circle of friends included Simon's younger sister, Caroline, who was Anne's best friend, Caroline's boyfriend, Jeff, and two other couples.

There wasn't a whole lot of entertainment to be found in Mount Evergreen. Since there wasn't even a movie theater in town, the young people had to invent their own fun. They often hung out at the hamburger emporium on Main Street, or at the teen recreation hall where they could play games from Ping-Pong to tennis or softball. Sometimes they simply lounged around someone's back lawn drinking soft drinks and munching chips. Some evenings they packed picnic hampers and spent their time beside the cool, inviting stream at the edge of town.

The stream wasn't deep enough for swimming, but that didn't prevent them from splashing around in the water and having a good time. Before sundown they'd set up a volleyball game in a nearby clearing and when dusk came, someone would build a camp fire within a circle of rocks that served as a pit. Then they would roast hot dogs and marshmallows and in the coolness of the evening, laugh and tease and simply enjoy each other's company.

Those innocent, pleasant summers during her teenage years were among the happiest of Anne's life. Now she marveled that she had ever been so carefree.

Anne spent the remainder of the morning going through her aunt's papers. It was deadly dull work. Except for bills and receipts of bills paid, some of which, incredibly, dated back to 1948, there were old letters, insurance policies and titles to various parcels of land. Anne was astonished to find even titles to cars that were no longer in existence. Clearly Aunt Rebecca had never thrown away any piece of paper she deemed important, not even years after it had become irrelevant. Once important, always important must have been her motto.

The wastepaper basket was soon overflowing.

At noon Anne took a break and made herself a sandwich and poured a glass of milk. While she ate, she dipped into another of Aunt Rebecca's journals she had brought up to the house from the playhouse the night before.

The pages were yellowed and brittle, and concerned about tearing the pages, Anne turned each one very carefully. This journal's script was done by a steadier, yet still adolescent hand than had written the first one. As she began reading, Anne soon learned that when these particular entries had been penned, the young lady who wrote them had been fourteen years old.

Anne merely read snatches here and there of the artless accounts of school and home life. Sometimes the tone was happy and bubbly, sometimes darkly despairing. Clearly Rebecca had been a girl of widely fluctuating emotions, as are most teenage girls. Sometimes she seemed to adore her papa, and at other times he seemed a monster bent on wrecking her life.

Anne smiled. The times and the girl were different, but Anne might have been reading about herself at fourteen and the up-and-down relationship she'd had with her father at that age.

She turned another page and found more interesting reading material. Here was a detailed account of the momentous occasion of Rebecca's sixteenth birthday. Her parents had thrown her a lavish dinner dance at the Tarrant Inn Resort Hotel.

Today Simon ran the luxury hotel that his great-grandfather, Jasper Tarrant, had built around the turn of the century. It was a large, rambling structure, nestled in the woods in the foothills of the Catskills, and city dwellers still came there regularly, particularly on weekends and holidays. Guests enjoyed the many diversions the grounds offered, from fishing and boating on a private lake to swimming, golfing, hiking and horseback riding. In the evenings there was dancing and headline entertainers. And the resort was as popular in the winter as it was in summer because it offered some wonderful slopes for skiers.

Anne could easily imagine the fair-haired Rebecca in her ecru lace dress, which according to the journal, *cost Papa a shocking sum*. She pictured a radiant young Rebecca sweeping around the ballroom dance floor to soft, romantic music in the arms of elegantly attired young men. What a thrilling evening it must have been for her.

It was that evening, too, that Rebecca received her first kiss. It was bestowed upon her by Douglas Tarrant during an after-dark stroll of the hotel grounds. Rebecca had been ecstatic. Later, she had confided to her diary, *Douglas kissed me tonight! I almost swooned! My pulse is still fluttering as I write this! Dare I believe he cares for me as much as I do for him?*

On that questioning note, Anne closed the journal. She popped the last of the sandwich into her mouth. The cat mewed plaintively at her feet, so Anne guiltily poured the last of her milk into his bowl. Then she decided to get away from the house for a while. She could use both the exercise and the change of scenery.

Anne walked briskly along the avenue, turning east at the corner. Two blocks farther there was a large park with playground equipment and picnic tables. The ground was littered with fallen leaves that crunched underneath Anne's feet as she walked across the park.

A half mile beyond the park Anne left the town behind. Past a sheltering screen of trees and brush ran the small trout stream where a few locals fished from time to time, including Simon. He had once confided to Anne that this stream was the best-kept fishing secret in town. Most people, however, drove five miles to another, larger stream when they wanted to do serious fishing.

This was the place where Anne and her friends had often come for picnics when they'd been teenagers. The stream was perpetually cold, but they were hardy and had plunged gamely into the icy-cold rushing waters. If anything, the coldness had energized and invigorated them.

Today the stream cast a strong chill upon the air, and before she sat down on the grassy bank Anne drew on the sweater she had brought with her.

Young Douglas Tarrant had given the sixteen-year-old Rebecca Lancaster her first kiss in an elegantly manicured hotel garden; his young great-nephew, Simon Tarrant, had given Rebecca's great-niece her first kiss here beside this wildly tumbling stream that meandered through the woods on the Christmas afternoon when Anne had also been sixteen. The wonder of that kiss, the sweetness of it, had snatched her breath away. Now she gazed almost hypnotically at the gray-blue waters and fancied she could still taste the flavor of Simon in that first shy kiss they had shared.

It was the day she had fallen headlong in love.

During all the years that she and Caroline Tarrant had been friends, Anne had always liked Simon. He'd been friendly toward her whenever she spent time at the Tarrant house, and he often teased her in an offhanded, brotherly fashion just the way he did his sister. And considering that Caroline and Simon's father, Joseph, and Anne's own father, Robert, had had some sort of falling-out years before, Mr. and Mrs. Tarrant had been extremely kind to Anne. They always made her feel welcome whenever she visited their home. When Joseph Tarrant ordered his son to stay away from Anne, it had been a shocking blow.

The memory was still painful. With an effort, Anne struggled to refocus her thoughts on that enchanting Christmas afternoon when Simon had unexpectedly kissed her, and the silent woods, the gray winter sky and the tumbling stream were their only witnesses.

Anne and her father had driven up from the city the day before to spend the holiday with Aunt Rebecca. Just after they'd finished a huge Christmas dinner, Caroline had telephoned and invited Anne to meet her by the stream to exchange their gifts. It was a rather strange location to exchange Christmas presents, particularly on a blustery, cold gray afternoon. But Anne agreed, and set out at once to walk there.

Caroline never showed up that day.

Simon came instead, grinning somewhat self-consciously, but walking toward her with a determined gait and bearing gifts in his hands, one from Caroline and one from himself.

His gift to Anne was a pretty, gold charm bracelet that must have set him back considerably. And next had come the kiss.

Anne had been surprised by both the gift and the kiss, but she wasn't surprised at the depth of her feelings for Simon. That day all her feelings toward him ripened into a sustaining love, a mutually committed love. It had been an exciting and exhilarating realization for both of them.

Tears of regret sprang to her eyes now...regret for all the might-have-beens. Slowly Anne got to her feet, turned her back on the stream and headed home.

That evening she decided to dine out. She didn't want to cook just for herself, and more importantly, she was finding the house oppressively lonely.

Mount Evergreen could boast of only one really nice restaurant, and the village was fortunate to have that. Most hamlets offered only fast-food outlets.

Anne was given a small table next to a picture window that had a fine view of a hillside and a few distant houses nestled amongst the trees. Their lights twinkled invitingly.

Anne ordered a glass of white wine and sipped it slowly while she studied the menu. When the waiter returned she ordered baked chicken with rice pilaf.

While she awaited her food, the restaurant rapidly filled with other patrons. It was, after all, the dinner hour. For lack of anything else to do to while away her time, Anne idly took note of each party of new arrivals. She always felt ill at ease whenever she had to dine out alone.

Just as the waiter brought her entrée and she politely refused more wine, her attention was riveted by a couple who had just arrived and who were following the hostess straight toward her table. Anne went rigid with shock and distress as the man's eyes fell upon her and their gazes met and locked.

The hostess swept past Anne's table, but Simon did not. He stopped beside her chair, and his hand on his companion's arm halted her, as well.

"Hello, Anne," he said softly.

Anne summoned a polite smile, but it felt stiff and out of place on her lips. She nodded. "'Evening, Simon.''

A short uncomfortable silence fell. Then Simon seemed to snap out of his daze and he introduced his date to Anne.

"Suzanne, I'd like you to meet Anne Ta—" At the hard, quelling look Anne threw him, Simon quickly covered his mistake and changed his introduction to, "Anne Lancaster."

The two women politely acknowledged each other. Then another awkward silence fell, but before it could become unendurable, the restaurant hostess finally realized that she'd lost her charges and came rushing back.

"Nice seeing you," Simon muttered in a low tone.

"Pleased to meet you," contributed Suzanne in a voice that told Anne she meant the exact opposite.

"Have a nice dinner," Anne murmured.

Unfortunately the hostess seated Simon and his date where Anne had a clear, unobstructed view of them. Whenever Simon smiled at the blond-haired beauty, Anne experienced a rush of pure jealousy that horrified her.

Yet how could that be? she asked herself angrily. She'd gotten over Simon a long, long time ago.

Simon's evening was ruined. Suzanne was an office supply rep who generally came through town once a month. Simon always tried to be free whenever she was here so he could take her out to dinner, either here or at the Tarrant Inn Resort Hotel thirty miles down the road. Likewise, whenever he paid one of his infrequent visits to Albany, Suzanne cleared her calendar so she could be with him. They enjoyed each other's company and always had a great time together. What made the relationship work—at least in Simon's opinion—was the fact that there had never been any strings attached for either of them.

Perhaps that wasn't strictly true any longer, though, Simon admitted silently. The past few months they'd been seeing each other more often than before, calling each other almost every day, and things had begun to get emotionally heavier. Being honest with himself now, Simon knew that his relationship with Suzanne was teetering on the brink of a serious commitment.

Yet now as he watched Anne picking at her dinner across the restaurant while trying to avoid contact with his eyes, he knew that any notion he might have had about planning for a permanent future with Suzanne was just so much smoke blowing in the wind.

"Who is she?" Suzanne asked in a strangely subdued voice.

"What?" Startled, Simon looked at the woman beside him and shrugged. "Just someone I've known since I was a kid. Until yesterday, I hadn't seen her in years. She lives in New York."

"And what is she to you?" Suzanne persisted in that oddly soft voice.

What is she to me? Simon ran the question through his mind. At one time he could've answered without a moment's hesitation. Anne had been the sun and the moon and the stars to him, the ocean and sand and sea air, the very breath of life itself.

But he couldn't very well tell Suzanne that. Besides, none of it was true anymore. Was it?

"What is she to me?" He repeated Suzanne's question aloud. "She's a youthful memory, that's all." And as he said it, he had a strong vision of Anne, dressed in a simple white dress, standing beside him in front of the minister who was marrying them in his study. Her face had been almost as white as her dress that day, and her hands had trembled badly. To him, she had never been more beautiful, before or since.

His bride.

Simon couldn't seem to stop himself. His gaze returned again and again to Anne. She'd given up pretending to eat, and was preparing to leave. She rose to her feet, swung the strap of her bag over her shoulder and for the first time since he'd sat down at his own table, she deliberately met Simon's eyes. A tiny smile parted her lips, she raised her hand in a brief goodbye gesture, and then she strode from the room.

It should have been easy to revive the evening once Anne was gone, but it wasn't. Everything had gone flat. Nothing Simon said seemed to please Suzanne, and nothing she said pleased him. His steak was too tough and his baked potato was undercooked. And though Anne no longer occupied the small table by the window, his brooding gaze kept returning there time and again. It was as though her very essence remained in the room and magically she would soon reappear. Most unforgivable of all, Simon had ceased to even hear Suzanne when she spoke.

He did hear her, however, when her fist suddenly came down forcefully on the tabletop. His cup rattled in its saucer and their neighbors swiveled in their chairs to stare. Simon himself gazed at Suzanne in astonishment. Her face was red and it was obvious that she was very, very angry.

She tossed her napkin to the table, picked up her handbag and thrust back her chair. As she surged to her feet, Simon did the same. "What's the matter? Where are you going?" he asked in sudden alarm.

"I'm leaving," she shot back. Suzanne's eyes smoldered. "You've been preoccupied with that other woman ever since we arrived, and she's not even here anymore! Well, I'm here to tell you, Simon, I don't play second fiddle to anyone!"

"Hey, I'm sorry." Simon exclaimed softly. He tried to clasp her hand, but Suzanne stepped away from him. "I'm really sorry. Sit down and eat your dinner. I was just woolgathering, that's all. It won't happen again, I promise."

"You bet it won't! Not with me, anyway!" Suzanne paused, then said in a milder tone, "Your lady friend didn't stick around long enough to finish her dinner, either. Maybe you ought to go after her, Simon, and straighten out whatever the heck's bothering the pair of you."

Simon didn't attempt to lie his way out of that one. He just ignored it and asked, "What about us? What about our dinner?"

"There is no 'us,'" Suzanne said sadly. "I see now there really never was. As for dinner, I'm not hungry anymore. Goodbye Simon. It was nice while it lasted."

Suzanne turned and walked away. In frustration and chagrin Simon was stuck at the table waiting for the check to arrive.

He wanted to rush after Suzanne and set things right with her, but on reflection, he supposed she'd already done that by calling it quits. She was a fine woman; unfortunately she just wasn't for him.

But neither was Anne, he thought angrily.

When Simon finally got away from the restaurant, his car drove as though of its own accord straight for Lancaster House. When he pulled into the driveway, he saw lights behind the curtains over the front windows.

Anne was home.

He parked, got out of the car and with long, angry strides, marched toward the porch. With every step his blood boiled hotter.

When Anne opened the door, he saw that she'd already changed for bed. She wore a pair of black silky pajamas with a matching robe trimmed with black lace. It wasn't a risqué outfit by any means, but it was ultrafeminine and very appealing. The lace at her throat plunged to the enticing dark recess between her breasts and the silky fabric draped her body with a sensuous intimacy he immediately envied. Her coal-black hair tumbled across her shoulders and framed her face like a billowy cloud, and despite his dark mood, Simon found Anne infinitely desirable.

"Simon!" she gasped. "What are you doing here?"

It was evident Anne was genuinely surprised and somewhat alarmed to see him. Alarmed, just as though he might harm her! Her conspicuous fear only intensified his anger.

Simon took a menacing step toward her and Anne stepped back. The unhappy little dance continued until they were both standing inside the hallway and he had kicked the front door closed behind him.

"What are you doing here?" she demanded a second time.

"I guess I can come to see my *wife* if I want to," he snarled.

"In your dreams!" Anne snapped. Whatever anxiety she'd felt evaporated with her rising anger. "I don't want to see you! I don't want you here, so go back to your *girlfriend!*"

The intonation on the last word was unmistakably a slur. Simon bristled. "And why do you say it like that?"

Anne shrugged. "Can't you see there's something a little fake about her—all that makeup and every hair glued perfectly into place? Even her speech seemed fake—a little too exaggerated, as though she was reciting lines in a play instead of just being spontaneous. She just didn't seem your style, somehow. You used to have different taste in women."

Simon tilted his head and his eyes glittered. "Don't you mean *better* taste in women?" he challenged.

"Well . . . since you ask," Anne replied. "Yes."

"Like hell I did!" he exploded. "I married you, didn't I?"

He had the intense satisfaction of seeing Anne blanch before hot anger scorched her cheeks. She raised her hand and started to swing it toward his face, but Simon was quicker. He blocked the assault by clasping her wrist and holding it firmly a safe distance away.

Their gazes clashed stormily, filled with concealed hostility, and for what seemed an endless moment neither moved. Then Simon did something that shocked him as much as it did Anne. Roughly he jerked her toward him with the hand that still grasped her arm while his other hand went around her waist, crushing her to his chest.

His lips took hers and the sizzling contact brought about an immediate and surprising change in them. Anger melted into passion and harshness into liquid softness as the kiss went on and on. Simon's touch had not been gentle, but now he removed his hand from around her wrist and began feather-stroking her cheek. Anne curled into his embrace the way she used to, with one hand caressing his neck and the other on his chest, over his heart. She used to tease him by saying when his heart raced erratically, throbbing against her fingertips, it proved he loved her.

Simon knew his heart was racing at this moment. Being with Anne again in this familiar way felt new and exciting, yet it also evoked poignant memories of a distant past. Her warmth seemed to billow and spread around Simon like a heated blanket, and he felt a deep stirring of desire.

But suddenly he realized it was a desire that he must not appease, no matter how willing Anne might be. He reminded himself that he had come here tonight to get her out of his life, not to get himself mixed up with her all over again.

Abruptly Simon dropped his hands away from Anne, stepped back and opened his eyes. She opened hers, too, and there was a slightly bemused expression on her face that tugged at his senses. He immediately felt the urge to kiss her again. The kiss they'd just shared had had a powerful effect upon both of them, and they were still slightly off balance. He realized with some alarm that he'd come dangerously close to sweeping Anne into his arms and carrying her upstairs to bed.

But he hadn't. Just in time he'd remembered the reason he had come here, and he was determined to carry through with his purpose.

"I want you to leave town as soon as possible," he told her in a hard voice. "My life was going along just fine until you came back into my territory."

Anne gasped incredulously. "You act as if I came back here for the sole purpose of making trouble for you. Nothing could be further from the truth, and you know it!"

Her eyes glinted into a furious glare and her hands went to her waist. One pajama-covered hip jutted out, and the stance infuriated Simon. It was angry, defiant and challenging; it was also sexy as hell!

The fact that he still desired her irritated Simon even more. "I realize you didn't return to Mount Evergreen on *my* account," he retorted heatedly. "I'm quite aware of how little I matter to you. But you've made trouble for me, all the same. Your presence at the restaurant surprised and distracted me, and it upset Suzanne so much she dumped me and went home to Albany. Your main purpose for having come back here is over and now it's time you left. You have no right to be interfering in my life, even if technically you still are my wife!"

"Why don't you say what you really mean?" she dared him. "You don't want me here messing up your love life!"

"Very true! And if you've got an ounce of decency in you at all, you'll finish your business here as fast as possible and get out of town!"

His cruel words stunned Anne into speechlessness. In unprotesting silence, she watched as Simon whirled and stormed out the door, vanishing into the night.

Chapter Three

Anne's high hopes were dashed as she showed the realtor out the door. Mr. Miller had been so pessimistic about the possibility of her selling the old house in the near future that in the end, she hadn't even signed the agreement he'd brought along that would give him the right to try.

She sighed raggedly and returning to the parlor, flopped down on the sofa in a dejected heap. Anne knew the realtor had been straight with her when he'd told her that in a place as small as Mount Evergreen there wasn't exactly a booming real estate market for old white elephants. The few houses that were moving were mostly the brand-new tract houses in the new development west of town.

So what was she going to do about Aunt Rebecca's house? She could go ahead and list it with Miller's Realty, and keep her fingers crossed that someone would come along who was mad for drafty old houses that need a lot of renovation. Or she could try to rent it to someone.

There was also a third option. She could move into the house herself.

The very notion astonished her.

Anne had a small studio in Manhattan where she photographed fashion models and still-life advertising layouts. Much of her work, however, was done in the field. She often got assignments for work in natural and outdoor settings, requiring frequent travel.

The more she thought about it, the more she realized it would be feasible to live in Mount Evergreen and commute to New York. She could cluster all her studio work into two or three days each week and spend the rest of her time here. She could even turn the playhouse into a studio for much of her still-life work.

Certainly the slower-paced life-style of a small town would be pleasant. But…there was Simon. He didn't want her here, nor did she relish the idea of living in the same town with him, either, always fearing she'd bump into him the way she had at the restaurant last night.

Feeling weak, Anne recalled how much Simon's angry kisses had aroused her. Her fingers touched her lips as though she could recapture the moment and she shivered at the memory of how intensely she'd wanted him. Her reaction was something she had not expected.

No, the last thing she needed to do was entertain an idea as wild as moving to Mount Evergreen. She ought to have her head examined for even thinking it.

Still, the notion of living here had a strong appeal. She loved the rambling old house despite its drawbacks. Who cared if the plumbing was antique, or instead of easy-care carpeting and tile, the floors were bare plank that required regular mopping and waxing? Who cared if living here meant raking leaves in the fall or mowing a huge lawn in the summer? At Lancaster House there was room to spread out, to breathe. She especially adored the huge old-fashioned kitchen. Even the closets were large and spacious, and if one ever did run out of closet space, there was always the attic. Her Manhattan apartment was so small and cramped it might legitimately have been leased as a large storage closet. It was also scandalously expensive, while this house had long ago been paid off. Of course, there would be the expenses of taxes, household maintenance and travel to and from the city, but even so she was still bound to come out ahead financially. That alone was a consideration worth thinking about.

As though pulled by some invisible force, Anne found herself wanting to return to the playhouse in order to assess its potential as a studio.

She decided to indulge herself and take a break from the boring, mentally fatiguing chore of sorting through the desk as well as the boxes of papers she'd discovered stowed away in a closet. She deserved to take the rest of the afternoon off.

Anne prepared a box lunch, also stashing a few snacks she'd bought yesterday at the supermarket inside the hamper. Then, with Aunt Rebecca's journal tucked beneath her arm, she walked across the backyard toward the playhouse.

Thunder was rumbling in the distance. The sky was dark and threatening over the far mountains, which appeared as though they were already being washed with rain. Here in her own backyard, however, slivers of sunshine still peeked around dark clouds making shadow and light patterns across the lawn and falling over Anne's head and shoulders.

Inside the playhouse, the old warm and comfortable feeling that she was completely isolated from the world and shielded from its problems stole over Anne. The feeling was comparable to the illicit pleasure of playing hooky from school. Here she could be totally alone to do whatever she pleased . . . eat, read the journal, nap or just daydream. No telephone or television or radio intruded here. It would be a sacrilege to bring such modern devices into the hideaway. Anne chuckled at herself over the lofty thought. When they'd been teenagers, she and her friends had kept a stereo here so that they could visit over the strains of their favorite music.

Anne sighed as she deposited her things on the small table. She had brought along a can of soup for lunch and while it warmed on the hot plate, she placed the rest of her meal on the table—cheese, crackers and an apple.

After she had finished her solitary lunch, Anne cleared the table and turned on the heat. The sunshine had completely disappeared and the rainstorm sounded as though it was drawing nearer. The air became definitely cooler, and the woolen afghan draped across the back of the sofa was a welcome sight.

Anne curled up on the sofa beneath the lamplight that was now needed against the dusky afternoon, drew the afghan over her knees and opened Rebecca's journal. At first she read about trivial happenings…church socials, school events, family outings. It didn't make the most exciting reading, but on the other hand, such detailed, first-hand accounts of life early in the twentieth century were historically illuminating. Life seemed so much simpler then.

But suddenly Anne sat upright and stared hard at the page she was reading. She'd already read the passage once, but had been unable to believe her eyes. Now she reread it slowly.

I feel so terrible sneaking around, lamented a distraught, seventeen-year-old Rebecca. *Mama will be so disappointed if she finds out, and Papa…Papa will be furious and punish me. But what else can I do? He has forbidden me to see Douglas, and I cannot abide by such an unfair order. Neither can Douglas. Just because our fathers had a fierce argument and ended their business partnership, why does that mean we shouldn't see each other? We're in love and our fathers demand too much. I've never disobeyed Papa before in my life, but this time he forced me to it.*

Seventy-five years ago, Rebecca's relationship with Douglas Tarrant had suffered beneath the same cruel, autocratic tyranny as Anne and Simon's! The parallel was so eerie that Anne was stunned, and a chill raced up her spine.

The summer following the Christmas kiss, the romance between Simon and Anne blossomed. They were together as often as possible, glowing with fresh young love. Other Mount Evergreen boys who'd been pursuing the pretty dark-haired girl visiting from New York and girls who'd entertained hopes about a relationship with Simon faded from the picture as it became apparent to them all that Simon Tarrant and Anne Lancaster were crazy about each other.

They didn't deliberately keep their newfound love from their parents. The subject just didn't come up. Simon rarely discussed girls with his parents and Anne's father was back in New York while she spent the summer in the mountains.

But Aunt Rebecca knew and never once expressed any objection. Nor did she reveal to her nephew that his daughter was seeing the son of his former friend. Now Anne saw that . . . and realized why Rebecca had been so compliant. By her silence, Aunt Rebecca had been protecting Anne and Simon from the same high-handed interference she and Douglas had met when they'd been young. As for Simon and Anne, they spent their enchanted summer blissfully oblivious of the fact that because their fathers held a grudge against each other, their own love was doomed.

In September of that year, Anne returned to school in New York, while Simon began his senior year at Mount Evergreen High. The storm, when it broke, took both of them by surprise.

Simon played football on the school team, and he invited Anne to return to Mount Evergreen on the weekend of the homecoming game and dance as his date. It never occurred to either of them to prevaricate.

But when Simon announced to his parents that Anne Lancaster was to be his date for the homecoming dance, his father, after an angry tirade against false friends and disloyal sons, ordered him to break the date and stop seeing Anne.

Anne got the same reaction from her father. Robert Lancaster also laid down the law...that Anne was never to date Simon again. "You can't trust a Tarrant," he'd flared. "Only trouble can come of it," he'd added direly.

Anne's father had been right. Only trouble had come of it. Years later, she was badly bruised when Simon put his family above her. The bald truth was that the pain of it was still with her after all this time.

But there was no point in dragging herself down into a pit of depression over it now. The past was past, and nothing could ever change it.

Anyway, for the time being, Anne had had enough of the past...Rebecca's as well as her own. She closed the journal, flipped off the lamp and fluffed up the sofa pillows. On an afternoon when rain threatened, she might as well try to snatch a nap. It beat going back to the house and cleaning out another closet or desk drawer.

The first hard, icy raindrops hit him just as he pushed through the shrubbery that concealed the playhouse from view. To Simon's disappointment he saw that the room was in darkness, which meant Anne wasn't here, either. He'd already tried the house.

Grimacing, he thought about trying to beat the rainfall back to his car out front, but it was already falling harder and he was about to get drenched. The playhouse, he hastily decided, would be as good a place as any to sit out the rainstorm. Besides, by the time the rain ended, Anne might have returned.

With a knowing hand, Simon reached behind the window shutter, located the key, and unlocked the door. Wet though he already was, he took time to return the key to its hiding place before he stepped through the door.

Just as he entered the dark, silent room, a strong gust of wind snatched the door from his hand and sent it crashing back against the wall at the same time as a ferocious clap of thunder assaulted from overhead.

He heard a startled cry from the darkness. "Who's there?" came Anne's anxious voice.

Simon was startled, too. Collecting himself, he flipped on the overhead light switch. "It's me, Anne," he said gruffly. "I'm sorry I scared you. The wind jerked the door from my hand."

Anne sat up on the sofa and stared at him. "What on earth are you doing here?" she demanded.

Simon closed the door against the wet, cold afternoon. "I was looking for you. What else? I'd decided you weren't here since the room was dark, but when it started to rain, I thought I'd come inside to wait it out." He smiled ruefully. "Do you mind?"

Anne ran her fingers through her hair in an effort to smooth it while she considered her answer. Did she mind? She supposed she ought to be indignant after the way Simon had behaved last night and just send him packing, rain or no rain. Instead, she found she was glad to see him. She'd been bored, lonely and sad, unable to doze off and too listless to get back to work. Simon's arrival seemed like the end of the rainstorm and the coming of sunshine, even though the rain still lashed furiously against the windows and thunder rumbled in the blue-black sky.

He looked so wonderful, she admitted to herself. Might as well be ruthlessly honest about it. He was damnably sexy. The rain had darkened his wheat-colored hair to the deeper shade of bleached wood, and those gorgeous blue eyes that had always done crazy things to her pulse held a question as he waited for her reply. His lips were crooked into the same slightly devilish smile that in the past had so often been her personal Waterloo.

As though to confirm her weakness, her heart was beginning to flutter. Anne dragged her eyes from Simon's unwavering gaze and lowered her own gaze to his chest. A thin brown sweater hugged his rock-hard chest and Anne caught her breath at how magnificently strong and fit he looked. And virile! She swallowed painfully as she took in his powerfully built thighs. No other man had ever tugged at her senses the way Simon Tarrant did.

Anne thrust aside the afghan and got to her feet. She clasped her suddenly unsteady hands behind her and avoided his eyes while she answered his question. "No, I don't mind," she said in a controlled voice that made her feel proud of herself. She turned toward the kitchenette counter and added over her shoulder, "There are towels in the bathroom. I'll put the kettle on while you dry off. Would you prefer coffee or hot chocolate? Bearing in mind, of course, that they're both the instant variety."

"I'll take the chocolate," Simon answered. "I don't think I've had any since that winter in Albany after we were married. You used to make it on really cold evenings."

The memory was unexpected, heartwarming, and oddly enough, somehow comforting to Simon. Those times with Anne had been some of the sweetest that they had shared.

Usually they'd both be studying in bed when Anne would decide they needed a break. Sometimes they would continue studying while they drank their hot chocolate; other times they would just talk. The best times were when the break would lead to the dumping of books and nightclothes on the floor—when forgetting everything except each other, they would make love.

Today, of course, there would be none of that, he reminded himself sternly. Still, he couldn't help but enjoy watching Anne as she prepared their drinks.

He didn't see much remaining of the innocent young teenage girl he'd first fallen in love with so long ago. This new, more mature Anne was someone he didn't know at all . . . a full-grown woman in every sense of the word. She was self-assured and dignified, and her movements were both competent and confident. Her body was at its feminine peak—lush and ripe, compelling the admiration of any masculine eye without making even the slightest effort to attract undue attention to herself. Today she wore neat, well-fitting but far from tight black slacks topped by a thick pink cable-knit sweater, which did more to obliterate all the attributes it covered than to emphasize them. And yet to Simon she looked knockout sexy.

A few minutes later they were seated at opposite ends of the sofa, discussing the rainstorm. The hot milk gradually relaxed Simon and the tension he'd felt when he'd seen Anne again the past couple of days was missing this afternoon. The atmosphere between them was comfortable, easy and pleasant.

Anne noticed the quizzical speculation in his eyes. "What?" she demanded. "Do I have a smudge on my face or something?"

Simon shook his head. "I was just wondering how you managed to grow more beautiful while everybody else merely adds a little more age every year."

Anne laughed, feeling inordinately pleased at his words. "Time has been good to you, too, Simon," she said softly. "Thanks."

Over the span of several heartbeats, they gazed searchingly at each other.

When the silence grew too long, Anne said, "You never told me why you came here today. Are you hoping to browbeat me into leaving Mount Evergreen the way you tried to do last night?"

Simon gave a short laugh. "Much good it would do me, huh?"

"Right. So... realizing that, why did you come?"

Simon took his time answering. While Anne's question was direct and brusque, she didn't sound particularly angry or defensive. Just straightforward. They were both in a different mood today from the passionately disturbed one of last night. Today they both simply wanted to get on with their business in a civilized manner. Simon hoped it meant they would succeed in coming to terms which they both could accept.

"I bumped into Darryl Miller at noon," he began.

"Ah." A spurt of anger shot through Anne. "Don't flatter yourself into thinking that the little scene between us last night had anything to do with my looking into the possibility of selling Lancaster House. I'd already set up an appointment with Mr. Miller before you ever showed up. And anyway, he had no right to be discussing my business with you," she added resentfully.

Simon held up a defensive hand. "Hey, take it easy! He didn't mean any harm."

Anne gazed at him sullenly. "What did he tell you?" she asked.

Simon shrugged. "He just mentioned you were considering putting the house on the market and that it was his opinion that you might be a long time unloading it. I came to make you an offer, that's all."

"You?" Anne was astonished. "Why do you want a huge old place like Lancaster House?"

"I don't particularly. I just thought it would help you out. It would be easier for me to keep an eye on the place and see to things like repairs and yard work than it would for you to try to manage all those things from New York. Eventually I'll put the house on the market myself, but I can afford to be patient while waiting for a sale. As for the price, I'll pay whatever an appraiser says is a fair market value. I'm certainly not trying to cheat you."

Anne tilted her head and gave Simon a long, searching look. "That's quite an offer," she said slowly. "It wouldn't have anything to do with the fact that if I sell the house to you right now, I'll have no excuse to keep returning to Mount Evergreen, would it?"

"The truth?" Simon's eyes met hers without wavering.

Anne nodded. "Please."

Simon set his cup on the lamp table and took Anne's free hand in his. He stared down at it for a long, long time. His voice was low and his words were measured when he finally did speak. "It's been hard, Anne, seeing you again like this . . . knowing the way things are between us. Look at your hand. You don't wear my ring anymore, or use my name. Not that there's any reason for you to, but still. . . . I just want there to be an end to the pain of it all so that I can get on with my life." He lifted his head and his sky-blue eyes had a dark, bruised look. "Surely you can understand that, can't you?" he asked softly.

A lump swelled in Anne's throat and her voice was raspy with unshed tears. "I understand perfectly," she said hoarsely, "because it's as hard for me seeing you. A lot harder than I'd expected. I thought I hated you, you see."

"And you don't?"

She shrugged and answered honestly, "I guess not. The good memories keep cropping up as often as the bad."

"They do, don't they?" Suddenly Simon grinned and glanced around the room. "We had a lot of fun in here when we were teenagers, didn't we? A bunch of us here dancing and playing music as loud as we pleased."

Anne laughed and nodded. "And Aunt Rebecca popping in and out constantly with refreshments."

Simon chuckled. "And at the same time checking on the goings-on out here and making sure we boys were behaving ourselves."

"You didn't . . . always," Anne murmured with a nostalgic smile.

"I know." All at once Simon was serious. His voice lowered to almost a whisper. "It was here in the playhouse that we came so close to making love for the first time."

"Yes," Anne murmured. "But I backed out. You were so furious with me."

"Can you blame me?" Simon winced as though he was still suffering from the pain of that rejection.

"Of course not!" Anne exclaimed. "My only excuse is that I was young and scared. Somehow I knew we were playing with a fire that could get out of hand."

"Fire is right!" Simon declared. "Every time we ever did make love, the very air sizzled and crackled with heat."

"Yes." Anne couldn't deny it. They always did shoot sparks off each other, whether they were making love or fighting.

When Anne graduated from high school, she followed Simon to college at Albany. And there, away from the prying eyes or interference of their fathers, the love they shared deepened and matured.

Just before the start of Simon's last year at college, they married. However, they agreed not to tell their fathers for another year and a half, at which time Anne would be finishing her studies. That would be soon enough to deal with whatever unpleasantness awaited them. In the meantime, they reveled in their newfound marital happiness, although it had to be kept a secret from everyone, even Caroline. Fortunately since Caroline was attending college in California at the time, the temptation to confide in her was considerably lessened.

Their lives had seemed right on track, heading precisely in the direction they had planned.

Without warning, everything went horribly wrong.

Only two months after their secret wedding, Simon was suddenly summoned home when his father suffered a debilitating stroke that left him incapacitated. Although in time Joseph Tarrant's condition would improve with therapy, it would come very slowly. Even at best, he would never be the same again. He was left partially paralyzed.

Since Caroline was on the West Coast, the entire burden of helping his mother run the family businesses in his father's absence fell to Simon. Simon began going to Mount Evergreen every Friday after classes and rushing back to college—and Anne—late Sunday nights.

By the time he graduated that spring, there was no question about Simon's future. He felt he had no choice except to go home and take over the management of both the hotel and the newspaper. It was out of the question for Joseph ever to return to work full-time, if at all, and Simon's mother had her hands full caring for her husband.

Anne remained in Albany. She still had a year of school remaining.

At first, Simon reversed his schedule. Now he spent weekdays in Mount Evergreen and traveled to Albany every Friday evening to be with Anne. But as time went by, Simon became so busy with his work that he'd skip a weekend, or Anne would be so engrossed in her studies when he came that she had no time for him.

The constant separations could not fail to harm the marriage. They found that they had less and less in common with each other, less to share, less to discuss as time went by. It was no surprise to Anne when Simon's weekend visits became infrequent, because by then they had reached the point where, when he did come, they quarreled frequently. Often when he left her on Sunday evenings they would both be feeling bitter and resentful. By the time Anne graduated the following spring, she and Simon were almost totally estranged.

The right time to announce to their families that they were married never came. As far as Simon was concerned, his father's precarious state of health precluded his being told the truth. There was no point in telling Anne's father as long as they were living apart and keeping their marriage a secret from Simon's family.

Simon even missed Anne's graduation ceremony. His father had suffered a second mild stroke and was back in the hospital.

That had been the official end to their marriage as far as Anne was concerned, although the real break actually took place a week later. Objectively she'd understood Simon's parents' need of him at that time, but she had needed him, too. She had needed his supportive presence on what was, after all, a very important day in her life. Once again, Simon had let her down, and she was crushed.

The following weekend Anne visited Aunt Rebecca for what was to be the last time, although she hadn't realized it then. She had gone to Mount Evergreen to confront Simon about their future.

She'd phoned, asking him to meet her in the playhouse that evening, and it was here in this very room that they'd agreed to separate. They had quarreled bitterly, and Anne had issued an ultimatum—either they would announce to both families that they were man and wife and live together openly, or they would go their separate ways. Simon had demanded more time, more patience, more understanding from her, claiming his father was still too ill to be told. The shock of it might bring on yet another stroke and Simon couldn't take the chance.

But Anne had no more time, patience or understanding left to give. They'd kept their love for each other under wraps since high school, and by keeping their marriage a secret for the past year and a half they'd been living a lie. Enough was enough. Simon had placed his family above his wife and she was too hurt and angry to be willing to wait any longer for the mythical "right time" to announce their true relationship to their families and the world at large.

Yet in all the years since, neither Simon nor Anne had initiated divorce proceedings.

Simon abruptly stood up and went to the window where the rain lashed fiercely against the glass pane. As though he had read her thoughts, he said, "You never filed for a divorce."

"No."

"Why not?"

Anne was glad he kept his back to her, that he kept gazing out at the rainy day. "I really don't know," she admitted truthfully. "There just never seemed to be any urgency about it. After that fiasco of ours, the idea of another marriage was distasteful to me. So I did nothing. I figured if you wanted a divorce, you could set the process in motion as well as I. But you didn't do it, either."

Simon turned and their eyes met. A rueful smile touched his lips. "I had no incentive for it, either," he told her. "I guess I've felt the same way you do about the prospect of remarriage." He shrugged and returned to sit beside her. His blue eyes were dark and earnest as he gazed at her. "Maybe we should have tried harder to make our marriage work. Maybe you were right and we should have bitten the bullet and told our fathers. I realize our breakup was largely my fault, since I refused to tell Dad about us at the time, but you . . ."

He broke off and Anne picked up the abandoned sentence for him. "I could have tried harder to be patient," she admitted. "After all, your father had just suffered a second stroke, so my timing couldn't have been worse for issuing an ultimatum the way I did. But our regrets come a little late, don't they, Simon? It's all water under the bridge now."

"That it is," Simon said with a sigh.

The storm had slackened considerably, but the rain still fell and the air was much cooler. Anne rose and carried their empty mugs to the sink. She made more chocolate and while she busied herself, she asked curiously, "Did you ever learn what it was that caused our fathers to hate each other so much they forbade us to date?"

"Not precisely, but it must have been something about business. Did you know that at one time they were in business together?"

Anne whirled in surprise. "I certainly didn't!"

"I found out several years ago when I was going through some old papers I found in Dad's office at the *Sentinel*," Simon told her. "I asked him about it and he admitted he and your father had once been partners. Dad bought out your father's interest in the newspaper. But when I asked him, he refused to tell me what caused them to split up. Whatever it was, it must have been one heck of a falling-out, since they both freaked out when we told them we were seeing each other."

"Yet neither of them ever objected to Caroline and me being friends. Why, we even used to stay overnight at each other's houses."

"I remember." Suddenly Simon grinned mischievously. "I used to eavesdrop on your girl talk through my bedroom wall."

"You didn't!" Outraged, Anne made a fist and struck his forearm. "You demon! You ought to be horsewhipped!"

Simon laughed and captured her assaulting hand, but then he became thoughtful and serious as he gazed down at it. "I suppose your friendship with Caroline didn't make our fathers feel threatened the way our interest in each other did. They must have been afraid that if we dated, we might just get serious enough to marry, which as it turns out, is exactly what happened in spite of their efforts."

"I suppose," Anne murmured, then shook her head. "I still can't believe they were business partners!"

"Why not?" Simon asked. "Since they grew up together and went to school together, it's not really surprising that they became friends. Sometimes old school friends grow up to become business partners."

"Of course," Anne said. She had recovered her hand from his and now waved it in a dismissive gesture. "That's not the point!" She picked up Rebecca's journal from the lamp table. "It's this."

"What?" Simon asked as she flipped it open.

"Aunt Rebecca's journal. She kept one all her life, and the parallels between her life and mine, and the man she loved and you, are absolutely astounding. Did you know, for instance, that our Tarrant and Lancaster greatgrandfathers were also business partners, and that they had a falling-out that ended their relationship, too?"

Simon stared at her in amazement. "I never heard about that."

Anne nodded. "They owned a logging company together. Did you know that your great-uncle Douglas and my great-aunt Rebecca were in love and were forced to hide their feelings because *their* fathers also forbade them to see each other?''

Shaking his head, Simon exclaimed, ''You're pulling my leg!''

Anne tapped the book in her lap. ''It's all in here if you want to read about it. Rebecca and Douglas saw each other in secret just as we had to do.''

Simon gave a low whistle. ''The only thing I've ever known about Uncle Doug is that he was killed in France during the First World War. Who would've thought he and your great-aunt went through the same thing we did? I wonder if they would have eventually married if he hadn't gone off to war?''

Anne shrugged, closed the journal and replaced it on the table. ''We'll never know for sure, will we? I always wondered why Aunt Rebecca never married. I guess all this explains it.'' She sighed. ''Poor Douglas. Poor Rebecca. He lost his life in the prime of his youth, while she was destined to a long, lonely life. They were both terribly cheated.''

The rainstorm had finally ended. Through the windows the world was freshly washed a vivid green. Raindrops glistened on leaves in the muted light of the now pale-gray sky.

Simon inhaled deeply. ''The rain's stopped. I should be going.'' Yet he made not the least move to stand up. Instead, he turned toward Anne and smiled. ''Have you made up your mind about selling me the house yet?''

She laughed. ''Eager, are we?'' She shook her head. ''How could I? I haven't had a moment to think about it.''

Simon rose to his feet, and Anne followed suit.

They stood facing each other, near enough to touch, but not touching. Simon's gaze swept over Anne, and something softened inside him, something that had been brick-hard for five years. The past hour had been wonderfully relaxed and casual, evoking memories of pleasant times when they'd lived together as husband and wife. The only difference was that then their comfortable conversations would often take place in bed, after lovemaking.

The thought of making love with Anne sent a swift, stabbing longing through Simon. At that moment the last thing he wanted was to walk through the door and leave her.

"Come to think of it," he heard himself admitting, "it's sorta nice having you around. Maybe I'm not as eager for you to be gone as I thought I was."

Anne was riveted by the suggestive tone of Simon's voice and the fiery light flickering in his eyes. The inside of her mouth went dry and she was rooted to the spot, unable to prevent his gaze from consuming her like a sudden wild-fire in a drought-dry forest. It had been so very, very long since he had looked at her like that . . . as though she were a treasure he coveted. It brought her close to tears, and it was all she could do not to fling herself into his arms and beg him to love her again.

Simon was mesmerized. His senses were stirred by the sweet womanly scent of her, by the questioning expression in her eyes, by the gentle rising and falling of her breasts as she breathed. Was it his imagination, or was her breath more rapid now than before?

He reached out and curled a lock of her dark hair around his finger. He stepped closer, eliminating the space be-tween them. Anne was gazing down now, as though she felt suddenly shy, and indeed her cheeks were a bright feverish pink when he moved his hand to cup her chin. Slowly he tilted her face toward his.

"Look at me, Anne," he whispered hoarsely.

At first she resisted, but finally Anne raised her eyes to meet Simon's. She saw no mockery in their blue depths...only warmth and tenderness and desire. Unmistakable desire.

"I've missed you," he said huskily. "I've missed everything about you, from the way you nibble on your lip when you're in deep thought to the way you sing along with the radio when you're happy. And I've missed holding you in my arms, missed kissing you and making love to you. Why, time was, on a rainy afternoon like this, making love was the first thing we'd have done."

Laughter seized Anne. She shook her head vigorously and her eyes twinkled with a teasing light. "Wrong. On a rainy afternoon like this, making love was the *only* thing we'd have done!"

Simon grinned broadly. "I stand corrected."

Anne sobered abruptly and her voice softened. "I've missed you, too, Simon. More than I can say."

"Have you?" Now his eyes were teasing. "In that case, how about giving me a kiss and let's see about making up for lost time."

With pleasurable anticipation, Anne complied. She stepped within the warm circle of his arms, wound her own arms around his neck, stood on tiptoe and pressed her lips to his.

Hot liquid desire raced through Simon's bloodstream as Anne curled her body to fit just so in his arms. It felt familiar and right. It was as though they'd never been apart, and yet he also felt as if he'd been deprived of her for a lifetime.

His breathing became raspy and uneven as his hands slid beneath her sweater. His fingers slipped inside her bra and touched the warm, soft roundness of her breast. Anne excited him as much as she ever had.

In the meantime, Anne's hands were snaking beneath his sweater, too. Her fingers tap-danced across his chest before sliding around to caress his back. Then, returning to his chest, her fingers began inching downward along his belly, slowly, ever so slowly, toward his belt.

Simon sucked in a sharp breath. He ached to have her! Anne always had been a provocative she-devil, driving him wild with desire by her bold playfulness. As her fingers dipped beneath his waistband, only to withdraw again, teasing him before creeping underneath once more, the urgency inside him came dangerously close to explosive.

He met no resistance from Anne when he pulled her down to the sofa. Their eyes met briefly and hers were smoky and passionate. From long past experience, Simon knew that at that moment, like him, Anne was all emotion, all feeling, all sensation.

He removed her sweater and paused to drop kisses along one creamy white shoulder and on the flesh along the edges of her lacy bra. Anne inhaled deeply as kiss followed kiss across the swelling mounds of her breasts.

She became impatient and tugged his sweater off, as well, and they came together and kissed again, long and deeply. Simon's fingers became engaged in unhooking her bra.

Suddenly they heard a voice shouting from the lawn beyond the screen of shrubbery and trees. Simon and Anne froze within their embrace.

"Anne! Anne, where are you?"

Profoundly shocked, Anne recognized the voice. It was Jack Harrison, the new man in her life. They'd been dating off and on for the past six weeks or so. The last thing she'd ever expected was for Jack to show up here in Mount Evergreen! As for his timing....

Anne's eyes met Simon's, and in them she saw a reflection of the same wild frustration she felt.

Chapter Four

"Who the hell is that?" Simon grumbled from deep in his throat.

Anne ungraciously thrust his sweater into his hands and in the next moment, she was pulling hers over her head.

"A friend from New York," she replied impatiently. She raked her hands through her hair, then patted it down to smooth it before she paused to glare at Simon. "Hurry!" she snapped. "Put your sweater back on so I can open the door and let him know we're in here."

Simon glowered at her, but he slipped on the sweater. As he straightened it at the shoulders, he demanded, "Why answer him? Keep quiet and if he thinks you're not home, he'll go away."

Anne shook her head resolutely, but at least Simon had the satisfaction of seeing a hint of the disappointment and frustration he was feeling in her gaze before she said, "He drove all the way up from the city, Simon. I can't just ignore him." She turned and stepped to the door.

Moments after she called out, Jack located the path between the thick shrubs and stepped into the clearing in front of the playhouse. "So this is where you are! A secret hideaway!" he exclaimed in wonderment. "Who'd have thought?"

"Hi, Jack." Anne tried to sound gracious, although despite what she'd said to Simon, she wasn't feeling at all hospitable. Only good manners had caused her to open the door and summon him. "What're you doing here?"

The question came out sounding more like an accusation than a simple inquiry, and Jack tossed her a quizzical look, as though he had caught the unwelcome tone in her voice.

"It's Friday," he declared as he joined Anne on the doorstep. "I decided to take off early to beat the crowds and drive up to be with you. I figured after almost a week of being stranded in a backwoods burg, you'd be glad of a little company."

"She's got company," came a hard, implacable voice from behind Anne's left shoulder.

Damn! Anne felt her face grow hot beneath the scrutiny of Jack's gray eyes. She felt like throwing something—at Simon for the insinuation plainly in his voice, at Jack for making the arrogant assumption that she couldn't get along happily without his company for more than a few days.

She sighed and suppressed the temptation to simply dart through the dripping bushes, jog to the back of the property and vanish behind a screen of trees and a neighbor's fence, leaving the two men alone to confront each other. Instead, she stepped back and allowed Jack to enter the playhouse.

Neither man offered to shake hands with the other when Anne introduced them. They eyed each other warily and their hellos sounded more like snarls than civility. The tension in the room was so thick it was almost suffocating.

In appearance as well as temperament and personality, the two men couldn't have been more different. Simon was large, with sun streaks in his hair, and the broad shoulders and ruddy complexion of a man who enjoys the outdoors. Jack, on the other hand, was a smaller, more compactly built man. He looked great in business suits and there was an air of nervous energy about him—energy he focused on courtroom juries.

"Er—Jack is a defense attorney," Anne volunteered when the conversation languished.

"Fascinating." Simon's response to Anne's statement just barely escaped being an open sneer.

Jack caught the tone of voice, and his face reddened. But glib attorney that he was, he got his own back. "And what is it *you* do in this hole-in-the-road place? Play checkers by the potbellied stove at the general store?"

"Nothing that would be likely to interest a big-shot attorney like you, that's for sure," Simon retorted. He turned toward Anne and his eyes glittered with pure fury. "I'll be going now. I need to milk the cows, gather the eggs and sweep the hayseed out of my house before chopping wood for the cookstove."

"Okay, okay, you've both had your fun," Anne declared irritably. Her hands were on her hips in a gesture of anger. "Now behave yourselves," she chided as though they were little boys. "And speaking of cookstoves, let's go up to the house and see what we can find to make for dinner."

Well, at least, Simon conceded to himself as the three of them marched smartly across the damp lawn toward the back porch, Anne had included him in that general invitation. That was a good sign, wasn't it? If she didn't want to be alone with the obnoxious city-boy, didn't that mean she wasn't all that romantically interested in him?

Jack Harrison didn't appear too pleased when Simon parked himself on a kitchen chair and it became obvious that he fully intended to stay for dinner. Simon secretly enjoyed the other man's displeasure enormously and he resolved to outstay Harrison's visit, no matter how late that might be.

That decision did a lot to keep his spirits up as the evening wore on and Anne and Harrison's chatter about people and events back in the city left Simon out of the conversation. Now and then Anne would remember that he was there, too, and she would direct a comment or a question to him in an effort to include him, but Harrison was always quick to change the topic to one that would leave Simon out.

By a quarter of midnight, both Anne and Simon were openly yawning and still, Jack Harrison had made no move to depart. Neither, of course, had Simon.

Anne finally faced the fact that Jack had come with the intention of being invited to stay the night. And why not? she asked herself. There was plenty of room and it was a long way back to the city.

But there was Simon. She could just imagine what he would think of the idea. Still, she reminded herself, despite what had almost happened between them that afternoon, what she did was none of his concern. Nothing she did was his concern anymore. It hadn't been in over five years.

And so, she did what she had to do…she invited Jack to stay the night. Jack accepted the offer with alacrity.

If looks could kill, the one she received from Simon would have cut her down on the spot. Anne might have laughed at his expression, except for the fact that she knew he was ragingly angry.

Somehow Anne finally got Simon out the door and then she turned to deal with her unexpected and unwelcome houseguest. She forced herself to smile. "I'll show you your room."

Jack followed her upstairs and Anne stopped at the first door she came to. "This is my father's old bedroom," she said as she crossed the threshold. "I think you'll find it comfortable."

Jack followed her inside and without warning, he clasped his arms around Anne's waist and drew her toward him. His gray eyes softened as he met her gaze.

"I was hoping I could sleep in your room," he said huskily. He bent his head, about to kiss her.

For a split second, Anne froze, but then she recovered from her astonishment enough to push him backward, freeing herself from his embrace.

He looked at her with complete surprise, and then anger surged into his cheeks. "What's this?" he asked gruffly. "You never minded my kisses before."

No, she admitted silently to herself. But then he'd never before kissed her on the same day as Simon had. It wasn't Jack's fault that he came in a poor second.

"Sorry." Anne tried to keep her voice light and casual. "I'm very tired and I just want to go to sleep. Alone," she added emphatically as she stepped around him and moved into the hallway.

Jack's eyes suddenly narrowed. "Is it because of that guy who was here tonight? What is he to you?"

Anne shrugged. She wasn't about to get into details about her relationship with Simon. "He's just someone I've known for years, that's all. An old friend."

"And I'm a new friend. But I think we've been going together long enough that my suggestion that we sleep together shouldn't come as a surprise. You must know I'm crazy about you, Anne. I thought you felt something for me, too."

"Of course I care about you," she murmured as she lowered her gaze to the floor. "And your suggestion's not a surprise, exactly."

"But it's unwelcome?"

"I…well, yes," she admitted. Anne knew she owed Jack the courtesy of telling him the truth about her feelings for him. During the weeks they'd been dating, he'd made romantic gestures toward her that she had somehow managed to fend off without affronting him. She'd always known that the day of reckoning would arrive. Well, now it had.

She lifted her gaze to his stern, somber face. He was clearly unhappy with her response, and she couldn't really blame him.

"Mind telling me why?" Now Jack's voice was cold as ice.

Anne shook her head. "I just… I don't know if I can explain."

"Try me."

"I simply can't…" Her voice lowered in frustration. How did you tell a nice man you'd been seeing that he simply didn't turn you on…that even his kisses left you cold…without hurting his feelings? The fact that she liked him tremendously in every other way except romantically bothered her, too. Anne *wanted* to want Jack. She just didn't, that's all.

"It's that other man, isn't it?" Jack asked harshly. "Simon. Are you in love with him?"

The question, hurled at her out of the blue that way, was like getting a bucket of icy water thrown in her face. Anne sucked in a sharp breath and squeezed her eyes closed against the sudden stinging tears.

"Yes." Her voice was raspy. She was admitting the truth to herself as much as to Jack. "I can't remember a time I wasn't in love with him."

"Then I was never in the running at all," Jack accused. "You were just leading me on."

"It's not like that," Anne insisted. "Until a few days ago, I hadn't seen Simon in over five years. I thought you and I had something wonderful going, too, Jack, honestly. But seeing Simon again..." She shook her head. "I'm sorry, but I think it's best if we don't go out together anymore. The last thing I want is to hurt you, and I can't promise you that things will ever be different in the future."

Jack sighed heavily. "If you're in love with someone else, I guess you can't help it, can you? Well—I'd better be going. Can you direct me to a nearby motel?"

"There isn't one. You'd have to drive twenty-five miles to get to a resort hotel." Anne carefully refrained from mentioning that the hotel belonged to Simon's family. "You'll stay here, of course. It would be silly for you to start searching for a room at this hour of the night. Just because we aren't going to date anymore, it doesn't mean we can't be civil and friendly, does it?"

Jack's eyes held sadness and disappointment, but he managed a wan smile. "I guess not," he replied. "Good night, Anne."

Simon danced to one side of a mud puddle, then gracefully hopped back to his original position without ever breaking stride. It was early Saturday morning and he had the street to himself as he jogged through the quiet residential neighborhood. All the other residents, it seemed, were sleeping late today.

It had rained again during the night, and this time the rainstorm had come with a lot of wind. This morning there were a lot of broken tree branches strewn haphazardly over lawns, sidewalks and in the streets, paper blown against fencelines and flattened plants in flower beds. The wind still had not died down completely; the air was damp and cold against Simon's face, although his body, covered by his sweatsuit, was warm.

The sharply cold, moist air was precisely what he needed to wake up fully and clear his head. Simon welcomed the chilly blast of wind that stung his face and reddened his eyes. He'd spent a terrible night, awake and brooding more often than asleep.

He'd been tortured all night by visions of Anne and Jack Harrison alone together in Lancaster House. He was tormented by speculation about whether they'd shared one bedroom. In light of the fact that it was obvious the pair had been dating for some time, it would be naive to hope they hadn't spent the night in each other's arms. After all, they were fully mature adults—and it had been five long years since Simon and Anne had parted.

Yet the thought of Anne making love with any other man filled Simon with such a jealous rage that it sickened him. He couldn't bear it if it was true.

But it couldn't be true, could it? After all, only yesterday afternoon Anne had been in his arms, sweet and flushed and wanting him as eagerly as he'd wanted her. Unquestionably they would have made love if there hadn't been the ill-timed interruption by Harrison. So, given that fact, it stood to reason she wouldn't have flung herself into the other man's arms last night after Simon left. If he knew anything at all about Anne, it was that she was not promiscuous. If she was in love with Harrison, Anne wouldn't have surrendered herself to Simon's caresses yesterday.

That thought was encouraging. Upon reaching the next intersection, Simon turned right and jogged toward the business district of town. Suddenly he felt there was firm purpose to the direction he'd taken.

But twenty minutes later as he approached Lancaster House, insidious fears, doubts and jealousies accosted Simon again. If Anne had slept with Harrison last night, did he really want to know it?

Simon reached the edge of the driveway, and still parked near the house was Harrison's gray compact car. Simon's heart sank and he had just about convinced himself to turn and go away—reasoning that whatever Anne did these days was none of his business—when Anne came around the side of the house.

She was picking up branches and twigs that had blown down during the previous night's storm and stowing the debris inside a large plastic trash bag. She didn't notice Simon standing at the foot of the driveway.

She wore sweats herself—in shocking pink—and except for her curvaceous hips and long legs, the rest of her dynamite figure was well concealed by the shapeless shirt. Although her dark hair was held back from her face by a bright pink band, it didn't seem to be doing a very good job. Numerous long black tendrils whipped against her rosy cheeks. She looked casual and slightly unkempt, and Simon thought she'd never been more captivating.

He began to walk slowly toward her, wondering what manner of greeting he would receive. Would she be glad to see him or angry that he had come?

What he deserved was a swift kick. Once he'd had all of Anne's love in the palm of his hand—a rare and precious gift—and he'd let it slip away from him. If anything, he'd pushed her away by being too afraid to stand up to his father and announce that Anne Lancaster had become Anne Tarrant, his wife. That he'd been terrified such news might cause his father to suffer a fatal stroke somehow didn't seem like much of an excuse after all these silent, empty years. There was perhaps an equal or better chance that his father wouldn't have had a stroke if he'd been told about Anne. There was no way of knowing. But Simon did know that his concern had been genuine. He'd never set out to hurt or alienate Anne...yet that was precisely what he had done.

But he'd paid for it. During the past five years his dreams had too often been filled with visions of Anne. He would awake in an agony of desire for her, a throbbing, painful ache for her that seemed destined to nag at him for the rest of his life. Those relentless dreams of Anne had kept Simon from ever committing himself to a truly close relationship with another woman.

He'd written to Anne twice during those years of separation, suggesting they meet, letting her know he missed her and longed for her. What he hadn't said in those letters was that he was willing to announce their marriage, but Anne, smart girl that she was, hadn't given Simon the time of day, much less the courtesy of a reply. By her deafening silence she'd made it perfectly clear that she wanted nothing whatsoever to do with him.

Until yesterday afternoon. If only Harrison hadn't shown up, Anne would've been his again.

Anne straightened and caught sight of him. Unexpectedly she grinned and there was a distinctive challenge in her voice. "Now why is it I'm not at all surprised to see you here this morning?"

"I don't know," Simon tossed back. "Were you expecting me?"

"More or less."

Anne's dark eyes were sparkling with good humor, and Simon resented the hell out of it. He had a sinking suspicion about what had caused such cheerfulness; it was awfully early in the morning to be in such a great mood without having a very good reason for it. All of the confidence he'd pumped into himself on the way over, that Anne wouldn't—couldn't—love another man, suddenly dissipated.

Simon wished he'd had sense enough to stay away. He felt like a lovesick fool who had let his jealousy get out of hand. He longed to simply turn and walk away, but he knew doing so would only make him look even more foolish.

Remembering the white paper bag in his hand, he held it out toward Anne. "Doughnuts," he announced. "Plain, cream-filled and chocolate-covered."

"All that sugar!" Anne chided. "All those empty calories! Simon, you know doughnuts are bad for you."

Simon shrugged. "These days everything you like is supposed to be bad for you. Give me a break! And anyway, you should be thanking me for bringing breakfast to help you entertain your houseguest. By the way, where *is* Harrison? Still asleep?"

"I don't know." Anne replied indifferently. She took the bag from Simon, opened it and peered inside.

"Do you mean you don't know because he was still asleep when you left him, or because you really don't know?"

Anne closed the bag and her eyes no longer sparkled as her gaze met his. "Are you asking me whether I slept with Jack last night?"

Simon tensed. "Yes. I guess I am."

Anne gasped and Simon sensed her growing indignation. "And you actually expect me to *tell* you?"

Simon clenched his teeth and stood his ground, shaky though he knew it was. "That's right."

"You're nuts, you know that?" she scoffed. "Whether I did or didn't is none of your business, Simon Tarrant! You've got one hell of a nerve for asking!" Anne turned and began striding away from him.

Simon caught up with her easily and grabbed her arm, swinging her around to face him. Her face was pink with indignation, but his own face was warm and flushed, too. "It most certainly is my business!" he declared in a low, menacing voice. "Whatever you do is my business as long as you're still my wife—particularly whom you sleep with!"

Anne snatched her arm free of his grasp. "Don't make me laugh," she snapped. "Wife? You don't understand the meaning of marriage, Simon. You only acknowledge the fact that I'm technically still your wife whenever it happens to suit your purpose, and you pretend I don't exist the rest of the time. So what's the big deal now? You haven't cared one whit all this time what I did or whom I saw. Why should it suddenly be so important to you now?"

"You're wrong about my not caring all these years," Simon insisted. "It was just that I felt I didn't have any right to interfere in your life."

"And you still don't!"

"Maybe not. I didn't get involved in your life when you were in New York, but now you're on my turf. It's a different matter if you're going to start carrying on a romance right here under my nose. A man can only be pushed so far, and then he's bound to push back if he's any sort of man at all."

For a long moment Anne glared resentfully at Simon. But then, unexpectedly, she began to laugh. "Come on into the kitchen, Simon. I'll pour some milk to go with these doughnuts."

Her abrupt mood change confused him. Simon stood still for a moment as she turned and mounted the porch steps, but then he rushed after her. He put his hand on her shoulder and turned her to face him. "Anne," he said earnestly, "I have to know this... are you serious about Harrison? Am I in your way by coming here this morning?"

Anne studied his face for a long time, as though by examining it she could see the essence of his soul there. She was no longer annoyed, or amused. Only searching.

She hesitated for a long time before she finally shook her head. "You're not in the way," she said at last.

Cheered immeasurably by the significance of those casual words, Simon followed Anne into the house.

Chapter Five

Anne shoved a plastic dishpan under the sink to catch the drip from the leaking pipe. She chewed her lips in consternation as she went to get the phone book so she could find a plumber.

She was still frustrated when she finished her conversation with the person at the only plumbing company in town. The plumber, she was informed, was out on a call and had several others ahead of Anne. He would see to her problem sometime in the afternoon and no, they weren't sure when she could expect him.

Having to hang around all day waiting for the plumber would be singularly dreary but there was little else Anne could do. Because she had to go to New York for a morning appointment the leak would have to be plugged today before she could return to the city.

Depression settled over her. Nothing was going right these days. She felt terrible about breaking off with Jack, and yet what other option had been open to her? She couldn't have gone on seeing him, feeling the way she did about Simon. That would've been dreadfully unfair to Jack.

As for Simon—the thought of him depressed her even more. She was angry with herself for being so disturbed by him whenever he was near; she was angry with herself for being so tempted by him; and she was angry with herself for almost having made love with him.

What good would have come of it had they made love, other than the obvious physical release it would bring? Nothing else would have changed. They would still be leading separate lives in separate places. Simon would still be a husband who wasn't a husband . . . she a wife who was not a wife. Could anything be more pathetic than to be so weak-willed she had wanted to make love with him again and stir up old sensations that were better left dormant?

She had admitted to Jack that she was still in love with Simon, but now, in her own mind and heart, Anne retracted the declaration. She would *not* love a man who didn't love her, who still put his family ahead of his wife.

He'd done it again this very weekend.

For all his seeming like a jealous bulldog come to stake out his territory Saturday morning, Simon hadn't stuck around long enough to claim her, if indeed that had been his original intent. That morning when Jack joined them in the kitchen, sipping black coffee but bypassing the doughnuts, the conversation was very general and a shade more cordial between the two men than it had been the previous night. Jack happened to mention that he hailed from Pennsylvania, and suddenly Simon was in a hurry to leave. He'd promised to drive his father to Philadelphia for the weekend to visit relatives, and his father was expecting to be picked up within the hour.

To this minute, Anne still didn't know whether she believed Simon's story, or whether he'd simply tired of playing the game of eager suitor and had concocted the tale as an excuse for a quick getaway. Whatever the reason, she hadn't heard from him since.

Not that it mattered, she told herself fiercely. She'd been finished with Simon Tarrant for years, and no matter how attractive he still was, or how much her heart raced whenever he smiled at her, she was not going to succumb to his charms again. He had rejected her once; he wouldn't get a second chance.

A few hours later, she discovered that her resolution was easier made than done. At around one o'clock, Simon telephoned, and predictably, her heart leaped inside her breast just at the sound of his voice.

"Hi. How are you today?"

"Busy." For the last forty minutes she'd been killing time while waiting for the plumber by taking pictures of the cat, but she would've died before admitting that to Simon. "I don't have much time to talk right now," she said ungraciously as she stroked Smoky's back. "I suppose you're calling to tell me what a delightful weekend you had with all your delightful relatives?"

"Sarcasm doesn't become you," Simon retorted mildly.

"Cowardice doesn't become you," Anne threw back at him.

"Is that what you think I am? A coward?" There was a short silence. "Maybe I am, at that," Simon said at last, "but I didn't keep our marriage a secret from Dad because I was afraid of him, and you know it. I was afraid *for* him. Then time just slipped by, and it was too late. Or so it seemed, with you in New York and me living here. But I'll tell him this very day if you want me to."

"Don't be ridiculous! What would be the point in telling anyone now?" Anne countered. "Anyway, I'm not in the mood for this discussion today."

"Neither am I," Simon answered briskly. "I called about dinner tonight."

"Dinner?"

"Yes. I'm working at the hotel today, and I'll still be here by dinnertime. How about driving down to join me this evening? I'll book you a room so you won't have to drive back after dark. I've missed you, Anne." There was a soft, seductive tone to his voice. "I'd really like to be with you tonight."

Simon had done it again. He'd gotten under her skin one more time. Anne didn't know why that should have surprised her. That provocative, suggestive note in his voice hinted at unlimited pleasures to be had in his arms... pleasures she knew for a fact he could deliver.

She shivered at the thought, weakly wishing she could accept his offer. It had been so many years. They were even married, so where was the harm in spending one final night of passion with him?

It was with genuine regret that Anne said, "I'm sorry, Simon. Your invitation sounds tempting, but it's impossible. I've got to return to the city today. I have a morning appointment tomorrow with a magazine editor about a photo layout."

Simon sounded as disappointed as she felt, and that made Anne feel a whole lot better. In spite of her resolve not to let herself care about him again, she was finding it harder and harder to be objective about him.

"Are you planning to come back to Mount Evergreen anytime soon?" Simon asked. "Or are you going away for good?"

Did it really matter to him, or did she just imagine that touch of anxiety and hope in Simon's voice? Anne wished she knew. It would make all the difference.

"Oh, I'll have to come back," she answered as casually as she could. "Probably next week sometime. There's still a lot of sorting out to do, and selling off the contents of the house."

"Have you made up your mind about selling the house to me?"

Anne's heart squeezed. His question certainly didn't sound lover-like. If Simon was still eager to buy the house so as to give her no reason to return to Mount Evergreen, then he obviously didn't want any long-term, not to mention permanent, relationship with her. She supposed his invitation for tonight had been tendered only so that they could satisfy their undeniable physical attraction for each other, nothing more.

"No," she answered finally. "I haven't yet decided what to do about the house." There was no point in telling him that she'd been entertaining the idea of moving into the house to live. For the time being she would keep that to herself.

Anne had a tiny efficiency apartment down near the Village, and it was stuffy after being closed up for over a week. She stashed her suitcase beside the beige upholstered sofa with the parade of colorful pillows that turned into her bed by night and went to open a window. While Smoky explored his new home, Anne tried to convince herself that it felt good to be back. The apartment had always seemed so welcoming whenever she returned from an out-of-town assignment, but today its silence was heavy and depressing. If things had been different, tonight she might have been staying in one of the elegant rooms at the Tarrant Inn Resort Hotel.

And not all alone, either.

Oh, stop it, already! she told herself. There was no sense in feeling sorry for herself. Truth to tell, she was darned lucky that her appointment tomorrow morning had interfered with her instant and instinctive desire to spend tonight with Simon. All he would bring to her was more heartache, and surely she'd already had enough of that. The fact that she'd had to return to the city this evening was the best thing that had happened to her in a long time. It had forced her to be disciplined against the temptation of Simon, even though her heart still traitorously longed to be with him.

Instead of a romantic candlelit dinner for two, Anne bought Chinese for one, came back to the apartment where she pulled on her favorite tattered T-shirt nightie and ate straight from the cartons by the flickering light of the television set. She was too depressed to even call her father to let him know she was back in town.

The following day Anne took care of business. She kept her appointment with the magazine editor and got her assignment. It was one of her favorite women's-magazine editors, who wanted a photo spread of two full pages, plus the magazine cover done with still-life Valentine mementos for the February issue. They agreed to meet soon for lunch and then they parted. Anne went next to her small studio, where she first dealt with her mail, collected messages from her answering machine, returned several important calls and finally set up cameras, lights and props in preparation for a live-model shoot scheduled for eight tomorrow morning.

Toward five o'clock, Anne left her studio and walked the ten blocks to her father's office. It was located in the heart of downtown Manhattan. The elegant marble and glass entrance to the building contrasted starkly with the old and worn red-brick-fronted building where her studio was situated.

WJL Publishing Group was the umbrella corporation for six highly successful magazines—one was a current events newsmagazine; a second, a women's magazine; another, sports. The others were a hobby publication, a children's magazine, and a health and diet periodical. Anne's grandfather had gone into partnership with two other men to establish the newsmagazine, and when it became successful they had gradually expanded by adding two more. Anne's father and the other original partners' heirs had kept the company intact and eventually added three more magazines to the group. Eight years ago Robert Lancaster bought out the other partners and became the sole owner.

Ever since Anne finished college, Robert had been badgering her to join the firm, but she wasn't ready to be swallowed up by her father. She adored him—but she also valued her independence, personally and professionally. However, she did take on a photo assignment for one or another of his magazines from time to time, and she visited the firm so frequently that she was on a first-name basis with everyone on staff.

Rosalind Mead, a tall, painfully thin woman, who covered her graying hair with shocking red, was Robert's longtime secretary. She had a rather sharp and brittle personality that masked a soft heart and a generous soul. Anne couldn't recall a time in her life when Roz hadn't been a part of the picture.

When she saw Anne, she closed a desk drawer with a little thud. "Well . . . fine time for you to show up. It's closing time, your father's out of the office, and now I suppose I'll have to wait here with you until he gets back."

Anyone else might have been put off by this brusque greeting, but Anne remained unruffled. "You don't need to stick around, Roz. I can entertain myself while I wait for

Dad. Do you have a hot date this evening?'' She grinned over the last words.

Roz heaved a sigh. ''Don't I wish! I was just trying to give you a hard time. Sit down, Anne, and fill me in on all your news. You haven't been around here lately. Your dad tells me you've inherited your great-aunt's house up in Mount Evergreen.''

Anne nodded and took a chair.

''My advice to you is to get rid of it quick,'' Roz said. ''The last thing you want is to get stuck with a house in such a dull little place! You'd curl up and die of sheer boredom. Nearly did myself.''

Anne looked at the older woman in surprise. ''You used to live in Mount Evergreen?''

It was Roz's turn to look surprised. ''Sure. I grew up there. I thought you knew that.''

Anne shook her head.

Roz took her chair, then went on. ''Bob and I were classmates. After we grew up and he became co-owner of the *Sentinel,* I became his secretary. Later, when he decided to come to New York and work with his father, I came with him—quite happily, I might add. Give me the city any day!''

Anne was suddenly struck by the possibility that Roz might be able to fill in some gaps for her. ''If you grew up with Dad, then you must've known my mother, as well.''

''Yes,'' Roz acknowledged. ''I did.''

''Was she as beautiful as she looks in her pictures?'' Anne asked wistfully.

''More so,'' Roz replied promptly. Her eyes narrowed as she gazed speculatively at Anne. ''You have her looks, you know...dark hair and eyes. But in your personality and mannerisms, you're more like your father.''

''What was she like? Were you friends?'' Anne asked eagerly. Her conversations with her father about her mother had never been very satisfactory, although she had never understood why. Robert had told Anne that Lorraine had loved her very much, but for some reason he'd never told her many anecdotes about her mother. In many respects, Aunt Rebecca had been more forthcoming about Anne's mother, although she'd never told her anything of real import . . . just a few trivial things . . . that Lorrie had loved fashion and always dressed in the latest styles; that she had hated cooking and hadn't been very good at it; that she'd sometimes played dolls with her young daughter; that she'd had a lovely, almost musical voice and had enjoyed singing Anne to sleep. They'd been nice snippets about a person Anne could not recall, but they were hardly revealing insights to her real character. Now, here was someone else who might be able to enlighten her about her mother.

But a wary distance crept into Roz's manner. "I didn't really know her well, Anne."

"Please," Anne pleaded. "I know so little about her. Just tell me what you do know."

Roz sighed. "It wasn't exactly easy to be friends with Lorrie. She sort of held herself aloof from everyone except Bob. And Joe Tarrant, of course." After a moment, she added thoughtfully, "Like me, she was another misfit in a small town."

Roz's comments only heightened Anne's curiosity about her mother. Why had she been a misfit in Mount Evergreen? Had she held herself aloof from most of her schoolmates, or only Roz? And why? Robert had explained to Anne that Lorrie had been orphaned and had come to Mount Evergreen to be raised by her grandmother. That information had always given Anne a feeling of especially poignant closeness to her mother's memory, because Lorrie herself had died young, leaving her two-year-old daughter without a mother.

Roz had brought up Simon's father's name, and it put Anne in mind of another question. "Roz, do you know why Dad left the *Sentinel?* Why he and Mr. Tarrant ended their partnership?"

The wariness flickered again in Roz's eyes. She hesitated. "I really couldn't say, Anne. Perhaps you'd better ask him that."

Anne could tell by the look in Roz's eyes that she knew the answer to the question, but out of loyalty to her boss, refused to speak. When the outer door opened just at that moment and Robert entered the office, the relief on Roz's face was almost comical.

But Anne wasn't laughing. And indeed she fully intended to ask her father about Joseph Tarrant.

"Why didn't you ever tell me you and Joseph Tarrant were once business partners?" Anne asked her father that very evening. She was having dinner with Robert in his tastefully elegant apartment overlooking Central Park. His housekeeper, Mrs. Gilmartin, had prepared rare roast beef with all the trimmings.

"How'd you happen to pick up that stale bit of news?" Robert asked sharply. He broke his dinner roll in half and began buttering it. "It appears that Roz's tongue has been a bit too busy."

"It wasn't Roz," Anne denied quickly, although Roz had indeed mentioned it to her. "Simon Tarrant told me."

Robert's head jerked up and he stared at Anne in astonishment. "Joe's son? What were you doing talking to him?"

Anne prevaricated. "We just happened to meet while I was staying in Mount Evergreen. He said that you and his father co-owned and operated the *Sentinel* until you sold out to Mr. Tarrant. It must've been before Mother died, because afterward we moved to New York."

Robert studied his plate, avoiding Anne's eyes, but his voice was casual enough when he finally spoke. "I needed a change after your mother died, so I chose to sell my share of the newspaper, join my father here in the city and work on the magazines."

The glib explanation was not entirely true, and Anne challenged it. "That's not the whole story, and we both know it! You and Mr. Tarrant had some sort of quarrel that was serious enough for you both to order Simon and me to stop dating each other years later when we were teenagers! What happened between you, Dad, that made you hate each other and that even drove you from Mount Evergreen? And why have you kept it a secret from me all these years?"

Robert raised his eyebrows at his daughter's harsh, challenging tone. "I never mentioned my relationship with Joe Tarrant because it wasn't any of your business," Robert replied bluntly. "You were only two years old at the time. It's all ancient history now. The past is over and done with, so why rehash it?"

"You can't blame me for wondering," Anne said. "Or Simon. His father's just as stubbornly closemouthed as you are, so naturally we're curious about what it is you're hiding from us!"

"Simon! Simon! You keep dragging his name into the conversation! Don't tell me you started seeing him while you were in Mount Evergreen!" Robert exclaimed.

"All right, I won't."

Anne got the reaction she wanted. Robert scowled and leaned forward, gruffly demanding, "You aren't, are you?"

"Can you give me one good reason why I shouldn't?"

"I can give you plenty!" Robert exploded. "Joe Tarrant is beneath contempt, and any son of his can't be any better. Believe me, you'll be doing yourself the worst turn you possibly can if you get mixed up with a Tarrant!"

Anne could only silently concur, but none of that answered her basic question. She decided to try once more. "Why, Dad? What did Simon's father do to cause you to despise him?"

Robert's eyes glittered with long-suppressed anger. "He took something important that belonged to me," he finally answered grudgingly. "I couldn't forgive him. It proved how contemptible he was. After that, I could never trust him again." He sighed. "So...I got out. And I've never had any regrets. WJL is where I belong, and it's far more challenging than a weekly newspaper could ever hope to be. WJL is where you belong, too, Anne, if only I could convince you."

Robert had adroitly changed the subject and once more he tried to recruit his daughter into the ranks of WJL's staff.

But as usual, Anne wasn't buying. "It's more interesting being a free-lancer. The assignments are more varied than they'd be if I was working for you alone, Dad. As long as I can pay the rent on my studio and keep myself fed and a roof over my head, I prefer to go it alone. At least for a few more years."

"And," Robert added, his eyes twinkling, "you like the feeling of pride in successfully operating a business that's entirely your own."

"Something like that," Anne conceded. "Much like you did when you first went into the newspaper game with Joseph Tarrant rather than going straight to work for Grandpa at WJL."

"So we're back to that. Let's drop the subject of Joe Tarrant, shall we? But yes...it's true. I wanted to prove my worth by going into business for myself and standing on my own two feet. I had accomplished that by the time I joined the WJL Publishing Group, so I guess I can't hold it against you for wanting to do the same.''

"How is it you grew up in Mount Evergreen, Dad, since your father had his business here in the city?"

"My parents chose to raise me there—countryside and fresh air and all that. There was plenty of room at Lancaster House, and Aunt Rebecca wanted the company, so we lived with her. Dad commuted most of the time, but we also had a small apartment here in the city for the times he needed to stay overnight or when Mother and I came to be with him for a few days." Robert sighed and his lips curved into a reminiscent smile. "I must admit Mount Evergreen was a great place to grow up. I loved it as a kid. Because it was so small, we children had immense freedom to roam all over the place. You can't turn a child loose in New York City that way."

"I guess that's why you allowed me to spend so much time there with Aunt Rebecca while I was growing up," Anne speculated. Robert nodded, and Anne went on, "I loved all the times I stayed with her. I always felt as at home with her as I did here with you."

Robert smiled. "She enjoyed mothering you."

"Yes," Anne agreed. "That's why it seems so tragic that she never married and had children of her own. All the same," she added wistfully, "I wish I could have known my own mother."

As always, an odd, inexplicable expression came to Robert's face at the mention of Anne's mother. It was a look that tantalized and baffled her—one of tender affection mixed with what appeared to be a spark of anger, both tempered by a haunting sadness that was heartbreaking to see. At the stricken expression in his eyes, Anne felt a twinge of guilt for having brought up the subject of her mother. Had Robert loved her so deeply that he still grieved to this day, or were the emotions his memories brought forth of an entirely different nature? Whatever his feelings were, Anne's father had never appeared to seriously entertain notions of a second marriage in all these years since her mother died. He had dated many women, even introduced a few of them to his daughter, but as far as she could tell, Robert was content enough with squiring a pretty lady to a party or an opening or a fine restaurant from time to time and leaving it at that. For the first time she wondered fleetingly if her father was ever lonely.

As she had been the past five years since she and Simon had separated.

Anne had so many questions about her father and his life and his marriage to her mother; so many questions about what her mother was really like; so many questions about the partnership he'd once had with Simon's father. But she also had an unhappy conviction that the answers would never be forthcoming.

Late Wednesday afternoon Simon was just reaching for the handle on the door of Anne's studio when a stunningly beautiful redhead opened the door. They nodded pleasantly and the girl asked, "You here to see Anne Lancaster?"

Simon winced inwardly at the use of Anne's maiden name, but that was silly. He'd known all along that she went by the name of Lancaster and not Tarrant. Since it was his own fault, he had nobody to blame but himself.

"Yes," he answered the redhead. "Is she inside?"

The girl nodded. "We just finished shooting."

"Then my timing is perfect, isn't it?"

The redhead nodded and favored him with a brilliant smile before she walked away.

Simon went through a small vestibule and entered a cavernous high-ceilinged room. A couple of dim lights illuminated parts of the room, but other areas were almost completely dark. Klieg lights faced a small raised stage, but they were not on at the moment. Neither was a large fan aimed at the stage.

On stage was a backdrop of a beach scene. Scattered around on the stage floor were beach-type props—a large ball, a blanket, a lounge chair and table with an umbrella, a bottle of suntan lotion, a paperback novel and a soft-drink bottle.

There was no sign of Anne, but toward the back of the room was a closed door with a red light above it. Simon had a suspicion that behind the door was a darkroom and that if he valued his life, he'd better heed the warning light and stay out of it.

While he waited, Simon killed time by wandering around the studio. Now that his eyes had adjusted to the dimness, he was able to make out a number of unrelated objects—a bicycle, an Oriental vase almost as tall as he was, papier-mâché flowers in bright, garish colors, a walking cane, a large box filled with fake jewelry, scarves, ribbons and belts. There were toys, ladies' wigs, a man's fur-lined parka, fake ice cubes.

This was Simon's first visit to Anne's studio and it amazed him that she could extract anything from such a hodgepodge of props, artistically arrange them and come up with a successful photograph, yet he knew full well that she could. He'd often seen her work in various magazines.

From time to time he glanced toward the door at the back of the studio. The red light still glowed. Simon fidgeted.

He wasn't entirely certain what he was even doing here, yet his desire to see Anne again—today—was so strong that he'd given himself the afternoon off from work and driven to the city. He hadn't paused to consider whether he would be welcome. He'd simply come. Now, while he waited for her to come out of the darkroom, Simon entertained doubts. Maybe Anne wouldn't want to see him. Maybe she had a date for the evening. Maybe...

Simon's weekend in Philadelphia with his father and his cousins had been agonizingly long and boring. While the family was engaged in catching up on everybody's news and telling all the children how much they'd grown, Simon had had to field the inevitable questions and comments about his state of bachelorhood and when he was going to do something about it. And all the time, all he could think about was Anne. He was tormented by the thought that if they'd announced to the world that they were married five years ago, and then had lived together openly from day one, he might very well have been sitting in his aunt's living room bouncing his own child on his knee instead of his cousin Shirley's one-year-old-son.

He had reached the stage in life where he wanted children. Simon wanted the sort of settled life with a wife and a family of his own that most of his friends already had.

Most of all, Simon wanted Anne.

At that moment, the red light blinked off and Anne walked out of the darkroom.

"Hello," Simon said.

Anne's head jerked around and she peered intently into the gloom. "Who is it?" she demanded sharply.

"It's me—Simon." He stepped forward into the light.

"Simon! What the blue blazes are *you* doing here? You scared me to death!"

"I didn't mean to," he protested. "I—"

"And anyway, how did you get in? The outside door locks itself. You didn't knock out a window or something, did you?" Now Anne glanced toward the walls as though she expected one of the heavily shrouded windows to be gaping open.

"Hey, calm down!" Simon exclaimed. "Since when have you known me to break and enter?" He stepped closer and touched her hand. Hers trembled slightly, but whether from fright or outrage, he couldn't be sure.

Anne snatched her hand away, sputtering furiously. "You have no right to be lurking in the shadows like that! What're you trying to do... give me a heart attack?"

Simon grabbed her hand again and took the other one, as well. He pulled Anne's quivering body close to his, keeping their hands clasped together between them.

"Hey," he whispered softly. "I'm sorry. Until I heard the alarm in your voice, I didn't realize the studio was so dark you couldn't see me. Or that my presence would disturb you so much." Anne trembled again and Simon released her hands and wrapped his arms around her, pressing her dark head against his chest. He rested his chin on the top of her head and began to smooth her hair with his hand. "I'm sorry," he repeated.

They were silent for some time. Anne remained locked within Simon's arms and neither of them moved. But gradually she began to relax and he was so attuned to her nearness that when she finally gave a soft sigh, he felt it as well as heard it.

"Better now?" he asked gently.

Anne's head bobbed up and down and she tried to step away, but Simon would not let her go. In the dim light that encircled them, he saw a new challenge ignite sparks in her eyes.

"You never did say... how did you get in here, Simon?"

He grinned as he traced Anne's jaw with the back of his index finger. "An exquisitely gorgeous redhead was coming out just as I arrived. She let me in."

"Oh. Liz. She was my model today."

"With that heavy makeup, those long painted fingernails and that to-die-for smile, I assumed as much," Simon commented dryly.

"Ah, so you fell for her, did you?" Anne asked sourly. She tried to pull away from him again, but Simon refused to let her go.

A chuckle welled inside him and he quirked an eyebrow at her. "What? Can it be that you're jealous?"

"Don't be ridiculous," Anne snapped. She tugged her hands but Simon's grip only tightened around her fingers. "Let me go, Simon!"

Simon ignored the demand. "Liz, hmm?" he drawled. "Well, she's certainly a beauty, no doubt about that. She also looks to me to be about sixteen beneath all that eyeshadow and lipstick. A little young for my taste."

"Seventeen," Anne corrected grumpily.

"Ah." Simon pretended to be considering. "Well, now, if only she were eighteen, I might be interested." At the fury he'd stirred up in Anne's eyes, he almost laughed out loud. As it was, he couldn't keep from grinning. In an entirely different voice, he said, "Anyway, here I am. Are you glad to see me?"

"Of course not," Anne groused. "You probably took ten years off my life and gave me gray hair besides. What *are* you doing here?"

Simon's eyebrows rose. "Isn't it obvious? I came to see you. I know it's unfashionably early, but I didn't get any lunch today, and I'm starving. Want to go get something to eat?"

He'd neatly sidestepped her question for the moment; nevertheless, a chummy expression abruptly replaced the stern suspicion in Anne's eyes. "Now that you mention it, I'm hungry, too. Make it Italian, and you've got a deal."

"Deal," Simon replied promptly.

"Just let me finish up a couple of chores first." This time Anne succeeded in extracting herself from Simon's embrace. She walked over to a wall, flipped a light switch, and suddenly the entire studio sprang into view. Mounted on the back wall were examples of Anne's photography that had previously escaped Simon's notice. "What sort of photos did you take of the redhead today?" he asked over his shoulder as he went over to inspect the wall display. He paused before a sharp commercial print of bakeware—various-sized pans filled with appetizing foods. He'd seen the same photograph in numerous magazine advertisements.

"It was a beach scene for a suntan lotion."

"Hmm." Simon was hardly listening. He was now studying a large, sepia-toned photograph of a scantily clad couple locked in a tender embrace as they gazed into each other's eyes. The woman wore a filmy negligee and the man, whose chest was bare, wore only pajama bottoms. The focus was somewhat hazy and dreamlike, giving the scene an enchanting and potent sensuous quality.

"Like?" Anne had come up behind him.

"Uh-huh," Simon murmured. "Very romantic."

"That photo was used in a magazine article dealing with how to achieve greater intimacy with one's partner."

"Aha. I'm all for that," Simon said huskily as he turned slowly toward her. "I came today because I missed you, Annie-girl."

It had been a long, long while since she'd been called that. Only Simon ever had, and the way he'd said it, it was a term of endearment. Anne's throat tightened as their eyes met, and for a timeless moment they were captured within the circle of their exclusive awareness of each other.

Simon's hot gaze swept over Anne. She stood utterly motionless, almost as though she were in a daze. Desire welled up inside him, fierce and insistent. He caught his breath as he drank in her beauty. God, but he loved Anne, from the top of her dark head to the tip of her toes. He'd been insane to think even for a minute that he'd gotten over her.

He stepped nearer to her.

But in that moment, she seemed to awaken from whatever state had paralyzed her. Neatly and deliberately sidestepping him, she moved back toward the stage. With quick, businesslike movements, she dismantled the beach scene, removing all the props, storing the small ones inside a large box and carrying the larger ones to a storage room. The last thing she did was roll up the canvas background photo of sand and sea before she went to a small desk in another corner of the cavernous room, where she opened a drawer and extracted her purse.

"I'm ready to go, if you are," she said in a crisp voice that belied the emotional tension that had sprung up between them. "Let's go eat."

But Anne's pleasure in Simon's company, and his in hers, couldn't be permanently disguised. Over dinner in the small, intimate restaurant they chose, they found themselves smiling and laughing frequently as they talked nonstop. As they filled each other in on their lives, it seemed as if they couldn't close up the chasm of five years apart quickly enough. Each felt a new closeness with the other that neither of them had expected.

When Simon's hand covered hers, Anne felt a tender warmth. When his shimmering blue eyes captured her gaze, the wall she'd erected around her heart began to crumble. It was as though all the years and events that had separated them had only been a long bad dream. Now she was with Simon, where she belonged, and happiness spread through her, warm and thick.

Since the restaurant was only a few blocks from Anne's apartment, they walked there after dinner rather than take a taxi. The evening was sharp and chilly, hinting of winter's approach, and they appreciated their jackets. But the cold fresh air was invigorating and exactly what they needed after the sleep-inducing food and wine.

When they entered Anne's apartment, she flipped on the switch of a lamp. She half turned toward Simon, about to ask if he wanted coffee, but when she saw the look in his eyes, the words stuck in her throat.

Slowly Simon reached for her, and as though she had no choice, no will of her own, Anne went into his arms. It was only as they closed around her that she realized this had been what she'd wanted all along.

His kiss took her breath away. It was fierce, roughly demanding and stirringly exciting. Anne's lips parted beneath Simon's forceful mouth and her senses began to swirl. His arms pressed her closer and closer until nothing separated them but their clothing.

Simon tugged Anne's silky blouse from the waistband of her skirt, his hands inching beneath the fabric and up her rib cage to her breasts. He caressed her for some time before his hands finally slid downward again to work at the zipper of her skirt.

After a moment, he groaned with frustration and lifted his head. "Help me, will you, darling? The zipper seems to be stuck."

His prosaic request brought Anne back to her senses. What was she doing? she asked herself frantically. Had she completely lost her mind?

She was ashamed of herself. It seemed as though at Simon's most casual beckoning, she responded; at his slightest attention, she melted; at his lightest touch, she was ready to make love with him. She was that weak-willed.

It wouldn't do! It simply wouldn't do! Suddenly Anne found the strength to pull her tattered pride around herself like a winter coat against the chill. She broke Simon's embrace, and with as much dignity as she could summon, she said, "You'd better go."

"Go?" Simon rasped. His eyes took on a shocked expression, and then his face became one of a man whose spirit was stricken. "How can you say that? Anne...we want each other. We need each other—we always have. We were just fooling ourselves that we didn't. Let me stay with you tonight. I want to hold you and love you and wake up with you next to me in the morning and—"

"No!" Anne shook her head vigorously. "No! Stop it and go away, Simon!"

"But why, damn it?" Simon grated. Anger had replaced injury.

"Because I've remembered what you said to me one evening in Mount Evergreen. You made it perfectly clear that you considered my presence there an interference in your life and you told me to get out of town. Well, Simon...the same thing applies here. Getting involved with you again would just bring new complications into my life that I don't need. So...I'd appreciate it if you'd leave now."

"Things have changed between us since that night," Simon protested. "We still have feelings for each other and—"

"I won't deny the old spark is still there," Anne conceded with an edge of bitterness in her voice. After all, it was useless to deny the obvious. "But nothing else has changed. Nothing at all." Almost in tears by then, she buried her face in her hands. Her voice was muffled. "I'm not a toy for you to pick up now and then to play with and put down when you're tired of it, Simon! I have feelings, and you've already dealt me enough pain for one lifetime. Now I'm asking you nicely one last time...please...just go away and leave me in peace." She nursed her temple with an unsteady hand and added, "I've got one horrible headache."

Chapter Six

"I told you—the man's name is Lassiter with two *s*'s, not one," Simon declared with exasperation.

"I'm sorry," Simon's secretary, Evelyn Green, said meekly. "I'll redo the letter at once."

"Please do," Simon growled.

As soon as Evelyn had eased out of the office, Simon felt ashamed of himself for snapping at her. He wasn't normally so irritable and impatient with others.

But then, he wasn't normally in such a black mood, either. Anne's rejection of him last night had cut him to the quick, and all day he found himself taking out his frustration on the hotel staff. As well as poor Evelyn, he'd also been surly to a busboy who hadn't been quick enough to clear a breakfast table and to one of the chambermaids whom he'd caught smoking in a public hallway.

After the wonderful evening they'd spent together, Simon frankly hadn't expected Anne to rebuff him. Her rejection had rocked his equilibrium. That afternoon at the playhouse before they'd been interrupted by Anne's friend Jack, she had clearly desired him, and Simon knew perfectly well that the message in her eyes yesterday in her studio had definitely been one of yearning. Never before had he had trouble reading Anne's emotions, and he was positive he hadn't been mistaken this time, either. She had definitely wanted him. He would stake his life on that.

She'd even admitted there was still a spark between them, but at the last moment, she'd changed her mind. Simon had been disappointed, angry, and deeply wounded. He still was. The ache filled his chest.

But so did the blazing fury he felt over her inexplicable about-face.

Maybe it was high time he seriously considered getting a divorce instead of just mulling it over as he'd been doing for the past five years. Actually it was ridiculous that he hadn't gotten a divorce years ago. He had given a lot of thought to it after they had first agreed to a separation. Anne had forced him to make a choice by insisting he announce their marriage or call it quits. Because Simon had believed his father still wasn't strong enough to withstand the shock of such news, he'd refused. He hadn't really believed Anne would walk away from him altogether, but she had. That was when he first thought of consulting a divorce attorney. But somehow the days and weeks just merged into months and years, and he'd never done anything about it. It hadn't seemed urgent. He'd known he could always initiate proceedings at a later date if he chose, or that one day Anne herself might put the process into motion.

In the end, neither of them had done anything toward making a final break to their marriage. Now, here he was five years later, still legally married, still entranced by Anne, still wanting his wife as much as ever and despising himself for it.

His telephone jangled. It was Evelyn. "Mrs. Mason calling from London, sir."

Simon's morose mood vanished in a flash. He pressed the illuminated button and with warm affection in his voice, said, "Hiya, kiddo. How're you doing?"

"Couldn't be better," Caroline Tarrant Mason replied cheerily. "And how's my big brother?"

"Fair," Simon allowed. Brushing off the subject of himself, he asked, "How are Neal and the boys?" Caroline and her British physician husband had too young sons, ages three and one.

"They're fine. Neal says hello. Nanny and I just got the little loves to sleep... we hope for the rest of the night. How's Daddy? I've called several times and each time there was no answer."

"He's okay as far as I know. I talked with him on the phone yesterday. He's probably just out taking his daily walk and Mrs. Potter's gone to the grocery or something." Mrs. Potter was their father's housekeeper. "Now don't start imagining things and getting yourself all upset," Simon admonished. "Dad's fine. He does get out of the house, you know."

Caroline sighed. "Oh, I know that. It's just that usually when I call and he's napping or gone out somewhere, I at least get Mrs. Potter. I can't help being anxious about him. It's so hard living this far away from him. And from you, too."

Simon chuckled. "I wondered if I rated a mention on your list. If it's any comfort, we miss you a little bit, too, you know."

There was a tiny sigh, then Caroline altered her tone and ordered sternly, "So, fill me in on the latest gossip."

"You know there's never any gossip in Mount Evergreen to report," he teased.

"Ha! Mount Evergreen's always a hotbed of gossip," Caroline retorted. "Everybody knows everybody else's business. So tell me, has Joanne decided who'll give her away at her wedding on Saturday?"

Joanne Charles was one of Caroline's closest childhood friends and by mail and phone, Caroline had been keeping up with the progress of the wedding preparations from Joanne herself and a couple of other girlfriends.

Simon chuckled. "I hear she's keeping it a secret until the big day, but most everybody's betting on her stepfather. My money's on her dad, though. You know the old saying, blood's thicker than water."

"You've got a point," Caroline conceded. She added wistfully, "I sure wish I could be there."

"I wish you could, too. All your old friends miss you. By the way, Bob Lawson was in town last week and he says hello. Oh, and guess who else was here and asked about you?"

"Another classmate like Bob?"

"Nope. It was Anne."

"Anne Lancaster?"

No. Anne Tarrant, Simon automatically corrected in his mind, but of course he couldn't say so.

"Yes," he replied. "When Miss Rebecca died, Anne spent several days at Lancaster House."

"I'd love to see her again," Caroline said warmly. "It's been years since we've seen each other, although we do still write occasionally. You know, back when we were all in high school, you two were so crazy about each other, all our friends thought you'd eventually get married."

Much as he loved and trusted his sister, Simon had never been able to bring himself to confide in her about his secret marriage to Anne. He still couldn't. Instead, he asked, "Have you forgotten how both Dad and her father forbade us to date each other?"

"Nope." Caroline laughed. "I also haven't forgotten how the two of you ignored that order. Anne even followed you to college at Albany after she graduated the following year. To tell you the truth, I believed you'd eventually get married, too. What happened?"

"We just...gradually drew apart," Simon answered carefully. "Anyway, there still would've been that unexplained objection from our fathers. Carrie, did you know that Dad and Anne's father once co-owned the *Sentinel?*"

"No. Really? When?"

"When we were all just babies. I found some papers at the office relating to their partnership. I asked Dad about it and he readily admitted he and Robert Lancaster had once been business partners, but he wouldn't tell me why they split up. I was hoping you might have heard something about it when you were a kid."

"Sorry, I haven't a clue. This is all news to me, too. It would be mighty interesting to know what happened between them, though, wouldn't it? I'll bet it would explain why Dad didn't want you dating Anne."

"I'm certain of it."

They chatted a few more minutes, mostly about the antics of Simon's nephews, and then hung up.

His sister's call had cheered him immensely. It had come just when he'd most needed something to distract him from his gloomy mood.

The country club was abuzz with guests for the wedding reception and Anne was pleased she had come. Although she'd never actually been a year-round resident of Mount Evergreen, through the years she'd gotten to know many of its citizens and she enjoyed meeting old acquaintances.

She'd almost skipped the wedding, knowing Simon was likely to attend, but she'd told herself it would be petty of her to stay away. Since Anne had always been good friends with Joanne Charles, she had chosen to come despite the danger of bumping into Simon. Fortunately there'd been no sign of him and that fact, plus a few bracing sips of champagne, had helped her relax.

Anne had a fistful of assignments that involved shooting stills, and impulsively and despite Simon's proximity, she'd decided to spend a few weeks at Lancaster House. She could use the playhouse as her studio and there was a spacious pantry inside the house that would make an ideal darkroom. When she'd arrived from the city last night, the car had brimmed with cameras, lighting equipment and props.

She was comfortable with the notion of working and living at Lancaster House because she considered it nothing more than a trial. She still had her studio and apartment in the city and she'd be working there when she had to use live models, so it wasn't as though she was burning her bridges behind her. If she found she didn't like living in the huge old house alone, or that the small-town atmosphere was too stifling, it would be easy enough to pack up and head back to New York for good.

As for Simon, he should be no problem. Surely even in a tiny community like Mount Evergreen, they could manage to avoid each other most of the time.

Anne turned away from a group of people with whom she'd been chatting. Only a couple of feet away, a familiar-looking man stood gazing quizzically at her.

Anne's fingers froze around the stem of her champagne glass. Her throat was dry and her heart thudded with alarm.

"Anne. It *is* Anne Lancaster, isn't it?"

It had been years since she'd seen him. His hair was graying and thinner now, and his mouth pulled slightly to one side, something it had not done before his stroke. But his eyes, piercing and deep blue, were still as keenly intelligent as she remembered. He wore a dark conservative business suit and he leaned heavily on a cane.

Although Anne had half expected to see Simon here today, she hadn't anticipated meeting his father. This was the man who stood between her and Simon, and seeing him jolted her. When she'd been small and had visited Caroline at her home, Joseph Tarrant had been good to Anne, treating her as kindly as he'd treated any other of his children's friends. Anne had felt entirely at ease around him and had taken it for granted that her friend's father liked and accepted her. Years later, it had been a terrible shock when he'd forbidden Simon to date her.

"Yes, Mr. Tarrant." Anne found her voice at last. "I'm Anne."

Tarrant hobbled nearer and solemnly regarded her for an uncomfortable length of time.

"You certainly grew up into a beauty," he said at last. "You're the image of your mother, God rest her soul." He paused and a smile softened his features. "Lorrie was so lovely and so lively. I was always very fond of her. Now, here you are—a charming, grown-up replica of her."

Anne found the statement utterly fascinating—that Joseph Tarrant had been fond of her mother, since he'd apparently come to hate her father. She wished she had the nerve to ask him about his relationship with her parents, but she didn't.

"Thank you," she said, responding politely to his surprising compliment. "How are you doing, Mr. Tarrant?"

"Fine. You may have heard about my stroke." Anne nodded, and Mr. Tarrant went on, "It's been a long, uphill battle, but I've recovered to a large extent. Of course I'm not going to be running any races—" he indicated his cane "—but I get around pretty well. My housekeeper and Simon do a good job of keeping me up and going."

"I'm glad to hear it," Anne murmured.

"Did you know Caroline's living in London?" he asked her.

"Yes, sir. We keep up with each other through Christmas cards and birthday letters, but it's been years since we've seen each other. I'd really enjoy a nice long visit with her and a chance to meet her husband and sons."

An unexpected sparkle flickered in the older man's eyes. "Yes, the boys! They're sturdy, energetic little fellows and they keep Caroline busy."

Anne smiled. "I can imagine. You must be very proud of them."

Tarrant nodded. "Yes. I am. Well...maybe you and Caroline can get together next time she comes home."

"I hope so. That would be very nice," Anne murmured.

An uncomfortable silence fell. They seemed to have run out of their pitifully skimpy supply of conversational tidbits. But then Mr. Tarrant startled Anne by asking, "How is Bob?"

"Dad's well," she replied after she got over the shock of his inquiring. "Working hard."

"Still running his magazines?"

"Yes, sir."

"How many does he have now?"

"Six. They keep him very busy."

Simon's father nodded. "He's got some of the best magazines on the stands. But then, I'm not surprised at his success. Bob was always sharp when it came to business." Mr. Tarrant paused, tilted his head slightly and squinted at Anne. "He never remarried, did he?"

"No, sir, he didn't."

"I guess he never got over your mother." He sighed softly. "I'd always hoped..."

Whatever Joseph Tarrant had hoped concerning Robert Lancaster was destined to remain unspoken. At that moment, another man interrupted them as he paused to exchange pleasantries with Simon's father. Anne was both frustrated and pleased. She'd wanted Mr. Tarrant to finish what he'd been saying about her father, but at the same time she realized with relief that the newcomer's arrival could facilitate her escape.

At the first break in the conversation, Anne began, "If you two will excuse me, I..."

She got no further. Suddenly she strongly sensed that someone was staring at her. Hard. The back of her neck prickled. Anne broke off what she was saying and turned sharply.

Simon was approaching, and at the expression in his eyes, she caught her breath. There was a blue flame in his gaze. She could actually feel the intense heat of it. But whether the fire was anger because she was with his father, or was something else entirely, Anne couldn't fathom.

"Simon, look who's here!" Joseph Tarrant exclaimed. "George Worth from Albany. And I'm sure you remember Caroline's old friend, Anne Lancaster."

Simon shifted his gaze from Anne to the middle-aged man standing next to his father. He made himself concentrate on greeting the man politely, but as soon as they shook hands and he could decently make the break, he returned his attention to Anne.

His heart was thudding hard and Simon only hoped nobody could hear it. It had begun racing the instant he spotted Anne. When he'd realized she was talking with his father, he was so shocked he couldn't even move for a time. What had they been talking about? And why was Anne here tonight in the first place?

She looked extraordinarily beautiful this evening. Her dark hair fluffed becomingly about her face and she wore a silk dress the shade of a gold autumn leaf. The delicate fabric skimmed lightly over her shapely frame. It stretched gently across to the tips of her breasts and fell smoothly around her hips, finally to flare gracefully around her slender legs. On her feet were elegant gold-toned high-heeled sandals.

Simon was so mesmerized by her loveliness that he was slow to become conscious of the expectant gazes of the others as they waited for him to greet Anne. When he realized they were staring, he took possession of himself at once, inhaled sharply, and mustered a polite smile.

"Hello, Anne."

"Hello, Simon." She sounded somewhat breathless. Suddenly Anne thrust her hand toward him, taking him by surprise.

Simon considered shaking hands with her for his father's benefit, but he quickly ruled it out. He couldn't bring himself to shake hands with his own wife. Instead, he took her hand in both of his and kept it there as he said, "I hadn't expected to see you here."

Anne's hand, captured between his, was cold, and now it quivered and fluttered like a sparrow's wing. Her eyes were overbright and her smile was definitely strained. She, too, was acutely conscious of their audience.

"I hope it's not an unwelcome surprise," she said with an uncertain smile.

"On the contrary," Simon assured her hastily. "It's wonderful to see you again."

"Thanks," Anne replied casually. "It's good to see you, too."

A combo had been hired to play at the reception, but for the past fifteen minutes the musicians had been taking a break. Now, suddenly they were back with a romantic slow tune.

Simon's gaze flickered in an appeal to Anne. "Care to dance?" he asked.

"That would be nice." Anne turned briefly toward Simon's father. "I'm glad to see you looking so well, Mr.

Tarrant. Give Caroline my love next time you talk with her."

"I will." Joseph Tarrant smiled. "It was good seeing you, Anne."

She and Mr. Worth exchanged brief "nice-to-meet-you's" and then Simon was tugging at her hand, urging her toward the dance floor.

He swept her into his arms and for a long time they were silent, each of them lost in the sweet sensation of touching and moving in unison.

Finally Simon murmured, "I never expected to see you here."

"You already said that," she reminded him.

"I know. But that was in public, in front of Dad. Now I'd like an explanation. What are you doing here?"

Anne raised her eyebrows. "The same thing you are, I presume...celebrating a friend's wedding. Next to Caroline, I was closer to Joanne than any other girl in town."

"How did it come about that you were talking with Dad? And what were you talking about?"

"Ah...worried, are you?" she taunted. "Don't be. I didn't give away any secrets. You know, I'm amazed you asked me to dance in front of your father. It might upset him, you know."

Simon whirled her around. "Maybe it's high time I began considering my own feelings instead of my father's."

Anne's heart skipped a beat at the intense light in his eyes. Careful, she told herself. It would be fatally easy to fall into the same quagmire she'd been in years ago...where she did all the giving, while Simon did all the taking. She couldn't allow that to happen again.

She wasn't a gullible young girl anymore. No, now she was a woman, full-grown and mature, and while her very natural grown-up desires and needs were drawbacks in this situation, she could not afford to weakly give in to those longings. She was still in love with Simon, but Anne had enough sense to know that the worst possible thing she could do for herself was to lose control, even for a single moment, and allow that love to be expressed.

Yet she couldn't quite steady her heartbeat, couldn't quite regulate her breathing. If only he wouldn't hold her quite so close; if only she didn't feel quite so warm and cherished wrapped within his arms. And if only he'd stop looking at her that way... as though she were the most precious jewel that ever existed.

They danced together how many more times... four or five? Anne lost track. Finally thirst won out over the next number the combo played and Simon led Anne toward the refreshment table.

They stood together, sipping champagne punch, with eyes only for each other, when a young woman approached.

"Simon! Sweetheart, it's me!"

Simon turned, and appeared startled. "Edie." Suddenly her arms were around his neck and she gave him a big kiss on the lips. Simon felt his face begin to redden as he tried to pull away.

When he was finally able to disentangle himself from her arms, Simon turned back to Anne. He cringed inwardly at the suddenly distant and withdrawn expression on her face. With a sinking spirit, he knew that everything he'd won during the past hour was now lost.

Dully he introduced the two. Then he attempted a hasty explanation. "Edie and I became friends about three years ago when she came here to live with her sister. Last year she moved to Florida. How do you like Tampa, Edie?"

"Come dance with me and I'll fill you in," Edie answered coyly. She pulled Simon's arm, urging him toward the dance floor while over her shoulder she tossed Anne a breezy, "You don't mind if I borrow Simon for a while, do you?"

Simon felt helplessly trapped. If he refused to dance with Edie, he would seem churlish and rude, but if he went with her, the magical time with Anne would be at an end.

"Hurry." Edie tugged harder on his arm. "They're playing one of our favorite songs. Remember?"

One of our favorite songs.

Old friend, indeed! Anne thought indignantly as she watched Simon head for the dance floor with the other woman. Obviously there'd been more to their relationship than mere friendship. Mere friends didn't plant X-rated kisses on another friend's lips; and a mere friend didn't have an *our song*.

For Anne, the evening was spoiled, but she had too much pride to slink away. That would be telling Simon loud and clear that she cared too much to stay. Even so, she couldn't bring herself to watch him dance away from her with his arms around another woman. Anne turned her back on the dance floor and became inordinately fascinated by a chafing dish full of Swedish meatballs on the refreshment table.

She was saved when one of the groomsmen asked her to dance, and for the remainder of the time she stayed at the reception, Anne was never alone.

Neither was Simon. Either he was strongly taken by his old friend, or Edie was the domineering type who refused to let him get away. The pair was still together every time Anne happened to catch a glimpse of them in the crowded room.

Anne mentally kicked herself for letting it get to her. A few evenings ago, she'd rejected Simon when he'd asked to stay the night with her. Now he was hanging out with another woman, and by the look of it, hugely enjoying himself, and she had no right to feel jealous and hurt. No right at all. One just couldn't have it both ways.

Yet she *was* jealous and hurt. Seeing Simon dancing with another woman, even as she herself danced with another man, hurt so badly Anne had to fight back the tears.

When all was said and done, Simon was still her husband.

As her dance partner swung her around, Anne lost sight of Simon and his companion, but another face swam into view...a face she singled out from the cluster of people milling around the sidelines of the dance floor.

Joseph Tarrant.

His eyes were on her and there was a questioning, pensive expression in his gaze.

Anne tensed. She hoped Mr. Tarrant hadn't caught her looking at his son as Simon had danced past with Edie. She feared her eyes may have given her away, and it would never do for Joseph Tarrant to suspect how she felt about Simon, or to question the nature of their relationship.

The time for telling Joseph Tarrant the truth about their marriage was long since past. No good whatsoever could come of his finding out now.

Chapter Seven

"It was good seeing you again, Edie," Simon said. "I enjoyed our afternoon." He was standing with her on the steps of her sister's home.

It was late Sunday afternoon and they had just returned from playing a round of golf.

"I enjoyed it, too," Edie replied. She smiled wistfully at him. "If you ever get to Florida..."

She left the remainder of the sentence dangling and Simon picked it up, nodding. "I'll look you up. Take care and have a safe trip back." Simon leaned forward and gave her a chaste kiss on the cheek, backing away quickly before she could try to turn the kiss into something more intimate.

When he drove away a few moments later, it was without regret. When Edie had first been divorced, she'd come to Mount Evergreen to stay with her married sister and had gone to work at city hall. Before long, Simon and Edie were seeing each other on a regular basis. But while they had enjoyed each other's company, there'd never been any question of their having a lasting relationship. She'd been wounded by her recent divorce, and he'd been secretly suffering over the demise of his own marriage. Neither of them had wanted anything from the other at the time except understanding, acceptance and companionship.

This time, though, Simon had sensed that things could be different . . . that Edie would've liked to have picked up where they had left off, which was as very warm friends, and then take the next step. That heated kiss with which she'd greeted him last night had been somewhat of a shock. Today, in subtle ways, she'd let him know that she would welcome his advances if he wanted to extend any.

He liked Edie, genuinely liked her a lot. She was a very nice person, and she'd become a special friend at a time when he'd been feeling very lonely and adrift. But liking wasn't love.

Love was . . . well, it wasn't Anne, either, he thought irritably. But the fact remained that the feelings he had for her were in a class of their own. Anne got to him, and without even seeming to be at all aware of her effect on him, she tripped his heart and sent his senses spiraling. He was, quite simply, crazy for her. Always had been.

He craved Anne the way another man might crave a drink or a cigarette; whenever a yearning for her set in, all Simon could think about was Anne. He could smell her sweet flowery scent, feel her incredibly soft skin, imagine her long dark hair threading silkily between his fingers; he could taste her lips on his; he would shiver with pleasure at the thought of her soft feminine body pressed to the hardness of his.

Okay, he said to himself as he drove toward his father's house, maybe he was addicted to Anne, to her beauty and appeal and the memory of how things once were between them when they were at their best, but what he felt definitely wasn't love. You simply didn't stay in love with somebody you hadn't been with, seen or heard from in five years. It wasn't possible. That old saw about absence making the heart grow fonder was just a bunch of stuff and nonsense. He wasn't fonder at all...it was just that his mind and body betrayed his logic by wanting her every time he saw her or thought about her, and that was all. And that was lust, not love.

Not that these assurances comforted him at all. Even though he was positive that he wasn't in love with Anne anymore, that didn't make it any easier for Simon to fall in love with someone else. If he could, he'd have done so long before Anne had come back on the scene. Either Edie or Suzanne would've made a great candidate. They were both lovely, warmhearted women. So why couldn't he have conveniently fallen in love with one of them?

Simon arrived at his father's house, parked in the driveway and, taking two at a time, dashed up the porch steps.

Mrs. Potter admitted him to the house. The aroma of ham permeated the front hall as Simon stepped inside.

"Mmm, smells great."

"I hope you brought your appetite with you," she stated as she closed the door behind him.

"That I did," he assured her.

Mrs. Potter nodded in the direction of the living room. "Your father's in there reading the newspaper."

"Thanks," Simon replied, moving toward the door. "Hi, Dad," he greeted as he entered the room.

The thick Sunday edition of the *The New York Times* lay scattered on the floor around Joseph Tarrant's recliner. He folded the section he'd been reading and dropped it atop one of the untidy piles of paper on the floor. "Afternoon, son," he said affably. "Where's Edie? I thought I made it clear to you she was welcome to come to dinner, too."

"She had other plans for the evening." Simon didn't know whether Edie had plans or not. The simple truth was that he hadn't extended his father's invitation to her, not wanting to mislead her in anyway.

"Mmm. It would've been nice to have a pretty face across the table from me for a change."

"What?" Simon teased. "Mine's not pretty enough to suit you?"

Joe grinned. "Unfortunately you've got a mug almost as ugly as your old man's."

"So is it any wonder we're two men alone for dinner this evening?" Simon said, laughing.

Joe chuckled. "When you put it that way, it's no wonder at all. How was your golf game this afternoon?"

"Let's just say I've had better days and leave it at that."

Joe laughed heartily. "A woman stomped all over you, huh?"

"Actually, no. Bad as my game was, Edie's was even worse."

"I suppose she'll be demanding a rematch, then."

Simon grinned. When Edie had stayed in Mount Evergreen, she'd soon become notorious with her friends for her love of sports and for an even greater fondness for winning. She was one gal who had never subscribed to the theory that a girl should lose at games with a boy so as not to damage his ego. In fact, whenever she could, she tromped a guy hard and laughed in his face while she did it.

"No rematch this time," he replied. "She heads back to Florida tomorrow."

Joe's eyes narrowed. "That right? You two used to have a pretty serious thing going, I thought. I even wondered if you were going to get married. What happened there, son? Why'd you let her go off way down there to Florida?"

Simon shrugged. "We just weren't right for each other, that's all. It was nice seeing her again, but I won't miss her when she leaves."

A silence fell between them for a little while, and then the elder Tarrant asked, "What about that young lady from Albany you told me you've been seeing lately? Sue? Susan, isn't it? When are you going to bring her around for me to meet?"

"Suzanne?" Simon shook his head. "That's over, too."

"And what was wrong with her, may I ask?"

"Nothing. The trouble was me. I just wasn't committed to building a relationship." On the defensive now, he asked somewhat sharply, "Why all these questions about my love life, Dad? You don't usually probe."

Joe shrugged. "I suppose I was just wondering why you're so hard to please when it comes to women. Here you are pushing thirty, but you don't show any signs of being ready to settle down, marry and start a family."

"Since when is that a prerequisite for reaching one's thirtieth birthday?" Simon asked irritably.

"Marriage may not be a prerequisite at your age, but it's the usual thing to do by now. Why is it so difficult for you to find a woman to suit you? It is because of Anne Lancaster?"

Simon felt as though the wind had been knocked out of him. Since when had his father become psychic, he wondered.

"Why do you ask that?" he asked cautiously, deliberately not answering Joe's question.

"I saw the way the two of you were looking at each other last night, and I remembered you were interested in her way back when you were teenagers and she used to come to Mount Evergreen to visit Miss Rebecca. Surely you haven't been carrying a torch for her all these years!"

Simon hesitated. He was tempted to unload the whole truth now that his father had asked. But in the end, he couldn't bring himself to do it. No good would come of it. A confession now would only open up a lot of old wounds. After raising his hopes and expectations that night at her apartment in New York, Anne had abruptly, without explanation, frozen him out. Last night she'd thawed again, seeming genuinely happy to see him. But then Edie had arrived and Anne had immediately turned to ice once more, reminding him that whatever feelings still existed between them were destined to remain unfulfilled. No . . . there was no sense burdening his father with the truth now. All the same, Joseph's observant gaze had not missed the desire in Simon and Anne's eyes when they'd first seen each other yesterday evening, and now Simon had to make some sort of a response.

"It's long past the time when there might have been the possibility of things working out between Anne Lancaster and me," Simon said at last. "You forbade me to take her to my senior prom or to go out with her at all, remember?"

Joseph remained silent for a long moment, and then he sighed heavily. "It was for the best, son, believe me. But I didn't stop you from going out with her because I had anything against Anne."

"Oh, that makes me feel a whole lot better," Simon said sharply. "As I'm sure it would Anne if you told her."

"You don't have to be sarcastic," his father chided mildly. "I did the right thing then, although I know it seemed unreasonable to you."

"I still find it unreasonable. Was it because of the bad blood between you and Anne's father?"

Joe nodded silently.

"Well... what was it?" Simon asked. "What happened between you that caused you to end your business partnership and step between Anne and me?"

"I really don't feel like talking about it," Joe stated firmly.

"I think I have a right to know," Simon maintained stubbornly.

Joseph's eyebrows raised. "Do you? Why? Just because you're an adult now?" He shook his head. "That doesn't justify your prying into my private business."

"Doesn't the fact that you ordered me not to have anything to do with Anne justify my wanting to know?"

His father appeared to consider the matter, but at last, he shook his head. "I can't see how talking about the trouble between Bob Lancaster and me would help anything," he said at last. With an air of firmly closing the subject, Joseph picked up the TV remote control and said in a completely different tone of voice, "Let's watch a little football until Mrs. Potter calls us to dinner."

Sunday evening after a light dinner and a long hot bath, Anne, wearing pj's and wrapped in a thick robe against the evening chill, plumped up the pillows on her bed, stretched out and leaned back against them.

She'd spent a busy day cleaning out closets and drawers, sorting, discarding and packing away family belongings. It was work she'd been dreading and putting off, but today had seemed like the right moment to get into something that would keep her busy for a long period of time. She'd needed any distraction she could find to keep her from thinking about Simon.

Simon and that other woman. Edie.

Jealousy simmered inside her as she thought once again of that kiss the other woman had greeted him with, of how he'd grinned sheepishly and, as though he had no will of his own, had followed her to the dance floor.

It hurt to remember how he'd remained with the other woman the rest of the evening, dancing and laughing and looking as though he were having the time of his life. That Anne had been quite a popular and sought-after dance partner herself had been gratifying to her bruised ego, but it hadn't alleviated the pain she'd felt over Simon's desertion. It was as if he'd totally forgotten Anne once Edie had arrived.

Anne shook her head, reminding herself not to think about Simon. Three musty books lay next to her on the bed and now she picked one up and opened it. They were her father's school yearbooks, which she had discovered in the back of one of the closets she'd cleaned out today. She decided to browse through it while she lay down to rest for a few minutes.

It was too bad Robert wasn't here himself so that he could tell her the stories behind the pictures…what brought about the tug-of-war contest between the French Club and the Science Club, for instance. Or what Old Baldy Prichart, the algebra teacher, did to correct a young and, no doubt, rowdy Bobby Lancaster, alias "Bucky," that seemed the subject of so many hand-scrawled notations on the flyleaves. She supposed she'd find out eventually since she intended to take the yearbooks to her father when she returned to the city, but for tonight she simply had to speculate about what trouble Bucky Lancaster had brought upon himself.

No doubt about it, Anne told herself with a smile as she flipped through the yearbook covering her father's junior year, he'd been a strikingly good-looking boy with a cheerfully cocky smile, mischievous eyes and thick black hair. He must've been the object of quite a few young girls' daydreams.

Anne put aside the junior yearbook and picked up the one covering Robert's senior year. Like she'd done with the previous one, she paused first to read the witty and not so witty scribblings on the flyleaves before she flipped through the pages.

One of the notations that caught her eye was written by "Cotton" Tarrant, and after several "Always remember..." anecdotes that were meaningless to Anne, it was signed Best Buddies Forever.

Some best buddies, Anne thought wistfully. The two boys' friendship had not been able to withstand the test of time. Whatever had happened between them had ended an apparently very special friendship that had begun at an early age and had even extended to co-owning a business as adults. It was a shame that such a long-standing friendship had not endured. Now they were two aging men afflicted with a festering bitterness toward each other.

Anne flipped a few pages and soon located the picture of her father in his cap and gown amongst all the other photographs of solemn, black-clad seniors. Again, she thought he looked quite handsome.

In the center of the yearbook there were at least half a dozen pages with informal snapshots of various members of the student body of Mount Evergreen High School. Anne paused to study each one; her patience paid off when she found a picture of her father. There were three people in the photo and Anne readily recognized two of them. She had never seen a picture of a youthful Joseph Tarrant before, but even without the caption identifying him, Anne would have figured out who he was easily enough. As for the other two, she needed no help in recognizing them as the people who would one day become her parents—Robert Lancaster and Lorraine Riley.

They looked like any ordinary fun-loving teens one would find on a high school campus, past or present. The grinning boys had their arms draped across each other's shoulders while the slender dark-haired girl wedged between them smiled prettily for the camera. The caption beneath read: *When The Best Man Wins, Who Will It Be, Cotton Or Bucky?*

Well, Anne had the answer to that. Her father had obviously won. Anne herself was living proof of it.

Had there really been a rivalry between the two boys for Lorrie's affections as the caption suggested? Anne frowned, considering the question. Many a friendship had ended as a result of a love triangle. Could that have been what had caused them to fall out with each other—that they were both pursuing Lorraine Riley?

But surely romantic jealousy couldn't have been the reason. Her father and Joseph Tarrant had remained friends until years later; they even became business partners. By then, both of them were married and had families. Simon was almost two years older than she, and Robert had told Anne she'd been two when her mother died in an automobile accident. It had been several months after the tragedy that Robert had taken his small daughter and moved to New York City. No, Anne concluded, whatever the cause of the two men's quarrel, it was most unlikely that it was connected to her mother.

It was dark and chilly Monday evening when Simon drove toward Lancaster House. A cold front had scooted down from Canada that morning bringing frosty air and the possibility of light snowfall during the night. The exquisitely beautiful Indian summer seemed to have come to an abrupt end.

Even as he approached the house, Simon had a strong impulse to drive by without stopping. His reason for wanting to see Anne tonight was not a pleasant one, and he hadn't entirely convinced himself that he was doing the right thing.

Tonight Simon intended to tell Anne that he wanted a divorce. The sooner the better.

His father's comments yesterday had struck a nerve. It was about time he was married and settled down. It was exactly what he wanted for himself, but as long as he was still married—yet not married—to Anne, he couldn't do a thing about it. Moreover, he had a growing conviction that he never would meet the right woman as long as it was in the back of his mind that he was still tied, however tenuously, to Anne. It was time, well past time, to get on with his life, and only by getting a divorce and freeing himself from Anne once and for all would that be possible.

Still, it was a hard thing to bring himself to do. He had loved her so much and for so long. A part of him always would. Anne had been the first love of his youth, and although it was unlikely she would be his last, the tenderest place in his heart would always be reserved for her alone.

Simon was tense as he rang the doorbell a few minutes later. He was still needled with doubts about what he was about to do. At the same time another part of him stoutly insisted he had to do this for both their sakes.

When Anne opened the door, she was silhouetted by the glow of firelight from the hearth in the old-fashioned parlor behind her. She was already dressed for bed in pink pajamas topped by a deep rose-colored velour robe. The robe was tied at the waist, starkly outlining her curves against the light.

"Were you about to go to bed?" Simon asked in surprise. It was only nine-thirty. It seemed awfully early for Anne to be wanting to sleep.

She shook her head. "Not yet. But I'm really not fit company for anyone tonight, Simon," she said with a ragged edge to her voice.

All thoughts of why he had come fled. Something had seriously distressed Anne. It was clear by her broken voice and moist eyes that she'd been crying.

Simon didn't pause to think. He simply stepped across the threshold, kicked the door closed behind him and pulled Anne into his arms.

"What is it?" he asked with sharp concern. "Has something happened to your father?"

"No." Anne shook her head and replied in a quavering voice, "It's Smoky."

"What about him?" Simon knew Smoky was Miss Rebecca's cat. He also knew that Anne had always had a great affection for the animal.

"He...he's dead," Anne cried.

"What happened? Did he wander into the street and get hit by a car or was he poisoned or what?"

Anne dashed her hand against her wet cheek, mopping away fresh tears. "The vet said it was old age and a variety of health problems. *I* think he died grieving for Aunt Rebecca. When I woke up this morning I found him semiconscious. He couldn't stand up, much less eat, so I took him to the vet, but there was nothing he could do to save him."

"I'm sorry, Annie-girl," Simon whispered gently. "I know you loved Smoky, but maybe it's for the best. As you say, he was probably pining terribly for Miss Rebecca. With her gone, nothing in his world was the same anymore. Besides that, he *was* old...how old, actually?"

He reached into a back pocket and produced a snowy white handkerchief that he presented to Anne.

"He was eleven, almost twelve." Anne accepted the handkerchief, blew her nose and immediately felt better. She inhaled deeply and sighed. "I know you're right. Smoky loved me ever since the day I found him, but not like he loved Aunt Rebecca. He seemed content enough with me as long as we were here in Lancaster House, but when I took him with me to my apartment in the city, he was utterly lost and miserable. I'd already begun to worry about what to do with him the next time I have an out-of-town assignment. I was worried that if I locked him up in a kennel, it would kill him for sure."

"So he took the best way out for all concerned," Simon assured her. "He went with his own dignity intact and secure in his own home."

"You're right, of course." Anne managed a wobbly smile. "Thanks for pointing that out, Simon. I'm glad you're here."

Anne's warmth turned Simon to mush. He smiled back. "I'm glad I was able to help."

Anne gently broke the circle of Simon's arms, asking as she did, "Why are you here, by the way?"

Simon had practically forgotten his original intentions. Now it came rushing back over him like an avalanche crashing down a mountainside. And he knew that he could not bring up the subject of a divorce. Not now. Not yet. Not tonight.

"I just...came," he said lamely. Then, with earnestness, he added, "I know you must be wondering about Edie. I admit I did date her for a while when she first moved to Mount Evergreen, but there was never anything serious between us."

"Oh, sure," Anne said dryly. "These days that's how all old friends greet each other, is it?"

Simon grinned. "Figured that kiss would make you jealous, if anything would."

Anne turned away. "I was not jealous," she maintained.

"No?" Simon stepped toward her, but she remained rigidly turned away from him.

"No!" she snapped.

Simon brushed Anne's hair away from the nape of her neck, bent his head and lightly trailed his lips across her sensitive skin. "Are you sure you weren't jealous?"

"Positive!"

Simon blew his warm breath against the place where he'd just put a kiss. "Are you very, very sure you weren't jealous?" he quizzed in a low, seductive growl. "I don't mind telling you, I was jealous as hell when it was the other way around...when your pal Jack came here, remember? I don't appreciate another man trespassing on my territory."

"I'm not your territory," Anne said, trying to sound harsh. "And you're not mine. Not anymore. Therefore," she declared as though the matter was settled once and for all, "I was *not* jealous! Do you understand me? *Not* jealous!"

"Oh, I understand you perfectly," Simon murmured. His warm lips moved against her skin, and he felt her shiver. "Why are you trembling?" he taunted softly.

"It's a cold evening," Anne had the presence of mind to point out. "I got chilled when I opened the door for you."

"Sure," Simon murmured in frank disbelief. "Sure. Whatever you say."

He'd traveled around her so that his lips were now at the pulse point of her throat while his hands dipped inside her robe and loose-hanging pajama top.

Anne quivered again when Simon's fingers lightly caressed her midsection as they slowly inched upward. Her mouth went dry and suddenly she was having a painful time breathing normally.

When one hand curved around her breast, the sweet sensation of it made Anne fear she was lost.

"Tell me," Simon's husky voice dared her, "that you don't want to make love with me right now."

Now Anne knew for certain that she was lost. But she valiantly tried to save herself anyway.

"I don't want to make love with you…now or ever!" she declared.

"I believe you, honey," Simon replied with faint mockery as he scooped her up into his arms. "I believe you."

Chapter Eight

Simon carried Anne into the parlor and set her on her feet in front of the fireplace. He pulled a couple of throw pillows and an afghan off the sofa and dropped them onto the carpet before tugging Anne down to the floor.

The blazing fire warmed them. Almost immediately Anne was wrapped snugly in Simon's arms while he kissed her again—soundly, roughly and most satisfyingly. His touch heated her more than the flames leaping in the hearth. It was all so achingly familiar, so potently exciting. Oh, but she had missed him!

Simon's hand threaded through Anne's hair and his fingers tightened around the nape of her neck. Her lips were parted slightly, tempting and inviting. He claimed them, his lips playing hungrily over hers.

His tongue sought and found hers and it was as though a bolt of electricity shot through them both at the intimate contact. The intensity of their kiss deepened, rendering them both breathless and shaken.

Anne's fingers crawled up Simon's chest and clutched his shoulders as though she needed to hold on to him to steady herself. Simon half turned her and pressed her downward until her head lay cushioned on one of the pillows he'd snatched from the sofa. Then he eased down himself, slowly stretching out full-length beside her.

"Now," he said, teasing her with a slightly wicked smile, "tell me again that you don't want me to make love to you."

"I don't! I don't!"

But Simon saw the playful gleam in her eyes. "Little liar," he whispered amiably. His fingers traced the V of her collar opening.

"I never liked making love with you," Anne insisted.

One thick dark blond eyebrow rose. "Never?"

Anne shook her head and declared emphatically, "Never!"

Simon tilted his head and looked at her with the skepticism her statement deserved. "Not even that night we were celebrating my finals being over? We spent half the evening in the bathtub trying to find each other under all the bubbles after you dumped an entire bottle of bubble bath into the water."

Anne giggled. "Well…that night *was* exceptional, wasn't it?"

"I'll say! Nothing could put out your fire that night—not even when the bathwater turned cold."

"Mmm." She closed her eyes. "You were pretty hot-blooded yourself. Practically *all* night, as I recall. What time did you finally let me go to sleep, anyway?"

"Sometime during the wee hours." Simon's thumb was sliding lazily back and forth over her throat. He leaned forward to drop a kiss there before his hand moved to the front of her pajama top and he began unfastening the buttons. "But as *I* recall, it was *you* who refused to let *me* go to sleep! You only permitted it, finally, when my batteries just plain ran down and I simply couldn't go anymore."

Anne giggled again. Then, slowly, piece by piece, her clothing came off as Simon's hands expertly stripped away every impediment.

Despite the chilly evening, by the time Simon had undressed her completely, Anne's skin was flushed the color of a very ripe peach; whether it was from the heat of the fire or because Simon was caressing her body, she wasn't sure.

She was sure about the tingles, however. Tingles were rippling all through her as Simon leisurely stroked her bare skin—her shoulders, her arms, the curving line of her waist and hip, and pausing longest over her sensitive breasts. His touch churned up deep sensations that had long been suppressed.

"Still don't want me, eh?" Simon challenged.

"Not one bit," she assured him. "Except...well... g-r-r-r-r!" Anne suddenly became the aggressor, a tigress, with Simon her hapless victim. She began to nibble at his earlobe while her fingers manipulated the buttons on his shirt.

When the shirt was open, she pressed both her hands to his bare chest, pushing him back so that she could sit up. She pressed him down to the pillow and bent over him. Her fingers slid languorously across his broad chest, sometimes disappearing beneath the dark gold hair that wound downward from his throat to his belly button. Not content, she began raining kisses over his bare skin while her fingers insinuated themselves beneath the waistband of his slacks.

Simon sucked in a sharp breath. Anne had turned the tables on him, but good. She no longer lay beneath him, quivering and vulnerable. Now it was the other way around. Somehow through the years, he'd managed to forget just how earthshaking, just how dangerous and exciting her touch could be—and that with him still half-dressed! But how he had managed to forget anything about Anne he couldn't imagine, since she always could set him off as easily as lightning igniting a fire in a drought-stricken forest. A powerful ache spread through his loins and he caught his lower lip between his teeth as he struggled to endure the delicious torture Anne's tongue was now inflicting on him.

When the tips of her breasts brushed lightly against his chest, Simon inhaled even more painfully. Anne's soft pliable flesh, feather-light, grazing his, teasing and tantalizing, heated his blood and stirred his loins even more strongly. She was so lush, so beautiful, so desirable . . . and she was his—his! he thought exultantly.

His arms wrapped around her, pulling her down on top of him. One hand caressed her curvaceous hips, then slid to the small of her back before traveling downward again. Next he reasserted himself, flipping her onto her back once more, filling his hands with the breathtaking fullness of her breasts. He bent his head and began to tease them with his mouth.

Simon's breathing was shallow and uneven when his eyes finally met Anne's. Hers were midnight black, dreamy and unfocused, while her lips were rosy and tender, just begging to be kissed again.

Simon did so promptly, then nuzzled her neck while Anne's hands slid into his hair.

"Ah, Annie-girl, I don't know how I've managed to do without you all these years," he murmured. "I've missed you so much!"

"Oh, Simon, no more than I've missed you," she whispered.

Simon drew back slightly in order to look into her eyes. "Ah, Anne, this is so good," he sighed.

"No," she contradicted. "It's not."

Simon went still and stared blankly at her. "It's not?"

The twinkle was suddenly there in her eyes again. "Well, you're still so formally attired, while I'm so...er... informal, shall we say? One of us is too dressed up and doesn't fit in at this party, and it's not me!"

Laughter erupted from deep in Simon's throat. He pulled himself out of Anne's arms and with quick dispatch, sent his shoes and socks sailing across the room. Then he got to his feet and just as speedily shed his slacks and briefs.

Anne gasped softly. Simon, naked, was a magnificent sight—so strong and virile. Wanton desire streaked through her, sizzling the blood in her veins. His masculinity was wildly exciting to her senses, and when he lowered his head to gaze down at her, her heart skipped a beat. She opened her arms wide and held them out to him.

Simon came down, kneeling over her, and by the passion smoldering in his eyes, Anne was certain he was about to take her. She couldn't have been more mistaken.

Instead, he began a thorough erotic assault on her. Pinning her hands at her sides, he made her his love prisoner, beginning his exquisite torture at the top of her head, and despite her pleas, refused to cease his sweet cruelty until he reached the tips of her toes.

Anne lay still, helpless to stop him, while his lips traveled slowly down her body. The potent power of the kisses left a wide path of destruction in the form of highly aroused flesh rendered achingly unsatisfied.

By the time he reached her toes, Anne was a throbbing mass of desperate need. If he didn't take her soon, she would lose all reason!

But still Simon postponed her fulfillment and took his pleasure at an agonizingly slow pace. He parted her legs and bent to kiss her tender, sensitive inner thigh. Anne arched her back and moaned.

"Not so fast, greedy," he murmured as he bent over her.

He was so close, and her feminine core cried out her urgent need of him.

Finally at the exact instant she'd decided she simply could endure the torture no longer, Simon kissed her deeply, giving her a tiny measure of the release she needed. Then he raised up and moved over her. She eagerly received him. Hearts, minds and spirits soared as they gave themselves to each other totally and with complete abandon.

Anne awoke the following morning to a feeling of blissful contentment and the most wonderful warmth. And why not? she thought, smiling into the shadowy early-morning darkness. Beside her in the bed Simon slept, his soft rhythmic breathing a tender morning song in her ears. Her body was curled and cradled into the curve of his body, and they lay as snug as a pair of spoons nestling together. Simon's arm lay across her hip, while one of his lanky legs stretched out over hers. She felt incredibly sheltered and cherished.

Last night had been incomparably glorious. For a long time, they'd lain drowsily in each other's arms, covered by the soft wool afghan, enjoying the afterglow of their lovemaking and the physical warmth of the fire in the grate while they recouped their energies.

After they'd been contentedly silent for some time, Simon had rolled onto his side, smiled into Anne's eyes and said in a low voice, "I want to stay the night with you." She had responded, "I wouldn't want it any other way."

Once they'd gone upstairs to bed, like that long-ago night after Simon's finals, they again made love until the wee hours.

Having been deprived of a full night's sleep, Anne was surprised she didn't feel tired, especially since it was so early in the morning. Instead she felt exhilarated, energized, totally alive.

From behind her right ear, she heard Simon yawn. Simultaneously his hand, draped limply over her hip, moved up to caress her breast. He kissed her shoulder and murmured, "'Morning, sweetheart."

"Good morning." Anne turned in his arms so that they were facing each other. They both smiled, as though they couldn't help themselves, and she asked, "How'd you know I was awake?"

"Your back."

"My back?"

"Uh-huh." Simon's face was flushed with sleep and an overnight growth of beard stubbled his jaw and chin. His pale hair was tousled, giving him the endearing innocent look of a small boy. But when his hand slid down to stroke her backside, Anne was swiftly reminded that she was dealing with an experienced man.

"When you first wake up," he explained, "you always stiffen your back and then you arch it before you yawn or stretch."

"Do I?" Anne asked in amazement.

Simon nodded. "Yep. You also make a little noise...sort of a snort."

"I don't!" Anne hotly denied.

Simon grinned. "Okay, that part might be an embellishment, but the rest is true. While we were living together you always did that little number with your back when you woke up, and you still do. It's nice to know some things never change." He leaned forward to kiss the tip of her nose. "Brr. Your nose is cold."

"I know. So is the bedroom. I'd better go turn on the heat. Want some coffee?"

"I'd rather have you," he murmured while his hands still explored her warm body beneath the covers, "but I've just spotted the time on your alarm clock, and I'd better get a move on. I've got an eight o'clock staff meeting at the hotel." Simon ran a hand over his raspy beard. "I don't suppose you've got a spare razor I can use?"

Anne nodded. "There are some disposable razors on the middle shelf of the bathroom cupboard." She turned from him then, scooted out of bed, shivered and quickly covered her nudity with her robe, as much to shield herself from the hot gaze she felt coming from behind her as to protect herself from the chilly morning air.

Downstairs, while she made coffee and put breakfast sausage into a skillet, Anne could hear water gurgling through the ancient bathroom pipes as Simon took a shower.

By the time he joined her, freshly showered, shaved and fully dressed, Anne had managed to find a moment to scoot into the downstairs bathroom, throw water on her face and run a brush through her hair. She didn't look impeccable by any means, and she still wore the robe with nothing under it, but at least she felt a little more presentable.

Breakfast was a pleasant interlude. The food was delicious and Simon and Anne were both inclined to keep the conversation casual and light.

When he'd finished his second cup of coffee, Simon reluctantly put down his napkin and thrust his chair away from the table.

Anne rose, too, as Simon came around the table to her.

He placed his hands gently on her arms. "We need to talk and decide what to do about us."

Anne nodded mutely.

"Tonight," he suggested. "I'll come back tonight and we'll talk."

Anne nodded again. As he drew her into his arms, she asked, "Why did you come in the first place, Simon? Last night, I mean." It had only just occurred to her that he hadn't told her.

Simon sighed. "Last night I was going to tell you I wanted a divorce."

"A—a divorce?" Anne's voice was barely above a whisper.

"But I couldn't go through with it after I found you in tears."

There was a long, frozen silence before Anne gasped, "So instead of following through with your original plan, you decided to have one last fling with me when you found me with my defenses down! What a cruel thing to do... taking advantage of me that way!"

Simon was caught off guard by her reaction. "It wasn't like that."

She jerked away from his hands as though his very touch was poison. "Of course it was like that! You just admitted it! Well, Simon, since we've had our *talk* now, there's no need for you to return tonight. I concur with you one hundred percent. Get your divorce, by all means—it'll be the best thing that ever happened to me!"

"Anne, you don't mean this," Simon said, his voice choked. "Give me a chance to explain."

"What's to explain?" she cried. "I understood perfectly. Get out, Simon, and this time, stay out of my life!"

Simon sighed. "I hate to leave you so upset."

"I'll only be more upset if you don't go!"

Simon studied Anne's pale, pinched face for another moment. There was a forbidding expression simmering in her dark eyes, a hostile jut to her chin. By trying to force an explanation now, he'd only be aggravating the whole sorry situation.

"All right," he said quietly. "I'll go for now. But I'll be back tonight after work. Then we're going to sit down and thrash out everything once and for all."

Before she could frame a retort, he was already gone.

As soon as she heard Simon's car backing out of the driveway, Anne became a frenzied whirlwind. She cleaned the breakfast dishes in record time and even swept and damp-mopped the kitchen floor before heading upstairs.

In the bedroom she stripped the bed and remade it with fresh sheets that would not bear the imprint of Simon's body nor carry the faintest hint of his masculine scent.

When the bed was made, Anne went into the bathroom, stripped off her robe and stepped into the shower.

She soaped her body vigorously, twisting and turning to allow the water to rinse away Simon's every caress, every kiss, every touch. And as she shampooed her hair, she wished there were also a way to wash him from her thoughts and scour him from her mind.

Simon had betrayed her... taken base advantage of her when she'd been in low spirits and was highly vulnerable. Anne stopped fighting the scalding tears that burned her throat and eyes and simply allowed them to flow, letting them mingle with the flow of warm water from the shower.

A terrible weight seemed to be pressing down on her heart. Last night she'd been so moved by Simon's passion that she'd forgotten herself, let down her guard and responded to him with the truth of her heart. She still loved him as much as she ever had, and she had freely given herself to him with that love, but Simon had paid her back by cheapening her feelings for him. He'd come to tell her he wanted to divorce her, yet he'd made love with her and even slept all night with her in his arms. Anne felt horribly used.

It was time she faced the unpalatable truth—she'd never meant as much to Simon as he had to her. Never. She'd loved him with all of herself... heart, mind, soul, body. Simon had loved her, too, enough to marry her. But in the end, she had been an inconvenient problem... and expendable.

Obviously she still was.

Anne had never wished Simon's father any harm, but all along she'd felt the secrecy surrounding her and Simon's marriage was dishonest and wrong. If Simon had genuinely loved her, he would have found a way to tell his father the truth. But he hadn't—not five years ago and not now.

Simon wanted to return tonight, but it seemed to Anne that all that needed to be said between them already had been said. He wanted a divorce; she had assented. Now it was over. Done. *Finis.*

She felt there was no point in even seeing each other again. It would only bring more pain. If Simon did show up tonight, Anne was determined he wouldn't find her there.

Anne finished her shower and dressed, then took her suitcase from the closet and began packing.

When she reached the city around midday, Anne went directly to the studio. She soon discovered she'd left one of her favorite cameras at Lancaster House. That meant a trip back to Mount Evergreen sometime soon to retrieve it. She also had to finish sorting through Aunt Rebecca's possessions.

Her brief experiment with living in Lancaster House was at an end. No matter how much she loved the old house and enjoyed the slow pace of village life, she knew she couldn't bear to live in such proximity to Simon. She'd always have to be on guard against running into him and she realized now she simply couldn't live that way. It had been foolish to even entertain the notion.

Anne was thoroughly exhausted by the time she reached her apartment that evening. She'd buried herself in work at the studio, experimentally arranging and shooting a bottle of perfume against various backdrops, from rich black velvet and bits of silk and lace to a poster-sized puffy-clouded sky.

Afterward she developed the film, and to her disgust, she didn't like a single shot. Tomorrow she'd have to start from scratch. The perfume was an expensive new fragrance that would be launched in time for Valentine Day sales and Anne didn't have a lot of time to play around with ideas for the photo setting. She needed to come up with a winning picture to show the advertising agency by the end of the week.

Tired, despondent and discouraged, Anne climbed into bed at eleven o'clock, but she felt far from sleepy. Bedtime tonight was so starkly different from last night. Tonight she was alone.

To distract herself, she picked up her great-aunt's journal from the lamp table next to the bed and read Rebecca's accounts of her own despair and unhappiness as she and Douglas Tarrant hid their love from their families. What she read only intensified Anne's despondency.

She soon put the journal aside and switched off the light. But as she lay in the darkness and thoughts of Simon came to torture her, sleep was farther away than ever.

Simon stared at the dark windows in mute frustration. It would be pointless to get out of the car and go to the door. Anne was clearly not at Lancaster House. The place had a forlorn, abandoned air.

She hadn't been here last night, either, when he'd stopped by. Simon knew with unshakable certainty that Anne had returned to New York, probably with only one purpose in mind—avoiding him.

He drove away and headed for his apartment. It was too late to follow her tonight, but tomorrow he would go after her. Simon was not going to allow Anne to simply walk away from him a second time.

The following morning he packed a change of clothes in a small bag and stowed it in the trunk of the car before going to the *Sentinel.* He put in a couple of hours of work there and left instructions and telephoned orders for the hotel staff at the Tarrant Inn. He would, he told them all, be back in a couple of days.

Simon finally escaped from his office at about eleven o'clock and headed straight toward the outskirts of town. His spirits alternated between high—because he'd soon be seeing Anne—and low—because it was entirely possible that she might not give him the time of day.

My wife. Simon clenched his fist and slammed it against the steering wheel. *And by heaven, she's going to remain just that!*

That business about his wanting a divorce had been nonsense. He'd been trying to convey that to Anne, but she'd flown off the handle and hadn't let him explain. Once he caught up with her, Simon was determined to make her listen whether she wanted to or not.

The night they had spent together had reminded him just how exciting life could be with Anne. Lovemaking with her was a torrid, exhilarating experience. She made him glad he was a man, and not for a single moment did she allow him to forget that she was all woman!

It had been a terrible mistake to ever let her get away from him in the first place.

Simon adored Anne, but he loved his father, too, and he'd been unwilling to do anything to jeopardize his life. While Joseph would never be one hundred percent healthy again, he'd recuperated remarkably well, and now, as Simon pondered the matter, he believed that his father's heart was more than strong enough to withstand the news of his son's marriage to the daughter of his former friend. Always supposing, a small doubting voice whispered, that Anne forgave him, returned to him and gave him a reason to announce their marriage.

Near the edge of town was the pride of Mount Evergreen—a whitewashed, tall-steepled, two-hundred-and-ten-year-old church. Simon's mother had seen to it that he and Caroline attended Sunday school there while they were growing up. Nowadays Simon rarely went to services, but he was still quite fond of the church and he sent a donation every month. He also generally found at least one Saturday morning each month to provide his own physical labor—or that of his hotel maintenance man or groundskeeper—to work around the church, whether it might be to repair the altar steps, add a fresh coat of paint to the vestibule, mow the grass or mulch the flower beds. It was a standing joke between Simon and Reverend Howard that the only way the minister could get Simon inside the church was if Simon had a hammer or a paintbrush in his hands.

One of the few traffic lights in Mount Evergreen was at the intersection just before reaching the church, which was on the right. The light turned red and Simon obediently stopped. While he waited for the light to change, he gazed at the churchyard and the shower of autumn leaves fluttering from the towering trees. He made a mental note to send Brewster, his handyman at the hotel, to the church with the leaf blower next week.

In the next instant, Simon was literally seeing stars, although it was broad daylight. His car leaped from the street and up onto the grassy edges of the church property, but Simon was helpless to stop it. His head fell forward, then jerked backward as his whole body was violently jolted.

For a few moments, he was disoriented and didn't know what had happened. Suddenly the door was pulled open and a man bent to peer inside. "Are you all right?" he asked.

Simon nodded and excruciating pain shot through him. He raised a hand to rub his neck. "I'm not sure," he admitted. "What happened?"

"You got rear-ended. Can you stand? Here...lean on me."

The driver of the car that had failed to stop for the light and had run into Simon from behind was unhurt. Simon was taken to his doctor's office while his car was towed to a garage. The other driver's car had smashed into the left rear tire of Simon's vehicle and his car was now undrivable. As for his own condition, Simon was suffering from whiplash and an absolute demon of a headache.

The doctor gave Simon some medication for the pain and advised him to go home and rest for a few days. Since he no longer had a car, he called Mary, his secretary at the *Sentinel,* to pick him up at the doctor's office and drive him home.

There he did exactly as the doctor prescribed—he took a pain pill and crawled gratefully into bed. He groaned as he shifted and turned several times, trying to find a comfortable position for his aching and bruised body; at this point he wished Anne had never come back to Mount Evergreen in the first place. All she'd brought him since her return was heartache and frustration. As for today, he thought grumpily, if he hadn't been on his way to see her, he wouldn't have been involved in that accident, and he wouldn't be in all this pain right now!

Somehow he derived a perverse satisfaction from laying the blame for all his misery on Anne.

Chapter Nine

During the following week, Anne kept on the go, slowing down only very late at night when falling into bed was an absolute necessity insisted upon by her exhausted body. She spent long hard hours working at the studio as well as dealing with clients. Her evening schedule was almost as rigorous as her daytime activities—aerobics classes, dining with friends or her father, the volunteer work she did one night a week at the hospital. When she finally did go home late at night, she found things to do around the apartment at the oddest hours. One night she washed her windows at one o'clock in the morning; on another sleepless night, at two in the morning she started baking a spice cake for her elderly widowed neighbor. Yet another night found her doing her weekly ironing while she watched a late, late, late movie on television.

It was consulting that divorce attorney that had sent her into such a tizzy. Anne had decided that since Simon wanted a divorce, he should have one as soon as it could be arranged. But since in over five years' time he'd been no better than she at starting the ball rolling, she would do it herself.

She had assured herself that visiting an attorney was just another mundane business matter and that it would be painless. After all, she wasn't visiting the dentist! But she'd been wrong. It had been very painful indeed to discuss her next-to-nothing marriage; it had hurt badly when the attorney had questioned her about joint property assets and she'd had to convince him that she wanted absolutely nothing from Simon except her freedom; and it had wounded something very deep, very fundamental within her soul when she'd finally signed the papers that would officially begin the process of divorce from the only man she'd ever loved.

Perhaps the only man she ever would love.

By the time the interview was over, Anne had felt almost crazy; it hadn't helped that immediately following it, she'd had a lunch date with her father. All through the meal Anne had been easily distracted and inattentive.

Robert had realized something was wrong, but when he'd inquired, Anne had put him off with vague murmurings about a heavy workload ahead of her. She longed to confide in someone, but clearly that someone couldn't be her father.

It was a relief when, the following Monday, Anne, along with several others associated with her father's woman's magazine, *Woman's Life Today*, boarded a plane for Denver. They were to spend a week there shooting a series of photos for a fashion layout. They were also planning to do a photo story on a family residing near Denver who'd experienced a miraculous escape from death following the crash of their private plane while flying over the Rocky Mountains. Everyone on the magazine crew was looking forward to doing the story. It would make a wonderful, upbeat feature.

Anne had worked a number of times with Jane Cassidy, the editor of *Woman's Life Today,* and they had become close personal friends as well as business associates. Jane was a couple of years older than Anne and, since her divorce three years ago, now claimed to be married to her job. Anne's father had told her privately that he hoped Jane never remarried, because since she'd become single, she'd been the best editor he'd ever had on any of his magazines.

As the plane took off and climbed, Jane's face drained of color and she gripped the armrests fiercely while her teeth ground into her lower lip. Anne knew better than to speak to her at this point, so she waited until the plane finally leveled off into a smooth horizontal position.

"You okay now?"

"Not really," Jane admitted. "You know, this job would be perfect if I didn't have to do so much traveling by plane. I've tried to convince Bob that it would make much more sense for me to stay at the office running things while my assistant went on these trips, but will he listen to me?"

Anne laughed. It was an old argument that needed no response. "Tell me what you've been up to lately. We haven't talked in ages."

"That's because you were holed up in that little burg somewhere upstate," Jane groused. "Or have you finally come to your senses and moved back to the city?"

Anne glanced at the puffy clouds outside her window. "I guess I've moved back," she replied. "I came back a week ago."

"About died of boredom there, did you?"

Anne shook her head. "I'm never bored at Mount Evergreen. Or at least not often. I've always loved it there."

"Then why'd you come back?" Jane asked. "Because of the long commute?"

"Nope. The commute didn't bother me, either, because I didn't have to do it every day."

"Then why?" Jane persisted.

Unable to hide her anguish, Anne merely looked at her friend. Jane was a perceptive person, and after gazing into Anne's sorrowful brown eyes for a long moment, she grimaced and stated flatly, "It's a man. Some lousy, good-for-nothing man."

Anne smiled feebly. "Why do you say that?"

"What else would put that expression in your eyes?" Jane snapped. "I'm an expert on the subject of being hurt by a man. So give already... who's the bum and what did he do to you?"

Anne hesitated. She and Simon had told no one about their marriage. Their friends at college had simply assumed they chose to live together the way so many couples did those days, and Anne and Simon had never considered it necessary to offer explanations to anyone.

But now, after all these years, after so much heartache, Anne felt a desperate need to confide in someone. The pain she carried was too heavy, and she needed an unbiased perspective. Mostly she just needed a friend.

Jane was neither shocked nor particularly sympathetic about Anne's deep dark secret. Instead, she was prosaically Jane, analyzing the situation as it was presented to her, sizing up Simon from Anne's description of him, as well as assessing Anne's own personality and motives. She did it with the cool calculation she used when considering a story idea for her magazine.

"Let me get this straight," she said when Anne had finished pouring out her heart. "You sneaked around to date this Mr. Wonderful, aided and abetted by his faultless judgment. Then you married him in secret and kept that fact hidden from the whole world until this very day as though it were something dirty or criminal. You actually agreed to live hidden away on the dark side of his life while Mr. Right shuttled back and forth between you and his family after his father became ill, until you finally got fed up and walked out. Are those the facts?''

''Well, more or less.'' Anne managed a wry smile. ''You make me sound like a first-class dunce.''

''What's first-class about being a dunce?'' Jane shot back. ''And I used to think you were so bright!'' They both laughed, Jane sharply, Anne feebly. Then Jane asked, ''And you never told Bob about your marriage, either?''

Anne shook her head. ''Since Dad had also forbidden me to date Simon, he would have disapproved of our marriage as much as Simon's father did. I was willing to brave his displeasure for the sake of living my marriage openly, but as long as it remained a secret from Simon's family, there didn't seem to be any reason to tell mine. So I never told Dad or Aunt Rebecca. And now that I've filed for divorce, there won't be any reason for Dad to know.''

''Maybe you should've had a baby,'' Jane mused. ''That would've forced everything out into the open. It's pretty hard to hide a baby.''

Anne would have adored having Simon's baby. A pang of regret for what would never be rolled over her. ''I guess it's best that didn't happen. I'm not sure even that would've made Simon tell his father about us.''

''Well, if you want to know what I think, you're better off without him. I can sympathize with his not wanting to bomb his father with that news at the time he had the stroke, but later?'' Jane shook her head. ''Any man who doesn't want to be open about his marriage doesn't deserve a wife or her love.''

''Thanks.'' Anne whispered softly. ''I agree. I just wish . . .'' She broke off.

Jane reached over and patted her hand. "I know," she replied gently. "You just wish you weren't still in love with the guy."

"Exactly." Anne sighed again.

"That's a tough one," Jane admitted. "I'm only now beginning to get over the stinker I was married to. All I can tell you is to give it time."

"How much time?" Anne asked wryly. "Until a few weeks ago I hadn't seen him in five years."

"I'd forgotten that. Poor Anne! You're really a hopeless case, aren't you? Ah, here come the stewardesses with refreshments," Jane said. "Let me buy you a drink and we'll toast to freedom from rotten marriages."

Rotten or no, the end of a marriage seemed to Anne a pathetic reason to celebrate. Besides, it was far too early to drink anything other than coffee or juice.

When they arrived in Denver, the group from *Woman's Life Today* rented two cars and drove to their hotel. The magazine crew, in addition to Anne and Jane Cassidy, consisted of three fashion models, a wardrobe manager, a hairstylist who also doubled as a makeup artist, and two strong young men who would assist with carrying and setting up lighting equipment and hauling the heavy wardrobe trunks that contained the clothes that would be modeled. That first afternoon was spent settling into the hotel and, for Jane, Anne and the two men, Hank and Barry, going with a local guide to look over the location for their fashion shoot.

It was a private ranch with a breathtaking view of the Rocky Mountains. Next spring's lacy fashions would be modeled against the backdrop of snow-peaked mountains, rustic barns, wagon wheels, fence posts and fields of placid, grazing cattle. Indoor shots would contrast elegant dresses with rugged stone fireplaces, colorful Indian blankets, woven baskets and rawhide leather chairs. Since this was a large working ranch, there would be the added attraction of the fall roundup, complete with horses, blue-jeaned ranch hands, and early-morning camp fires. The magazine crew huddled to consult one another about sunrise and lighting angles, which colored dresses showed up best against which background, and the composition of the scenes. Although Anne was the only photographer on assignment and was accustomed to working alone and making all her own creative decisions, every shot of the current project would be the result of team effort. It offered an interesting challenge, in addition to the human interest story they'd be doing. Anne was grateful that she would be so busy during the coming week.

Busy was what she needed most, anything that would demand all her thoughts and attention and would consume all her energy; anything that would keep her mind off Simon and the utter finality of divorce.

That evening, although the members of the magazine crew dined together, nobody lingered over dinner. It had been a long day and everyone was tired and more than glad to make it an early night.

Anne treated herself to a long, relaxing soak in a hot bath. After sliding into a nightgown, she turned on the TV. There seemed to be nothing on that she wanted to watch, so after a few moments of channel-flipping, she settled on the tail end of a detective show. Anne fluffed up the pillows, got into bed and found herself not only wide awake and not the slightest bit interested in the television show, but bored and desperately lonely.

She had brought along one of Aunt Rebecca's journals and now Anne climbed out of bed once more to dig inside her carry-on flight bag until she found it. This was journal number seven, and she hadn't yet found time to even open it. Journal number six had ended with Rebecca's high school graduation.

Sometimes Anne felt ashamed and voyeuristic peeking
into the pages of her aunt's life, yet she found she could not
stop herself. There were so many ironic similarities with
Anne's own life. In addition, she was sincerely fascinated
by the thoughts, ideals and daily activities of a young lady
living around the turn of the century.

Much of what she read this evening was dull, however,
and no more engaging than the detective show she still eyed
periodically. There were accounts of volunteer church-work
and afternoon teas and weddings Rebecca attended.

Anne yawned and started to close the book, but then it
suddenly became more interesting.

It was spring, 1917, and there was mention of several local young men who had joined the army and expected to be
shipped to Europe now that the United States had joined
the Allies in their war against the Kaiser. Heading the list
of names of the local young men who had joined the army
was Douglas Tarrant. Rebecca and the other young ladies
in town immediately had set to work collecting linens to
turn into bandages and procuring yarn for knitting scarves,
socks and gloves to send to the soldiers before winter came.

Suddenly Anne's attention was riveted on the journal and
she could scarcely believe what she was reading.

*The past few days have been the most glorious—and
the most agonizing—of my life. Douglas was on leave
before shipping out and I met him secretly in New York
City, where we were married. My parents thought that
I was spending a few days at a girlfriend's home. I hate
having deceived them, but what else was to be done by
either Douglas or myself? Our fathers still hate each
other and telling them we had married would only
bring forth their wrath. Douglas didn't want to leave
me subject to their condemnation alone after he went
away, and the little remaining time we had to spend*

*together was far too precious to be marred with anger
and recriminations. Selfishly we wanted it to be filled
only with our love and our joy in each other. We will
tell our families only when Douglas is home once more
and we can finally begin our life together as man and
wife.*

*He left today for France, and I am bereft! Like so
many other of our country's finest young men, he is
being sent into battle. How my heart cries as I think of
it! Oh, God, please bring him back safely to me!*

*I touch my beautiful new gold wedding band and it
draws me closer to my dear husband in spirit and I can
feel his love surround me like warm golden sunlight.
But I can only wear my ring in the privacy of my bedroom. During the day I must hide it away carefully, so
that Papa and Mama won't see it.*

*If only I could tell them the truth! If only I could be
open with Douglas's family! I could both give and receive comfort during this anxious time, but as it is, I'm
isolated and alone with my fears.*

Anne closed the journal and stared unseeingly at a car chase
scene on television. She was stunned to learn that Rebecca
Lancaster and Douglas Tarrant had been secretly married,
just as she and Simon were all these years later! It was
downright spooky!

The passage she'd just read explained the wedding band
Anne had inherited along with Aunt Rebecca's other jewelry. It had been Rebecca's own, a treasure she was never to
wear in public, because Douglas Tarrant was killed during
the war. All these years people had believed she was a
spinster, and all the time Rebecca had kept her secret locked
in her heart, revealing it only within the confidential pages
of her journal.

Anne picked up her own handbag from beside the bed and opened it. From the inner zipper pocket she took a knotted handkerchief. Slowly she unwrapped the object inside the linen and gazed at it through a rainbow haze of tears.

It was her own gold wedding band—the simple ring Simon had so tenderly placed on her finger five years ago. For some ridiculous reason she'd never had the heart to tuck it away in a jewelry box and forget it; instead, she'd always carried it with her. It had been a long time since she'd looked at it.

Her heart ached as she thought of Simon and their failed marriage, but at least she could be glad of one thing: Unlike Aunt Rebecca, she hadn't lost Simon in the slaughter of war, in the finality of death. As hard as it was to deal with the reality and pain of divorce, surely it was nothing compared with Aunt Rebecca's loss. Anne was thankful that Simon was alive, even though he no longer chose to be married to her.

The woman behind the desk at WJL Publishing Group seemed painfully emaciated, yet she obviously had enough money to buy food, because the suit she wore was expensive and it was obvious her flaming red hair had been styled at a salon.

"May I help you?" she asked as she gathered up several pages on her desk and stapled them together. Her long fingernails were bright crimson.

Simon nodded. "I'm here to see Mr. Lancaster."

"I'm sorry, but I'm afraid that's impossible. He's very busy this morning and his appointment schedule is full."

"I don't care if he's busy interviewing the President himself." Simon walked over to the secretary's desk and bracing his hands on the edge of it, leaned toward the woman on the other side of the desk. "I intend to see Mr. Lancaster and I'm not leaving until I do."

The skinny woman drew her shoulders back so that she was ramrod straight and she glared at him. "And just who are you, please?"

"My name's Tarrant. Simon Tarrant."

The woman's eyes widened. "Tarrant. Are you any relation to Joe Tarrant of Mount Evergreen?"

This time it was Simon's turn to widen his eyes in surprise. "Why, yes! He's my father. How did you know?"

The secretary extended her hand. "I'm Rosalind Mead. Joe and I went to school together. How is he, anyway?"

Simon smiled and shook hands with the woman. "Fairly well. A few years back he suffered a bad stroke, but he's recovered remarkably well."

"I'm glad to hear it." Rosalind Mead frowned slightly as she eyed Simon. "Are you sure you want to see Robert Lancaster?" she asked.

So... this woman knew something about the feud between his father and Robert Lancaster. Simon didn't waste time pretending not to get the gist. Instead he nodded grimly. "I'm sure."

Rosalind sighed. "He really is terribly busy this morning, but I'll tell him you're here. He's not expecting you, is he?"

"No, he's not."

Rosalind nodded, and instead of using the phone to announce Simon, she turned, knocked on the door behind them and softly entered the other room, closing the door firmly after her.

She returned a moment later, gave Simon a thumbs-up and held the door open while he went into Robert Lancaster's private office.

After the secretary had closed the door once more, Simon and Robert Lancaster took a long moment to silently assess each other. Finally Robert spoke.

"Tarrant? Joe's boy?"

"That's right, sir," Simon answered.

Robert walked around the desk and the two men shook hands, assessing one another again. "I've got to admit," Robert said, "you have my curiosity aroused. I haven't seen you since you were small. How long's it been, anyway?"

Simon shook his head and chuckled. "I'm not sure, sir. But you looked a lot bigger the last time I saw you."

Robert chuckled, too. "Have a seat," he invited.

"No thanks. I don't want to take up much of your time."

"All right," Robert said agreeably. "How may I help you?"

"I'd like to know where to find Anne."

"Anne?" Robert appeared taken aback by the question. He sounded as though he'd never heard the name before in his life.

Simon nodded. "Yes, sir. I've been trying to reach her for a week and a half. I've called her studio and left messages on her answering machine, but she never returned my calls, and I can't phone her at her apartment because her number's unlisted. Today I went to both her apartment and the studio, but apparently she wasn't at either place. I'd be extremely grateful if you can tell me where she is."

Robert tilted his head and gazed at Simon with open curiosity. "Why are you looking for her?" he asked bluntly.

Simon had anticipated the question. Nevertheless, he had no intention of revealing the reason he wanted to see Anne. "It's a private matter, sir," he replied politely. "It's between the two of us alone. Can you tell me where she is?" he asked again.

"I'm not sure that I should," Robert replied. "How do I know she wants to see you?"

"She doesn't," Simon admitted honestly. "But it's very important that I see her all the same. Please," he added more urgently. "If you have any compassion at all, you'll tell me where to find her."

Robert fell silent for a long moment as he eyed Simon. Finally he nodded and said, "She's in Denver on an assignment. My secretary has the name of the hotel where she's staying. You can get it from her."

Simon felt immense relief. "Thanks, Mr. Lancaster. I really appreciate this."

"I hope I've done the right thing," Robert said dryly as they shook hands again.

"You have," Simon assured him. "You definitely have."

He turned toward the door. Then Robert stopped him with a question. "How is Joe?"

Simon turned around slowly to face the older man who'd once been so close to his father. "He's doing very well these days," he answered.

Robert nodded briskly. "I'm glad."

And then Simon opened the door and walked out.

On the flight to Denver, Simon brooded. Would Anne be glad to see him when he showed up at her hotel, or would she cold-shoulder him? Regardless of the outcome, he was compelled to make the effort. He had to do all he could to save his marriage. When the letter from the New York attorney had arrived last week, it was as though someone had slammed a fist into his face.

Divorce! Anne had really gone and done it! She had formally filed for divorce. Just thinking about it again spread pain through Simon's chest, and his throat went dry.

How could Anne do this after all this time, and after the way they had made love that night? How could she?

Yet even as he asked himself the question, Simon knew he had no one to blame but himself. *He* was the one who had the idea in the first place. *He* was the one who had made the monumental mistake of telling her, after the night spent in each other's arms, that the reason he'd come to see her was to tell her that he'd wanted a divorce. *Idiot! Idiot!*

He hadn't told her in order to hurt her, as she believed. He'd told her because he'd felt so close to her again that he'd thought he could be completely honest about his feelings. Simon had been about to tell her that after their passionate night together, he'd faced the irrefutable truth... that he was still madly in love with her and that all he wanted now was to give their marriage another try. If only she would give him the chance, he wouldn't blow it this time.

But Anne had been so wounded by his disclosure that she'd taken it as a sign that he still wanted a divorce. She'd believed that he'd gone to bed with her to take advantage of her when she was vulnerable. The moment the words were out of his mouth, Simon had known it was a mistake to have told her, that he had hurt Anne deeply, but it was already too late to make amends. She'd gone pale and then turned on him bitterly, refusing to listen to anything more he had to say.

She had run away from Mount Evergreen... and him... before he could return that evening to try to explain. When he'd started to follow her the next day, he'd been prevented by the car accident.

As the plane sped westward, Simon hoped with all his heart that he could get Anne to listen to him now. Somehow he had to find a way to reverse all the mistakes he'd made in the past and win his wife back. And this time their marriage would be open, proud and forever. He would never let her go again.

Still, Simon was a realist. He knew his chances were slim to nonexistent. The mistake he'd made five years ago had only been compounded by his most recent ones. There was a hell of a lot to forgive, and he wasn't sure Anne had it in her to forgive so much. He had serious doubts that she would even hear him out, much less that he would be able to reason with her and convince her to give him a second chance. If he didn't...

But he couldn't allow himself to think of defeat. He was going to fight this divorce to the bitter end, if need be. He simply had no choice.

Anne was still damp from her shower as she padded out of the bathroom, shrugging into her robe. She walked over to the television and switched it on. It was time for the evening news.

Wearily she plopped down on the bed while she watched the newscast. A towel was wrapped around her wet hair. She knew she really shouldn't take time to rest if she intended to meet the others downstairs in time for a drink before dinner.

The day had been an exhausting one. Now that she was stretched out, the bed felt so soft and pleasant that she seriously contemplated ordering a sandwich from room service and spending a relaxing evening watching TV.

The problem with that was that she would be alone, and whenever that happened, Anne had a tendency to choke up with tears. All week she had driven herself to stay busy in order to avoid thinking about Simon and to try to end the excruciating pain that he was now lost to her forever. Last week he'd been served with the divorce papers. She hadn't heard from him since, probably because he was too busy celebrating his imminent freedom.

A commercial flashed on the television screen. Anne closed her eyes, trying to relax and put away thoughts of Simon. It had been a long hard day at the ranch in which nothing had gone right. They'd been working on the fashion shoot, and the weather had turned extremely cold and gray. It hadn't been easy working with shivering, complaining models wearing gauzy spring fashions. One of the models had the beginnings of a cold and had been in frequent need of the services of the makeup artist. She hadn't cooperated with Anne because she'd felt so lousy. Jane, also, had been in as rotten a mood as the weather. By late afternoon when it began to rain, nobody was surprised: the rain seemed only fitting to top off an already miserable day. Everyone had been glad to get back to the warm hotel.

There was a knock at the door. Anne grimaced as she swung her legs off the bed and went to answer it. She supposed it was Jane or one of the other women in their group. She hoped she wasn't in for a long visit, because she wasn't in the mood.

She was stunned when she opened the door and saw Simon standing there. She caught her breath and blinked, convinced that because she had thought of him so often and so intensely, she had conjured him up.

But he was flesh and blood and this was reality. His face was grim and dark as he gazed at her.

"Aren't you going to invite me in?" he asked her somberly.

Too surprised to refuse, Anne stepped back and let Simon enter the room.

He was dressed casually in tan slacks and a brown leather jacket over his shirt. He carried a duffel bag, which he dropped to the floor. Then he turned toward Anne. For a long, electric moment, they gazed silently at each other. At last, Anne asked feebly, "What...what are you doing here, Simon? How did you find me?"

"I went to see your father," he answered.

"My father?" she asked incredulously. Alarm surged through her. "You didn't tell him about us, did you?"

Simon shook his head. "Relax. I didn't tell him a thing, although he was very curious about why I wanted to find you."

"I'm sure he was!" Anne exclaimed. "What did you tell him?"

"I told him that it was an urgent, private matter, and that I needed to see you. He hemmed and hawed a bit, but he finally told me where you were."

"And just what is this urgent, private matter?" Anne asked with a touch of sarcasm. She brushed past Simon and went over to turn off the TV. Suddenly it seemed deafeningly loud and raucous.

"I came to tell you that I am totally against this divorce action you've filed, and I intend to fight you tooth and nail over it if I have to."

Anne turned sharply around from the television and stared at Simon in disbelief. Her dark eyes flashed with indignation. "Have you gone crazy?" she demanded. "You're the one who wanted the divorce! Remember? So why are you complaining now?"

Simon stepped toward her and grabbed her arms, giving her a little shake. His blue eyes were as stormy-gray as the day itself. "I do not want a divorce," he said in a slow, measured voice. "I'll admit I went to you that night thinking that's what I wanted, but it was because I was so miserable and unhappy without you, being near you and not able to have you. But after that night, everything changed for me. I was trying to tell you the next morning at breakfast how much I love you and want you back, but you wouldn't give me the chance, Anne. The next thing I knew, you had gone. I tried to go after you the next morning, but I was bashed up a little in an accident, and my car was undrivable."

"An accident?" In spite of herself, Anne's concern burst forth. "How badly were you hurt?"

Simon was heartened by her concern, but he rushed to reassure her. "Whiplash... fierce headaches, a couple of bruises and a stiff neck for a few days, but it wasn't serious. I'm fine now. It's just that for more than a week, neither I nor my car were in any shape to travel. I repeatedly called your studio, as I'm sure you're quite aware, but you wouldn't return any of my calls, and I didn't know your home number. Not," he added bleakly, "that you'd have talked to me there, either, of course. I only got my car back from the garage late yesterday, and this morning was the first chance I had to get to New York. When I couldn't find you, I went to see your father. I didn't know what else to do."

His fingers tightened around Anne's arms and slowly he drew her toward him. His voice was raspy and harsh. "Tell me you don't mean this divorce business, Anne. I can't bear it if you do. Tell me you won't go through with it!"

Anne started to argue, but the words died in her throat. The agony in Simon's gaze matched the pain she'd seen in her own reflection these past couple of weeks.

"Simon," she whispered. "I..."

His arms slid down her back, and in the next second, she was cradled firmly, yet gently, in his arms. Her head rested against Simon's shoulder.

"I love you, Anne," he said gruffly. "Oh, God, I love you so much, and I just can't bear to lose you. Give me another chance, and I'll prove how much I love you. I want to go home and tell both our fathers that we're married, and that no matter what their quarrel is, it's not our quarrel and that we're not going to allow it to interfere with our love another day. I should never have allowed it to happen at all. I should've insisted upon telling my family, no matter what, but I honestly thought it would be just a short, temporary secret! Forgive me, Anne! If you'll take me back, I swear I'll never deny you again as long as I live."

His voice trembled. "I'll spend the rest of my life making it up to you."

"Ah, Simon," she whispered, near tears. "Why are you doing this to me? I've been trying so hard to get you out of my system, and I was doing a pretty good job of it until you sailed in here. Go away and . . . and . . ."

Simon took heart at the feebleness of her protest. His arms tightened around her, so that both of them were breathless even before his lips fell upon hers. "Say it once more with meaning," he murmured against the softness of her lips, "and maybe I'll consider going, Mrs. Tarrant."

"Mrs. . . ." Anne was diverted from her resistance to his persuasions by the charm of the name she'd never had the opportunity to use; she was even more distracted by the thrilling vibrations that coursed through her as his warm lips moved over hers and his hand sneaked beneath her robe.

In a moment she would put a stop to such insanity, of course. One didn't welcome lovemaking from the man one intended to divorce, did one?

Definitely not! Quite rationally Anne mentally answered her own question. Any second now she would break the contact of their burning lips, withdraw from the comfort and happiness of being in Simon's arms, and she would send him away.

Any . . . moment . . . now . . .

Chapter Ten

Anne did not send Simon away. When he kissed her again, she found herself incapable of telling him to go.

Simon loved her! He wanted her, not a divorce!

All the depression she'd suffered the past week and a half since that last morning with him suddenly lifted. She returned his kiss with a fervor that surprised them both.

After a moment, Simon drew back and gave her a quizzical look, then joyfully scooped her up into his arms and swung her around. They were both laughing as he carried her to the bed, tossed her down into the middle of it and then came down on top of her, still fully clothed.

They rolled over, wrapped in each other's arms, and they laughed again. Simon nuzzled Anne's neck and whispered, "You're adorable, Mrs. Tarrant. You do know that, don't you?"

"You're not so bad yourself, Mr. Tarrant," she replied huskily.

Simon flipped her over onto her back again, and then levered himself off the bed. While he shed his jacket, his face suddenly turned serious and he said, "I don't know about that. If you ask me, I was a jerk for hurting you, for letting you go, and just plain stupid for actually thinking I might ever be happy without you."

Tremendous joy bubbled up inside Anne and it was impossible to hide it. She grinned and her eyes began to twinkle as she teased him. "You know what, Simon? This is a very boring conversation. There are more interesting things we could be doing besides talking."

He tossed his head back and roared with laughter. "Is that a fact?" he asked. "Well, let's see now. We could go to a movie," he suggested.

Anne propped her head on her hand and squinted her eyes, pretending to consider the idea. "Nooo," she drawled at last. "I don't feel like getting dressed and going out."

Simon scratched his chin. "Hmm. That seriously narrows down our options, then. Well…how about a game of cards? They've probably got decks of cards at the front desk. Want me to call and find out?"

Anne shook her head. "I'm not really in the mood for a card game, either," she told him.

"What then? An evening of television? Or reading?"

"Nope." Anne crooked a beckoning finger. Simon stooped and she whispered something outrageous in his ear.

"Eeeyowwee!" Simon exclaimed. He straightened again and quickly shed his clothes, all the while not taking his eyes off Anne. Then he came down beside her, opening and removing her robe himself.

He unwound the towel from her hair and ran his fingers through the damp, silky strands. He bent his head, sampling her lips and lingering over them. Finally Simon drew away from her a little, just enough so that he had an unhampered view of Anne's exquisite body.

It was perfectly proportioned. Her milk-white breasts were so beautifully sculptured, it scarcely seemed possible they belonged to a living, breathing woman; below the narrow band of her rib cage was the indention of her tiny waist. His gaze moved lower to her flat stomach, her gently flaring hips and at last, to that dark, mysterious and inviting triangle between her legs.

Simon's throat tightened. Oh, God, she was beautiful! And she was his, all his! His throat tightened and he swallowed hard before dropping a kiss to her bare shoulder. At the same time, his hand slid down her throat to pause finally over her breast.

A faint hint of the fragrance of her bath soap lingered on Anne's skin. Simon enjoyed the fresh, clean scent mingled with her own very feminine scent. And her skin...it was so delicate and soft beneath his hard fingers. Like an explosion, hot desire flared within him.

Anne held Simon's head with her hands and her fingers combed slowly and luxuriously through his thick blond hair. Her dark eyes met his deep sky blue ones and a silent message of fervent desire sparked between them. Slowly she brought his head lower until their lips met.

She was conscious of waves of heat spreading through her—sensuous, erotic heat generated by the touch of Simon's lips on hers, his searching tongue, his exploring hands, his hair-roughened chest pressed to her breasts, his long, muscular legs covering hers. Anne reveled in the red-hot blaze within her; it seemed as though before this she had been frozen numb, without feeling, and only now, lying beneath Simon's hard masculine body and basking in the firelight of his love, was she at last thawing out.

Anne quivered involuntarily as Simon's hands stroked her gently. His touch had brought her quiescent body to life with a powerful intensity.

She wrapped her arms around Simon so that she could caress his back. Then her fingers slid down to move slowly over his muscle-hardened buttocks. The feel of his body pressed against hers, and knowing it was her right to freely touch him when she'd believed she'd never have that privilege again, was almost overwhelming.

Abruptly Anne wanted Simon. That very instant! If it were up to her, he would take her now, without delay, but she knew from past experience that his way with her would be slow, a sensual torturing until she reached a frenzied peak of excitement.

As though he had read her mind, Simon's mouth and tongue began to pay homage to her breasts, first one and then the other. A burning simmered deep within Anne and she writhed against him, her body demanding more, more.

But Simon took his own sweet time. As though he were ravenous for the taste of her, he kissed her everywhere...her throat, her earlobe, her breasts again, her lips again, her rib cage, her navel, her breasts once more, all the while ignoring the lower half of her body, which was on fire.

Anne's fingers dug into his hips as her need for him surged through her. She was intoxicated by his kisses, but they weren't enough. They were far from enough and Simon knew it. He still avoided touching her below the waist, knowing that in its own special way, that abstinence generated a greater degree of tension in her than a caress. He knew she couldn't endure it much longer.

"Simon...please," she moaned. She embedded her teeth in her lower lip as she strained for control.

Simon's eyes met hers briefly. His were dark, smoldering with his own tightly controlled passion. In answer to her desperate plea, he moved lower, now tantalizing her by dropping brief kisses along her thigh and ending at her toes.

"Simon!"

He grinned devilishly and began to kiss his way up the opposite leg, only this time, he paused at her tender, highly sensitive inner thigh before at last turning his attention to her very essence.

Anne's pulse raced and her senses clamored for release. If he didn't take her soon, she was certain she would lose her mind.

She moaned again in agony. Simon ceased his sweet assault on her and she thought that at last he would take her. She was wrong.

"Now it's your turn," he whispered hoarsely. "It's your turn to make love to me."

Anne's eyes widened and the words stuck in her throat as she tried to object. At last she squeezed them out, protesting, "No. I can't wait anymore. Take me now."

Simon grinned, but shook his head firmly. "Not yet." He plucked her up from the pillow as though she herself weighed no more than the pillow, and then he quickly rolled over, taking her former passive position.

"Simon!" Anne playfully struck his rock-hard shoulder. "You can't leave me this way!" Her entire body quivered with need.

"Oh, yes I can, Miss Greedy. No more lovin' for you until you give me my fair share."

"You're a cruel man," she accused, kneeling beside him. "But now you're going to pay for it."

Simon crossed his arms behind his head, closed his eyes and smiled, waiting.

A moment later he realized that Anne had been quite serious when she said he was going to pay for it. She began to slowly tantalize and torment him in every way imaginable. She touched him, feather-light, teasing, teasing, and when he reached for her, she withdrew, leaving him grasping at air. She kissed and nibbled and stroked and nuzzled and massaged; she stirred his blood boiling hot and when he moaned, she laughed at him.

At last, when he could bear it no more, Simon grasped her firmly beneath her arms and drew her up from his midsection. She fell upon him, full-length, and when her face drew level with his, they both suddenly became quite serious.

His mouth captured hers as she moved against him, and a moment later they were together, wafting, drifting, flying, soaring. It was an extraordinary flight, an exhilarating journey into the highest, most exquisite realms of joy.

They returned to earth in a slow, gradual descent and found themselves wrapped snugly in each other's arms.

Simon's eyes were like two blue pools beneath brilliant sunlight as he smiled. "I love you, you know," he told her in an emotion-roughened voice. "I really love you, Annie-girl."

Anne smiled back and murmured, "I love you, too."

Simon's smile became a rueful grin. "I'd also love to have a steak right now. I'm starved."

Anne laughed at him. "Men!" she said derisively. "How unromantic can you get? Don't you know there's more to life than food?"

Simon's grin broadened. "Don't I ever? You just proved that, didn't you? All the same, I'm spent. It's been a long day, and I didn't eat much of that dry sandwich they served for an afternoon snack on the plane. If I don't get something to eat soon, you're liable to have a fainting man on your hands."

"Well, we can't have that, can we? Do you want to get dressed and go downstairs to the restaurant for dinner, or would you rather have room service send something up?"

Since neither of them were in the mood to be around other people, they opted for room service. Before the hour was out, they were sharing a leisurely private dinner. Their conversation was alternately serious and lighthearted, like that of any young couple in love who are planning their life together.

"We'll keep your apartment in New York," Simon stated. "That way you'll always have a place of your own to stay in whenever you have to be in the city on assignments. You don't mind living in Mount Evergreen, do you?" There was a sudden anxious quality to his voice.

Anne shook her head. "You know I love Mount Evergreen. In spite of the way things were between us, I'd just about convinced myself to stay there as my permanent base. But where will we live? Do you want to live in Lancaster House, your apartment or get one of those new modern houses on the west end of town?"

"That's entirely up to you," Simon told her. "But I think you'll find we'll need more room than my small apartment for the two of us. If you want to live in Lancaster House, I'm perfectly happy to do so, but if you'd rather have a new home with all the modern conveniences, we'll do that instead. There's a couple of acres for sale at the north edge of town that would make a beautiful homesite. We could live in Lancaster House while we build a home of our own, if you'd like. Whatever you want, Anne. I'll be happy with whatever makes you happy. My only requirement is that wherever we live, the house must be big enough for a family."

"A family?" Anne echoed softly.

Simon nodded, reached across the table and took her hand. "We've wasted enough years already, don't you think? I'm ready for us to start a family immediately if you are." His voice dropped a notch. "We used to talk about having children. I hope you still want them as much as I do?"

"Yes," Anne replied huskily. "I do."

"When will you be returning to New York?" Simon asked over dessert.

"Day after tomorrow, we're hoping."

"Good. How about if I stay over with you and we go back together? As soon as we get to the city, we'll visit your father and tell him about us, and then we'll go straight to Mount Evergreen and tell mine."

Anne's eyes suddenly filled with doubt. "Are you sure you're really ready to tell your father, Simon? To tell everyone? Because when it's done, it's done, and there's no taking it back."

Simon rose from his chair and came to Anne. Taking her hand, he lifted her to her feet and then he cupped her face with both his hands. "I've never been more sure about anything," Simon declared. "No more secrets! I want everything out in the open and aboveboard. I want *you* in my life. Whatever it is between our fathers, they're just going to have to rise above it and accept that we love each other and are married and that we're planning to stay that way."

That night Anne enjoyed her best night's sleep in a long time. Nestled within the crook of Simon's arm, warm, happy and secure, she dreamed of them together. In the dream, they were old, and there were children and grandchildren around them. It was a lovely, lovely dream.

In the morning, she awoke refreshed, filled with joy and energy, excited by the new day ahead. From the bathroom she could hear Simon's shower running. It hadn't all been a dream after all! The part about having children and grandchildren had been, of course, but it wasn't a dream that he was here with her! It wasn't a dream that they were together at last and that she was finished with loneliness for good!

The sound of water ceased and a moment later the bathroom door opened. Simon entered the bedroom damp and handsome and enticingly dressed in nothing but a towel.

"'Morning." He padded across the carpet to the bed, bent down and gave her a kiss. "How did you sleep?"

"Mmm! Wonderfully." Anne stretched her arms lazily.

"Me, too." Simon grinned. "Probably the best night's sleep I've had in months."

Anne's glance fell on the clock. "Oh, dear!" she exclaimed, swinging her legs off the bed. "I'd better get a move on," she said over her shoulder as she scooted toward the bathroom. "I'm supposed to meet the rest of the crew downstairs in half an hour."

"Must you?" Simon eyed her bare backside with leering approval. "I was hoping we'd have a bit of snuggle time before you got busy with your day."

"Sorry." Anne paused and blew him a kiss. "What will you do all day while I'm working?"

"I thought I might tag along with your crew if you think they'll let me," Simon replied. "I can be a handyman, hauling things or helping out in any other ways you need. I promise to stay out of your way while you're working."

Anne flashed a sleepy smile. "Fine with me," she answered. "And I'm sure it'll be all right with Jane and the others."

When Anne had finished with her own shower and returned to the bedroom to start dressing, Simon was dialing the phone. "I'm calling the *Sentinel* to check on things," he murmured to her. Then he addressed all his attention to the telephone.

"Thank goodness you called!" Mary, his secretary exclaimed. "I've been calling everywhere for you! Where are you, anyway?"

A cold chill rippled up Simon's spine. "What's wrong?"

"It's your father," came the answer. "He had a heart attack yesterday. He was taken by air ambulance to the hospital in Albany."

Simon sucked in a sharp breath. "How bad is it?"

"It's very serious. I'm sorry," Mary replied. Then, she asked again, "Where are you?"

"I'm in Colorado."

"Colorado?"

Simon didn't waste time satisfying his secretary's curiosity. "Who's with my father?" he asked.

"Mrs. Potter. She said she'll stay at the hospital until you arrive."

"Good." Briskly Simon asked, "Has anybody notified my sister?"

"I did," Mary answered. "Mrs. Mason's on her way to New York."

"Good. I'll take the first plane home. I'll be there as soon as I can."

Simon hung up the phone and slowly turned to face Anne. There was a stricken expression in his eyes.

Anne made no pretense of not having listened to his side of the conversation. "Another stroke?" she asked.

"A heart attack. Bad." Simon paused, then said sadly, "Anne, I'm sorry. I never anticipated this. It seems I lied to you about never leaving you again. But I have to go."

She nodded. "Of course you do."

"As much as I hate to say this," Simon continued, "we'll have to postpone the announcement of our marriage."

"I know that, too," Anne said quietly. "Well..." She managed what she hoped was an encouraging smile. "I'd better finish dressing while you call the airport."

Simon came to her and put his hands on her shoulders. "Anne, I don't know when I'll see you again."

She nodded again. "I understand that," she replied with a heavy heart. She turned away from him quickly so that he wouldn't see her tears. "Call the airport," she reminded him.

A half hour later they parted at the door with only the briefest of kisses. Both of their gazes were filled with agony.

"I'll call you tomorrow and let you know how things are."

He started to walk away, but then he turned back once more. "Anne . . . ?"

"Just go, Simon," she said in a tear-filled voice. "Just go, now."

He hadn't been able to make any promises about the future. How could he? Almost the exact same thing that had happened five years ago was happening all over again. Simon's father was gravely ill; Joseph Tarrant hated Anne's father, and the knowledge that his son was married to Robert Lancaster's daughter might be so upsetting that it would kill him. Once again, Simon couldn't risk it.

Anne understood that, perhaps even better than she had five years ago. After all, she loved her father, too.

But understanding didn't make acceptance any easier. Her heart was as leaden as the gray skies the remainder of the time she spent in Denver. When she returned to a drearily wet and cold New York, it was with an aching emptiness.

Simon had lost track of how many round-trips he'd made to and from Albany these past couple of weeks. He pulled into his parking space at the hotel and walked stiffly toward the entrance. What he wouldn't give to be able to go back to his apartment and grab a couple of hours of sleep, but there wasn't time. He had a lot of work to get done both at the hotel and back in town at the newspaper before returning to Albany tomorrow. He'd promised he'd be back there sometime tomorrow afternoon to give Caroline a break from the hospital. She desperately needed some rest, too.

Joseph Tarrant's condition had been touch and go for the first week after his heart attack. When the doctors finally felt he had stabilized enough to endure it, he'd undergone a heart bypass operation. Now, it was touch and go again. It was anybody's guess whether his father was going to survive and Simon and Caroline both felt bound to be at the hospital every moment they could.

Simon was worried and exhausted. He also missed Anne. Although he'd talked with her a few times by phone since she'd gotten back to New York, she hadn't returned to Mount Evergreen, and Simon hadn't had a free moment to go to the city to see her.

He felt so frustrated. He wanted to be with her, to love her, to share his troubles with her, and have her share hers with him, but given the situation it was impossible. Simon sensed, just from their telephone conversations, that Anne was drawing away from him again, and he was helpless to stop her withdrawal. Their plans to establish a life together seemed further away than ever, and he couldn't offer her any assurances that things would change anytime soon. Right now, as before, his father's needs came first.

When he was alone within the privacy of his office, Simon delayed diving into the work that awaited him. Instead, for a moment he gave in to his overwhelming sadness. He crossed his arms on his desk and dropped his head onto them.

Would his and Anne's needs ever be met? he wondered in quiet despair. Or were they always destined to yearn for the unreachable?

Chapter Eleven

When the telephone rang Anne knew it was Simon. She simply knew without knowing how she knew.

It was a dismal, drizzly Thursday evening. She had been preparing a simple meal of soup and a sandwich when she heard the ring. Now she abandoned the task and went into the living room, where the telephone was.

She listened to the sound of her own recorded voice on the answering machine. Then came Simon's familiar voice.

"Anne? It's me, and I know you're probably there, damn it, so pick up the phone."

Anne stood frozen, mute, like a statue.

"Anne? Please." Simon's voice came again. "Pick up the phone and talk to me. What's happened with you? I've been trying to reach you for three days."

Three days. That was how long Anne had managed to avoid talking to Simon. Before then, she'd spoken with him a few times since he had returned to Mount Evergreen.

They had been short, unsatisfactory and far from lover-like conversations with Simon describing the seriousness of his father's condition and talking about his own workload. During those conversations, Simon had neither suggested Anne's returning to Mount Evergreen to be with him, nor mentioned any plans of his own for making a trip, however brief, to New York City to see her.

Neither had he referred to anything remotely related to their previous decision to reconcile. It was as though that night in Denver had never happened, as though their discussion and plans to live as husband and wife had never taken place at all. It left her feeling strange, almost as if she had dreamed the whole thing.

Anne knew that Simon couldn't help his situation right now, that his father was gravely ill and needed him at the moment more than she did. But she had needs, too, and she felt vulnerable and uncertain now that they were apart. It didn't help any that Simon was silent about the future of their relationship.

She needed a sign from him . . . anything that would indicate that he hadn't abandoned their plans to reunite, that she was still important to him, that he still loved her. She needed to be reassured that this latest separation was only temporary.

But no such reassurance had come through during their brief telephone conversations. Its absence filled her with ever-increasing despair and doubt...so much so that for the past three nights, Anne had not answered her phone, ignoring the messages Simon had left on her machine.

Not that there had been a great many of them. Anne knew that Simon was too busy to spend much time on the phone trying to reach her, what with running two businesses and driving back and forth to Albany to visit his father in the hospital, and that suited her just fine, given her present mood. While Simon kept a physical and emotional distance from her, she had concluded that she also needed an emotional distance from him. She needed time in which to think more clearly. Maybe the promises they'd made to each other in Denver had all been a rash mistake that Simon now regretted.

As for Joseph Tarrant, Anne was genuinely sorry that he was so ill, but as hard as she tried, she could not help also feeling a bit sorry for herself. Joseph Tarrant had come between her and Simon twice before and now he'd done it again. It was history repeating itself, only this time Anne was neither a young teenage girl nor an insecure bride, easily intimidated and shunted aside. This time she was an adult, a woman with needs and expectations, and she didn't intend her future to be left dangling any longer.

Numbly Anne walked away from her unanswered telephone and returned to the kitchen. Mechanically she resumed her dinner preparations. But somehow Simon's call and her thoughts of him robbed her of her appetite. She decided against the sandwich altogether and was able to sip only a few spoonfuls of the soup.

A half hour later, Anne was not surprised when Simon called again. She would have to talk to him sooner or later, and she supposed she might as well get it over with. Resigned, she picked up the phone.

"What the hell's going on?" Simon demanded irritably. "For the past three days I've left messages both here and at your studio, and you've never called back."

Anne didn't bother making up any excuses. "I just didn't have anything to say to you," she answered truthfully.

There was a short silence, and then Simon asked in a weary tone of voice, "What's the matter now, Anne?"

"Nothing new," she replied. "I just needed a little time and space to think things over, that's all."

"Seems to me you've had plenty of time for that without ignoring my calls, too. After all, we haven't seen each other in three weeks."

"Exactly!" she answered sharply. "The truth is that I've just plain run out of the stamina to deal with this impossible situation. I'm tired of hoping and waiting, Simon, and I just can't do it anymore."

She heard an exasperated hissing sound at the other end of the wire. "Don't you think I'm tired of it, too?" he challenged. "Look! We're both just frustrated because we haven't been able to be together. You know I can't take time out right now to go to the city. I have my hands full here, and with running constantly back and forth between Mount Evergreen and Albany, but surely you can arrange to come here, can't you?"

"I don't think that would be a very good idea right now," Anne returned.

"Why not, for God's sake?"

"You're too busy, too anxious, too tense. You'd hardly have an hour to spare for me, if that. Besides, although you may not realize it, I have a life, too. I'm stacked up with assignments here. I don't have time to waste hanging around to be at your beck and call until you decide you can afford to grant me a few minutes of your precious time."

"You make it sound as though I don't want to be with you."

"Maybe you don't!"

"That's not true, and you know it!"

"I'm not so sure about that!" Anne returned swiftly.

"Why are you acting this way?" Simon demanded angrily. "You know my situation here and—"

"I'm sorry, Simon, but that's how I feel. I've made allowances for your situation, and I know this is a tough time for you. But I can't make allowances for the change in your attitude toward me since you got back home. You've been treating me like a second-class person, and I've had quite enough of it!''

"Don't be ridiculous! For some reason, you're just determined to be stubborn and unreasonable tonight!''

"Is that right?" she retorted. "Then I suppose you'll just have to put it down to my Lancaster blood, won't you? It seems that Tarrants and Lancasters just can't get along in any generation, doesn't it? What arrogance made us believe we were any different from those that went before us?''

Angrily Anne hung up the telephone, and this time Simon didn't call back.

Later that evening when she was in bed, Anne began to read from Aunt Rebecca's diary again. This time, she reached the place that she'd been expecting to find for some time now . . . the anguish and grief that Rebecca suffered in secret over the news of Douglas Tarrant's death. He had been killed during the Battle of the Meuse-Argonne, a massive tragedy which involved 1,200,000 American soldiers. When the dust had settled, one man out of every ten had become a casualty.

Rebecca's agony over Douglas's death was compounded by never being able to openly acknowledge that she was his wife. Her grief, poured onto the pages of her journal, was heartbreakingly vivid and painful to read even so many decades later. In some places, the pen strokes were blurred, and Anne knew that those splotches had been made by Rebecca's tears.

Anne felt a deep compassion for the blighted love that Rebecca and her Douglas had shared. How had Rebecca done it, she wondered. How had she hung onto her sanity, when she couldn't even openly admit that she was Mrs. Douglas Tarrant and that she had a right to grieve as much as his family did?

The following day, Anne met her father for lunch. It was the first time they'd seen each other since before Anne had gone to Denver, although they had spoken on the phone a couple of times.

Robert, who was trying to diet off a few pounds, had ordered a chef salad, and he stared at it resentfully as he asked, "What was all that about with Simon Tarrant? He showed up at my office one morning demanding to know how to find you. I didn't know whether to tell him or not, but in the end, I did. Did he call you while you were in Denver? What did he want?"

Anne shrugged and did her best to appear nonchalant. "It was just a business matter, that's all."

"Important enough for him to storm into my office and demand to know where you were? He seemed pretty agitated." Robert's eyes were lively with curiosity.

"Apparently he thought it was important at the time," Anne replied lightly. "Speaking of Simon," she said, changing the subject, "did you know that a few weeks ago his father had a massive heart attack, and since then has undergone bypass surgery?"

"Joe?" Robert's eyes darkened with genuine concern. "Oh, my God! Is he going to make it?"

Anne was taken aback by her father's distress and she was glad she could reassure him. "Apparently it was touch and go at first and his condition was critical until a few days ago, but he's doing better now."

Robert inhaled raggedly and nodded, but said no more. The waiter arrived, interrupting their conversation. Reassured that everything was satisfactory, he went away again. Anne gazed curiously at her father. "What happened between you and Mr. Tarrant that made you turn against each other, Dad? I've seen your high school yearbooks. You used to be best friends."

"Best friends?" Robert said disdainfully. "We were more than that! We were thicker than thieves!" He gave a short chuckle. "There wasn't much one of us did that the other didn't do also. I guess we were about as close as any two kids can be." His eyes took on a distant, reminiscent expression.

"So what happened to end such a tight friendship?" Anne asked insistently.

Robert's gaze returned to Anne's face. With a tiny jerk, as though pulling himself back to the present, he shook his head. "I really don't feel like talking about the past, Anne. Joe and I were friends once, and I have some fond memories of when we were growing up, but what's over is over. Let's just drop the subject."

"I know you became business partners after you'd grown up, so it wasn't just a childhood friendship," Anne persisted.

Robert's lips pressed together tightly. Then he took a bite of his salad, frowning as he chewed.

Anne plunged on, unwilling to let the subject die. "Did you know that your grandfather and Mr. Tarrant's grandfather were also business partners at one time?"

Robert nodded and took a sip of his coffee. "When I was a boy, I heard that my grandfather and Andrew Tarrant had fallen out, ended their business relationship and stopped speaking, but I never did know the particulars."

"Did you also know that their quarrel interfered with their children's love affair?"

Robert's eyes widened and he stared at her. "What on earth are you talking about? Joe's father, Peter, and Aunt Rebecca?" he asked incredulously.

"Not Peter," Anne declared. "It was Douglas Tarrant and Aunt Rebecca."

Robert's face took on a thoughtful expression. "Douglas? He's the one who died very young, I believe...in France, during World War I."

Anne nodded. "That's him. He and Aunt Rebecca were forbidden to see each other because of their fathers' quarrel. But their love was too deep to submit to that veto, and they were secretly married shortly before Douglas shipped out. Remember that wedding band I received along with Aunt Rebecca's other jewelry? Dad, that was her own wedding ring."

Robert shook his head wonderingly. "I had no idea," he murmured. "I always thought of Aunt Rebecca as a tragic, lonely figure. Apparently she *was* tragic and lonely, if what you've said is true. How did you come by this information, anyhow?"

"From her journals," Anne explained. "I found them locked in a cupboard in the playhouse, and I've been reading them."

"Well, I'm sorry for her," Robert said.

So am I, Anne thought. So am I.

She came close at that moment to telling her father that his own falling out with Simon's father, like that of their grandfathers, had brought about a similar tragedy for their children, but she couldn't quite bring herself to do it. Robert might be sorry to hear that Joe Tarrant was in poor health, but they were still enemies. She just couldn't tell him the truth, that she'd been secretly married to Joe Tarrant's son for the past five years.

Since the night she had refused Simon's request to visit him in Mount Evergreen, she had not heard from him. But a few days later, wanting to retrieve the camera she had inadvertently left behind at Lancaster House almost six weeks ago, Anne decided to make a short trip to Mount Evergreen after all.

She drove up late one afternoon and intended only to stay that night. She would not let Simon know she was there. What good would it do either of them?

Anne had left no food in the house the last time she'd returned to the city, and so she was forced to go out for dinner.

She stopped at a fast-food restaurant and had a hamburger and a soft drink, and then she decided to make a quick stop at the supermarket to pick up a pint of milk and a small package of cereal for tomorrow's breakfast.

It didn't take her long to conduct her business in the store. It was dark now, but the store's parking lot was well lit as Anne hurried back to her car.

A woman emerged from the car next to hers, about to go toward the store, and they nodded to each other politely. Then both of them stopped, as though struck by a bolt of lightning, turned and stared at each other.

"Anne!"

"Caroline!"

The two women fell into each other's arms, laughing.

"I don't believe this!" Caroline exclaimed.

"Neither do I!" Anne answered breathlessly. It had been several years since she had last seen Caroline Tarrant Mason. Now Anne gave her old friend an extra hug, then stood back so that she could look at her. Caroline was a feminine version of Simon. Just now her blue eyes twinkled with delight and her blond hair, as silky and lovely as ever, swung loosely from shoulder to shoulder in a casual pageboy style.

"How are you?" they both asked at once. They laughed again, and then Caroline insisted, "You first."

Anne smiled. "I'm fine. But how are you and your husband and children?" She sobered instantly and added, "I know why you're here . . . your father."

Caroline nodded. "How did you know?"

Since Anne didn't want to bring up the subject of Simon, she shrugged lightly and said, "Everyone in town knows," which was perfectly true. "The last I heard, he was recovering nicely. Is he still?"

"Yes," Caroline agreed. "Until today Simon and I've been taking turns staying with Dad at the hospital. Of course I've stayed more than Simon, because he has the businesses to run, but today for the first time, Dad's there alone. It was his idea and his doctor backed him up, so I came home this morning." A touch of anxiety stole the twinkle from her eyes. "I hope I did the right thing by leaving him. Dad can sometimes be too stubborn for his own good."

Anne gently touched Caroline's shoulder. "Don't worry. I'm sure the doctor wouldn't also have told you to come home if he were afraid your dad was in imminent danger of a setback."

"You're right, of course." Caroline nodded. "What are *you* doing in Mount Evergreen?"

Anne looked down, tossing the car keys in her right hand. "I wrote you that Aunt Rebecca died." She looked at Caroline once more.

"Yes," the other woman replied. "Simon also mentioned it to me. I'm sorry, Anne. I know you really loved Miss Rebecca. All of us kids were very fond of her—she was so good to us."

"Yes, she was," Anne replied. "Very good to us. And to me. She left me Lancaster House."

Caroline's blue eyes rounded. "You don't mean to tell me you've moved here?"

Anne grinned and shook her head. "No. I gave it some thought, and I even came and stayed a few weeks, going back and forth to my studio in the city, but I've decided it won't work. I'm going to try to sell the house. I just drove up today to retrieve my best camera. The last time I was here I accidentally left it behind.''

"I'm thrilled you did," Caroline said. "We wouldn't have bumped into each other if you hadn't. How long will you be here, Anne?"

"I'll be going back to the city tomorrow morning."

Caroline looked crestfallen. "So soon? I was hoping we could get together for a visit. Day after tomorrow I'm due to return to the hospital."

"What about tonight?" Anne asked eagerly. "I'm at loose ends. If you don't have other plans, why don't you come to the house so we can visit and catch up on our news?"

"Great!" Caroline exclaimed. "I was only going into the store to buy myself some midnight snacks and a magazine before going back to Dad's lonely house."

Anne grinned. "Forget the magazine. Just get enough junk food for two."

"Will do." Caroline laughed, and turned away and hurried toward the store's entrance.

Anne watched her go for a moment and then she opened the door of her car and slid beneath the wheel.

Forty-five minutes later, with cups of hot apple cider, a large bowl of buttered popcorn, a bag of cookies and a couple of candy bars on the coffee table, the two old friends lounged comfortably on the sofa. They'd kicked off their shoes and wearing jeans and sweaters, they sat cross-legged at opposite ends of the sofa. A warm fire crackled in the hearth.

Caroline was plumper than she'd been the last time Anne had seen her, a legacy, no doubt, from carrying her second son, who was now a year old. But her lively personality and vivaciousness was still intact, and her lighthearted laughter made Anne feel like a young girl again.

Caroline glowed as she talked about her British husband, Neal, and their children. While she admitted she missed living in the States, she said she also loved her adopted country, and except for having to live so far away from her family, she was perfectly content in England.

She scooped up a handful of popcorn, and said, "I've been doing all the talking. Tell me about your life, Anne. I know you're a smashing success at your work. Some of your photos even show up in British magazines. But what about the important stuff?"

"The important stuff?"

Caroline's head bobbed as she giggled. "But of course. Your love life, silly!"

Anne chuckled grimly. She'd known all along what Caroline meant, of course. Even in her letters, Caroline never failed to ask how Anne's love life was going. Now Anne shrugged. "There's no love life to talk about."

"I don't believe that for a second," Caroline retorted. "A looker like you? What's the matter? Aren't there any eligible men in New York?"

Anne grinned. "There are a lot fewer of them than you might believe. Oh, I go out occasionally, but there's no one serious in my life." Just as she'd done when she was a child and she'd told a whopper, Anne crossed her fingers behind her back as she spoke. *Liar! Liar! Liar!* her conscience shouted. But the last thing she could do was to admit the truth to Simon's sister about her feelings for him.

Almost as though she'd read Anne's mind, Caroline brought up that very subject. "You know, when we were in high school, you and Simon were so crazy about each other, the rest of us had bets that you'd end up married someday."

And so we were, Anne's heart acknowledged silently. *And so we were.*

She shrugged, and said as casually as she could, "Some things just don't work out the way we think they will, do they?"

Caroline sighed. "No, they don't. Well," she added briskly, "tell you what... come visit me in London next summer and I'll see what I can do about introducing you to some nice eligible British men."

Anne laughed, shook her head and accused, "You're only thinking of yourself. You want to fix me up there so you'll have an old friend living near you."

Caroline grinned devilishly. "Of course! That's the whole idea! Anyway, there are worse places in the world to live than London."

"I'm sure there are," Anne agreed. "I've always thought I'd enjoy visiting England someday, but I'm not sure I'd care to live there permanently, as you do."

"You wouldn't care where you lived if you found the right man," Caroline stated astutely.

"Touché." Anne nodded. "Anyway, at the moment I'm not in the market for any man, American or British or any other nationality. I'm just trying to concentrate on my career."

It was long past midnight when they finally said goodnight. "I didn't mean to stay so late," Caroline said apologetically as they parted at the door. "I'm beat, and I'm sure you must be tired, too, but..." She shrugged.

Anne smiled affectionately. "We had no choice," she insisted. "We only had tonight to do all our catching up!" They hugged each other, and Anne murmured, "I'm so happy I had the chance to see you, Caroline."

"So am I," Caroline replied. "I just hope it won't be so many years before we get together again. I'm serious about your coming to visit me, even if you won't marry one of my British bachelors."

"I'll give it some thought," Anne replied, smiling.

Caroline gave a tiny yawn, and laughed. "It's been a long day. Well . . . good night."

When the telephone receiver was picked up at the other end of the line by Caroline, Simon was both relieved and irritated.

"Where the hell have you been all evening?" he demanded. "I've been worried sick about you! I was almost about to call out a search party! Do you realize it's almost two in the morning?"

"So what?" came the indignant reply. "I'm a grown woman, for goodness sake! I don't have to report my comings and goings to *you,* big brother, so you can just climb down off your high horse right now, Simon Tarrant!"

Simon grimaced and struggled to control his temper. Their sharp exchange was reminiscent of the squabbles he and Caroline used to get into as children. He knew from painful experience that his sister was quite capable of verbally wrangling with him all night long if he didn't back off a little.

And she would win. She was better with words than he was.

Besides . . . she was right. She *was* a grown woman and he wasn't her keeper. Still . . . Traces of an anxiety that had steadily increased all evening still quivered in his veins.

"Okay," he finally conceded. "Maybe I did come on a little too strong just now, but . . ."

"A little? Simon, what's got you so stirred up? Didn't Evelyn tell you I called the hotel this afternoon to let you know I was back from Albany? She said you were busy, so I just left a message."

"Of course she told me. How else would I have known you were supposed to be at Dad's house? And how is he, anyway? Do you think it was wise to leave him alone at the hospital for a few days?"

They spent a few minutes discussing the subject of their father's health, and that drew the fire out of them both. Simon's mood calmed as Caroline reported the doctor's latest judgment. When she'd finished, he asked in a much milder manner, "So where were you tonight, Sis? I was late getting back from the hotel, but as soon as I got home I started calling you. I'd planned to invite you to my place for pizza. Naturally I also wanted to get the latest news about Dad's condition, but when it got so late and you still didn't answer the phone, I was beginning to think you'd been in an accident or something."

"You borrow trouble, Simon," Caroline chided gently. "I'm sorry you were so concerned. It just never occurred to me that you might worry about me. It was inconsiderate of me. I suppose I was enjoying myself too much to think about anybody else."

"Whoa!" Simon exploded. "That sounds like you were out on a hot date! Tell me it's not so, kiddo! Think of your husband and your babies!"

Caroline giggled. "Don't be silly. My virtue's still intact, so relax. I was visiting an old girlfriend. Come to think of it," she added in a teasing voice, "she's one of your old girlfriends, too."

There was only one person he knew who might fit that description. Simon's fingers tightened around the receiver. "Who?"

"Anne Lancaster," Caroline said, confirming his suspicion. "I spent the evening visiting with her and..."

Simon interrupted without compunction, another suspicion coldly coiling up his neck. "Anne? She lives in New York. Did you drive all the way to the city and back tonight?" he asked.

Caroline chuckled. "After first driving down from Albany? You've got to be kidding! No, it was just one of those happy coincidences. We bumped into each other in the supermarket parking lot.''

So... Anne was here! Simon kept his tone casual as he asked, ''What's she doing in Mount Evergreen?'' He hoped the true depth of his interest in Anne wasn't apparent to his sister.

''Something to do with a camera she left at the house the last time she was here, I think,'' Caroline answered off-handedly. ''She got here late this afternoon and she was only here for tonight, so we spent the evening together. We had a lovely visit.''

Simon inhaled silently. At last he murmured, ''How nice for you. Your visit with Anne must certainly have beat spending a boring evening with your brother.''

''Now Simon...'' Caroline began.

He laughed shortly, concealing the boiling anger that simmered just beneath the surface. ''Just teasing, little sis,'' he assured her. ''It's really late and you must be tired. I know I am, and I have to get to the office early tomorrow. I'll say good-night now.''

''All right. But... Simon?''

''What?''

''I'm really sorry I worried you. How 'bout the pizza tomorrow night?''

Simon didn't want to commit himself—not until after he'd spoken to Anne. ''I'll have to get back to you on that,'' he answered.

The clock showed that it was just past two a.m. It was a heck of a time to be paying a call on anyone, but Simon had no choice if Caroline's report was correct that Anne would be returning to the city in the morning. As soon as he'd said goodbye to his sister and hung up the phone, he grabbed his keys and wallet from the top of the bureau and headed out the door, ignoring the protests of his body, which yearned for sleep.

While he expected to find Lancaster House dark, Simon doubted that Anne would be asleep yet, since Caroline had only left her a short while ago. But when he pulled into the driveway, he saw the glimmer of a light peeping through the draperies on the windows of the old-fashioned parlor.

When he reached the door, he pounded on it loudly, since now that he was on the porch he could hear the sounds of the television.

A moment later the porch light flared, but Anne remained firmly out of sight behind the door. "Who is it?" she asked. Her voice betrayed alarm.

"It's Simon. Open up!"

The door opened. "What—what are you doing here this hour of the night?" Anne asked in astonishment. "Do you realize what time it is?"

Simon stepped forward, forcing her backward into the tiny front hallway. When he was inside, he kicked the door closed behind him, and the racket it made vibrated a mirror on the wall to his left. Automatically he reached out a hand and steadied the object.

"I can't believe you came to town after I'd asked you to, and yet you didn't even bother to let me know you were here!" he fumed. His eyes flashed with both pain and fury.

Anne inhaled deeply. Her eyes met his for the briefest instant, then quickly lowered. She turned away from him and walked into the parlor. "Obviously you've spoken with Caroline," she murmured.

"Did you think she wouldn't tell me?"

Anne shook her head. "I'd hoped... but no, I really didn't count on her not telling you she'd seen me. But I was counting on being out of town again by the time she did it."

"Why?" Simon's voice trembled with anger. "You know I haven't been able to get to the city to see you because of the way things have been around here, but when I asked you to come to see me here, you turned me down flat. Now you sneak into town and plan on sneaking out again without my ever knowing you were here! Why? What's changed you since that night in Denver?''

Anne stuffed her hands into the pockets of her faded jeans. Simon sensed that she did it to hide their unsteadiness, but of course he didn't know that for sure. All he knew for certain was the evidence before his eyes. Anne didn't appear at all happy to see him.

She turned away from him again, switched off the television and went to the fireplace where she withdrew her hands from her pockets and held them out toward the warming fire.

''What's changed?'' she echoed in a cracked voice. ''You've changed, Simon. You've changed since that night. That's why I refused to come up here to see you, even for an hour or two. I couldn't see any profit in it.''

''You're wrong,'' Simon insisted. Anne still had her back turned to him, but Simon knew she felt his nearness the moment he stepped up behind her, even before he touched her. From behind, he slid his arms around her waist, drew her back to lean against his chest and rested his chin on the top of her head. ''Nothing's changed. I love you. That hasn't changed, Anne, I promise you.''

He turned her gently in his arms and he saw the doubt and uncertainty in her beautiful brown eyes. ''I love you,'' he added again, in a whisper. ''And you love me. You can't turn away from me... from *us* ... not after we've finally committed ourselves to each other again.''

Simon drew her closer and placed his lips on hers. She was warm and soft, but for a moment Anne was as rigid as a rock in his arms. Gradually, beneath the pressure of his kisses, some of her tension eased and she at last began to respond.

Her lips parted receptively beneath his and her hands lightly caressed his chest before sliding around his midsection. Simon crushed her more tightly to him now, as the sweep of passion, so familiar whenever he was with her, began to inflame him. He had been miserable without her; he'd missed her terribly, and he was so desperately hungry for her.

But he also knew that until they'd broken down this new barrier between them, Anne would not give herself readily, despite her yielding response now.

In that, he was correct. An instant later Anne pulled back to gaze at him with unnerving somberness. She would have attempted to step out of his arms, but she couldn't because Simon held her more tightly than ever, determined not to let her escape.

"What is it that's bothering you so much... that's filling you with doubts, Anne?" he asked softly. "We were so close in Denver. I thought we had things all ironed out between us. You say I've changed, but how? I'm still the same man who loved and needed you then. I still love you and need you terribly. You can't tell me you don't still love me, too!"

"Of course I love you, more's the pity!" Anne replied, sounding and looking miserable. She pressed her hands against his chest, and this time she was able to break free of his embrace. She stepped away hastily, and her eyes were troubled as she met Simon's gaze.

"Anne, what *is* it?" Simon asked in desperation. "Why are you putting this distance between us?"

Her eyes widened. "*Me?* It's *you* who put a distance between us... just as you did five years ago."

"I don't follow," Simon said. His voice hardened, for he was beginning to believe Anne was merely taunting him.

"Don't you?" she responded. Anne didn't sound as though she was trying to taunt him. She only sounded hurt, bitterly hurt. "Then tell me this, Simon," she challenged him. "Are you ready now... tonight... to start telling the world that I'm your wife? I know it's very late, but I don't think either Caroline or my dad would mind if we called to tell them. Tomorrow we could drive up to Albany and visit your father and—"

Anne broke off what she was saying and Simon felt the color drain from his face. He stared at her in misery. "You know I can't do that," he said quietly after a long silence. "Dad's just beginning to recover from his surgery. He almost *died*, Anne! You know I can't give him any news that might disturb him right now. It might bring on another heart attack!"

Anne nodded. "Yes. I thought as much. You see, Simon…it's the same old story." She sighed heavily. "I don't want to be the cause of bringing any harm to your father, but I'm also not willing to be just a shadow behind your life, a secret you're ashamed of."

"Ashamed of! Never!" Simon exploded. He took a step toward Anne. "Just give me time," he pleaded. "Be patient a while longer. When the time is right, I'll…"

Anne held up a hand and Simon's footsteps halted as she shook her head. A short space stretched between them, but Simon could clearly see the unshed tears glazing Anne's eyes.

"Maybe I'm being unreasonable," Anne admitted. "In fact, I know I am. I realize your father is seriously ill. But telling him that we're married could bring on a heart attack years from now as well as today. And how much longer *is* later? Later never came after his stroke five years ago. Am I to wait another five years before you decide it's safe to mention me to him?" She shook her head once more, then impatiently raked her fingers through her hair. "By then, it would be something else, and the right time will never have come! Well…I won't put the rest of my life on hold while you bide your time, waiting for the right moment to come. I'm not trying to hurt you or to be vindictive or to force you into doing something against your will. I'm just . . . tired . . . and I want to get on with my life. So I've made my decision, and that is not to sit around hopelessly waiting any longer for a someday that doesn't exist."

"You can't mean this, Anne," Simon said in alarm. "You must—"

He was wildly frustrated when there came an insistent pounding on the front door.

Anne looked startled. "Who in the world . . . at this hour?"

"Better let me go with you to the door," Simon insisted.

"Be my guest," Anne replied, sounding grateful.

It was elderly Mr. Benson from across the street. "My wife is running a high fever and coughing," he said. "The doc called Jim Black, and he promised to meet me at the pharmacy and fill a prescription for her, but now my car won't start. I saw your light, Anne, so I knew you were still up. Would you be kind enough to drive me to the drugstore?"

"Of course I will, Mr. Benson. Just let me get my purse."

Simon was terribly upset at having to leave things at such an impasse with Anne, but there was nothing else he could do. He left the house with Anne, and mindful of Mr. Benson's presence, he said, "Stay through tomorrow night, Anne. We need to finish our discussion, and I can't get away tomorrow until the evening."

"We'll see," she murmured noncommittally.

But she didn't have the slightest intention of waiting here for Simon to return the following evening. She'd meant it when she'd said she was tired of waiting, and she'd already said all that she intended to say.

The headlights clearly pinpointed Simon standing next to his own car as Anne shifted gears and prepared to back her car out of the driveway. He stood still, not even seeming to breathe as he watched her go. When Anne finally wrenched her eyes from him and turned her head to back up the car, her heart felt as though it were breaking in two.

Chapter Twelve

The first moment he could get free the following evening, Simon headed straight for Lancaster House. But the place was in darkness and Anne didn't answer when he pounded on the door. He had a sinking feeling that she had gone back to the city, deliberately avoiding him, but just to make sure he went across the street and knocked on Mr. Benson's door.

Mr. Benson opened the door, and recalling the older man's anxiety last night, Simon politely inquired about Mrs. Benson's health. He was assured that she was much better now that she had proper medication, so Simon got to the point of his visit. Did Mr. Benson know where Anne might be right now?

"Oh, sure," the other man replied cheerfully. "She stopped in to say goodbye before she left. She headed back to the city about midmorning."

"I see." Simon felt cold, and suddenly very, very tired. "Did she say anything about when she might be back?"

Mr. Benson scratched his chin and nodded. "Just that it would probably be a good while, and would we keep an eye on the house for her."

"Thanks." Simon nodded. "I hope Mrs. Benson keeps improving."

Mr. Benson nodded in return. "And I hope the same for your father."

Simon headed back across the street, greatly frustrated. As he climbed into his car, he knew without a doubt that if he tried to call Anne, all he would get was her answering machine.

She had slipped away from him once more.

Instead of returning to his lonely apartment, he drove to his father's house, where Caroline was staying.

"Hi," she greeted him. She stood on tiptoe and kissed his cheek as he entered the house. "I've been trying to call you, but Mary said you'd already left the newspaper for the day. Then I tried your apartment, but you didn't answer."

"I didn't go home," Simon explained without explaining. "Are you ready for that pizza?"

"More than ready," Caroline laughed. "I'm starving."

"Do you want to go out to the pizza parlor, or order in?" Simon asked.

"Which would you rather do?" she asked.

"Let's order in," Simon said after a moment's thought. "I'm in a mood to really relax. Besides, it's threatening to rain."

"Getting colder, too." Caroline rubbed her arms. She was wearing jeans and a gray sweatshirt. "Why don't you build us a fire while I call for the pizza? Oh," she added. "I bought some beer on the chance that we ended up eating here tonight. Want one?"

"I'd love it." Simon sighed deeply and rubbed the back of his neck. He was more exhausted than he'd thought. Last night he'd had precious little sleep. It had been extremely late when he'd seen Anne, and once he'd gotten home to bed, he'd been so distressed by their conversation that his thoughts had kept him awake. Today he'd been constantly on the run. There'd been crises at both Tarrant Inn Resort Hotel and at the *Sentinel* that had required his attention. Finding that Anne had gone away again just seemed to bring the weight of fatigue down on his shoulders more firmly.

Once he had the fire started, Simon pulled a large pillow off the sofa and tucked it behind his head while he leaned back against the sofa. He stretched out his long legs.

Caroline returned, handed him his beer and then curled up into a ball on the sofa.

Simon took a long draft of his beer and sighed deeply. It was the first time he'd relaxed all day. "How was your day?" he finally thought to inquire of his sister.

Earlier in the day Caroline had spoken to their father in the hospital, and now she related the news to Simon. "He's still getting stronger, so much so that he insisted I not return to Albany for at least another day. I think I ought to go back tomorrow, though. He'll get lonely, and maybe even depressed if we're away from him too long."

"It's my turn to go," Simon reminded her. "I'm planning to go first thing in the morning. You stay here and take another day to rest up. I'm sick of making trips to that hospital, and I know you must be twice as tired of it as I am. After all, you've had to stay there the most."

"Thanks," Caroline said gratefully. "I could use another day's break, to be honest. Why is it that sitting with someone in the hospital is so exhausting?"

It was a rhetorical question, and for a long moment they both stared into the fire, lost in their own thoughts.

"I just called home an hour ago," Caroline said a bit later.

"Oh?" Simon pulled himself out of his reverie and tried to exhibit a proper interest in his sister's family. "How're Neal and the boys?"

"Fine. Missing me," Caroline said wistfully. "I miss them, too."

"Well, let's hope we'll get Dad home from the hospital soon, and Mrs. Potter will come back from her sister's and you can go back to your family where you belong. We sure can't have the boys forgetting what their pretty mom looks like!" Simon reached up and patted Caroline's knee.

"Thanks for the compliment." Caroline smiled. "You make a pretty handsome uncle yourself."

Simon frowned. "I'm just sorry we have to live so far apart that I don't have a chance to get really acquainted with my nephews on a day-to-day basis. I'd like to be able to be close to them."

Caroline sighed. "I'd like that, too." She fell silent for a moment, running her finger around the rim of the beer stein she held. "You need children of your own, Simon," she murmured. "Why don't you find yourself a nice wife and settle down and start a family?"

Simon gazed at her thoughtfully. He had never breathed to a living soul the secret that he and Anne shared, but now he badly needed someone in whom to confide, someone who could advise him, someone he could trust.

Finally he said, "Caroline, I have something to tell you, and it's going to be sort of a shock."

Her eyes were fixed on his, but she remained silent, waiting.

"I've got a problem and I thought you might be able to help me."

She nodded. "Sure. If I can. What is it, Simon?"

Simon sucked in a deep breath, and then finally let go of it. "Anne…Anne and I have been married for the past five years."

Caroline stared at him with almost comical disbelief. Her reaction might have been funny to Simon if it concerned any other subject.

"Married?" his sister shrieked. "To Anne?" She threw him a skeptical look and insisted, "Oh, come on, Simon! You're pulling my leg."

Simon shook his head and gazed at her glumly. "It's no joke, believe me."

Caroline gave him a long, considering look, and finally she gave her own head a little shake. "You're really serious, aren't you?"

Simon nodded. "I wouldn't joke about something like this," he replied.

"You and Anne are truly married? Why didn't you ever tell us?"

For the next half hour Simon told his sister almost everything about his relationship with Anne. The closer he came to the present, however, the harder the telling became. But Simon forced himself to continue. If Caroline was to be of any help at all, she had to know the whole story.

"Now Anne's walked away from me again," he said despondently. "I haven't been able to go to the city to see her since the news about Dad, and she refused to come to see me here. I didn't even know she was in Mount Evergreen yesterday until you told me. She wasn't going to let me know she was here at all!"

"But why?" Caroline asked softly. "She obviously has a reason. Did you quarrel?"

"Not exactly. But obviously I can't tell Dad about us right now, not with him in such a precarious condition. Anne says she's not trying to force my hand, that she understands why I can't speak out right now, but she also says she's simply tired of waiting . . . that this is just like the last time and she's unwilling to keep on waiting indefinitely." He spread his hands in a gesture of helplessness and shrugging, said, "That's it. That's the whole dismal story."

Caroline rose from the sofa and moved restlessly around the room, touching first one object, then another. Simon eyed her morosely as she prowled about. Finally she swung around to look at him.

"You've gotten yourself into a fine mess, haven't you?" she asked.

"I'd say that's the understatement of the year." Simon rubbed his hand across his forehead and looked at her beseechingly. "What am I going to do? I can't let her go, but I can't be open about our marriage and tell Dad right now, either."

"I don't know," Caroline replied slowly. "I feel for you. I really do. But I have to tell you, Simon, as a woman I also have an enormous amount of sympathy for Anne's side of things."

"But she's being unreasonable!" Simon exclaimed. Now he got to his feet and began striding agitatedly around the room.

Caroline shook her head and said gently, "No, Simon, she isn't."

He opened his mouth to argue, but Caroline lifted a hand, stifling his unuttered protests. "No woman would want to continuously live in limbo as she's done the past five years, or be treated like a back-street mistress when she's a legal wife. How much to do you expect from her, for God's sake? There's a limit to how much any woman can or is willing to take! Anne wants a life, Simon, a rich, fulfilling life, and I don't blame her. She wants everything out in the open and aboveboard. You have to understand that

or else you cheapen your entire relationship and the whole
ideal of marriage."

"I understand what you're saying," Simon responded.
"But how can I tell Dad the truth right now when he's not
well enough to accept it? Telling him might kill him! But if
I don't tell him, I'll lose Anne altogether!" He paced the
length of the room and back, pausing in front of Caroline.
His voice was bleak when he said, "I have no choice. I have
to let her go."

"I'm sorry," Caroline murmured.

Later, when their pizza arrived and they were eating it,
Caroline asked, "What was the feud about between Dad
and Anne's father, anyway?"

"Who knows?" Simon replied. "I've asked Dad, and
Anne has asked her father, but neither one of them will say.
Not only were they business partners, but the two of them
were best friends while they were growing up, and now
look! Whatever their quarrel, it's wrecked mine and Anne's
lives!"

"Whatever happened," Caroline speculated, "it must've
been pretty serious to have created such a final split between two men who'd been best friends all their lives. I hate
to say this, Simon, but it's a real pity you and Anne had to
go and fall in love with each other."

"Don't I know it!" Simon muttered morosely.

Anne put in some long difficult hours the next few weeks,
both working at her studio and making calls on magazine-
photography editors and advertising agencies. At other
times when she'd had too many things going at once, she'd
wished she wasn't just a one-woman show; that there was
someone with whom she could share the work. But lately
she'd been grateful to have a lot of work to do because
staying busy kept her mind and her body occupied. Today
as she hurried along the sidewalk from the subway stop to-

ward her apartment, she remained preoccupied with her current project. She'd been assigned to photograph a collection of new skin-care products. She was to come up with a unique way to display the bottles and jars as a change from the usual satin-and-lace approach, while maintaining the required image of a beautiful woman who has flawless skin as a result of using the contents of those jars and bottles. So far, she hadn't been pleased with any of her ideas.

Yesterday had been Thanksgiving. Anne and her father had spent the day with friends who lived on Long Island. It had been a pleasant day filled with warm companionship and too much turkey and dressing and pumpkin pie. Unusually mild, sunny weather had invited them all outdoors to walk off the heavy midday meal, and Anne had tried to remind herself of the many things for which she had to be grateful; somehow this year it was extremely difficult to count her blessings.

All she could think of was her loss.

She loved Simon so much that it was like a wound in her heart to think of him and to know that his presence in her life was finally over and done with. There was almost nothing she would not do for him, except wait any longer. No more hope lingered in her. Thinking that Simon would announce their marriage had been a foolish and vain hope for far too many years already, and she wasn't going to waste anymore of her time waiting for something that was never going to happen. It was time to turn the page and begin a new chapter in her life, one without Simon in it.

It was more than time to put the past behind her. Her life was speeding by, and yet she seemed to be standing still, her progress arrested by an illusion, by a dream that would never be realized.

Most of her friends were married and starting families; their lives were filled with purpose and meaning. Anne wanted those things for herself, but her life felt empty and meaningless. She had her career, of course, and she was pleased that she had achieved some success with it by giving it her all, but in the end what did she really have? A hollow achievement. Simply a means of earning a living. Enjoyable and rewarding though her work was, it couldn't bring her life and light and love and joy, the way a husband and children and a commitment to family life could. Although her career as a photographer gave her a gratifying creative outlet, it didn't allow for the expression of her most profound desire to be a vital part of another person's life.

Anne yearned to share her being with her husband in that special closeness that only exists between two people who give all of themselves to each other, a relationship that encompasses but goes far deeper than just sexual passion, wonderful as that was. She wanted the sort of kinship that speaks a private language between two people even without a word being said by either of them. She wanted the kind of closeness that makes the one incomplete without the other, that gladly uplifts the other through the hard patches of life and joyfully celebrates the glorious moments. She ached to hold children in her arms, *her* children, to soothe a tiny forehead with her hands, to hug a teary-eyed child back to smiles, to be there always to offer a supportive hand, encouragement, security and confidence. In short, Anne wanted her life to count in the most profound ways a woman's life can count, and with Simon that was just never going to happen. It was time she dealt with that fact, however painful. It was time to let go and move on.

Anne rounded the corner at the end of the block. Her apartment was in the middle of the next block, and she was eager to get there. It was almost dark, and the temperature was dropping. A blast of frigid air from Canada had swept over the city with numbing rapidity and now a steady, freezing drizzle had begun. It was a drastic change from the previous day. Anne looked forward to getting inside her apartment and out of the inclement weather.

From a distance she could see a dark masculine form hunched on the stoop of her apartment building, but Anne thought nothing of it. Sometimes Mr. Wickers sat there, smoking the smelly cigars that his wife forbade him to enjoy indoors. Still, it was strange for him to be sitting outside in such foul weather.

She'd almost reached the steps before the man, whose head had been turned away from her, heard her approach and twisted around to look in her direction. Surprised, Anne stopped dead in her tracks.

"Simon!"

He swung to his feet. "Thank God you're here at last!"

"Why?" Her heart began to thud. "What's happened?"

Simon was running down the few steps to meet her. "Happened?" he echoed, sounding puzzled. "Nothing's happened. I'm merely freezing to death, that's all. I've been sitting here for over an hour. Thank God you're here with the key to your warm apartment! You *are* going to let me in so I can thaw out, aren't you?"

Simon shivered, and he looked so miserable and pouty, like an unhappy little boy, that suddenly laughter bubbled up inside Anne. "All right," she said. "I might even throw in a cup of hot coffee."

"Bless you!" he exclaimed with heartfelt gratitude. "You're a saint!" He followed her up the steps and into the vestibule of the building.

"What brings you here, Simon?" Anne asked as she collected her mail before mounting the stairs.

"I took Caroline to JFK to catch a plane back to London," he replied as he climbed the stairs behind her.

"I see," Anne murmured. "Then your father is doing better?"

"Much," Simon replied. "We got him home from the hospital a week ago, and he seems to be getting stronger every day. Actually Caroline could've left then, since Mrs. Potter is at the house to take care of his needs during the day, and I can stay over at night until he gets strong enough to be left alone, but Dad asked her to stay through Thanksgiving, so of course she did."

They had reached Anne's second-floor apartment. She slipped the key into the lock, and moments later, they were inside.

"Make yourself comfortable," she told Simon as she shed her coat. "I'll go put on the coffee."

While she was alone in the kitchen, Anne wondered why Simon had bothered to come to see her. She couldn't decide whether she was glad to see him or not. True, her heart had leaped at the sight of him waiting for her outside. When his eyes had lit up and he'd smiled and come dashing down the steps toward her, she hadn't been able to stop the rush of gladness that spread through her.

But now, alone in her kitchen, she had a moment for reflection, and she concluded that it was not a good thing that he was here. His visit merely prolonged the agony of trying to get over him. It was a quietly thoughtful Anne who carried the coffee tray into the living room a few minutes later.

Simon stood at her window, gazing out at the rain-slick street.

"Coffee's ready," she said.

He turned and smiled at her, rubbing his hands together. "Ah, wonderful!"

For the next half hour they were careful to speak only on neutral subjects that did not affect their own precarious relationship. The air was charged with suppressed tension as they both attempted to behave in an easy, relaxed way

Like acquaintances, they each gave brief, meaningless accounts of how they'd spent Thanksgiving Day, and then they moved on to talk about the upcoming Christmas holidays.

Simon mentioned that among other gifts he'd sent home with Caroline, he'd included New York Giants T-shirts for his young nephews. "It's never too early to start teaching them about the truly important things in life," he declared.

Anne laughed. "I suppose that's true."

After skirting the issue of their relationship for as long as he could, Simon dropped all pretense, looked at Anne gravely and asked, "You didn't really mean goodbye, did you?"

A tortured expression came into her eyes, and the pain of it made Simon glance away.

"Yes," Anne answered after a long moment. "I meant every word of it, Simon."

"But you can't end things like this!" he insisted gruffly. "I won't let you!" He set his coffee cup on the table and got up, going to her chair. He knelt beside her, and took her hand in his. "Please, Anne, can't you be a little more patient? Give me a couple more months? Just until Dad is stronger. Then I promise I'll tell him about us. I need you, darling! Just a little more time, that's all I'm asking!"

A bleak, distant look entered Anne's eyes. Simon saw that she was not angry with him, maybe no longer even hurt. Her expression was just infinitely sad. She seemed terribly disappointed, and above all, she seemed tired.

Now she shook her head, and tears welled in her beautiful brown eyes. Her voice was husky when she finally spoke. "I'm sorry, Simon. There've been too many fallings-out between our families, too many secret marriages. It just won't work. I don't think our relationship was ever meant to work. Fate is against us."

"What are you talking about?" Simon got to his feet and stared down at her uncomprehendingly.

Anne began to tell him about the secret marriage that had existed between Rebecca Lancaster and Douglas Tarrant, and how difficult it had been for Rebecca, never to be able to openly acknowledge her love for Douglas, nor to be able to openly show her grief as his widow when news came of his death. They had planned to announce their marriage to their families after he returned from overseas, and because of that, she'd refused to allow him to rewrite his will in her favor, or to list her as his legitimate next of kin. She'd felt that because she hadn't yet had a chance to live with Douglas as his wife, she had no right to benefit from his possible death, so of course, she neither received widow's benefits from the military, nor did she inherit Douglas's personal assets and possessions. Whatever he'd possessed went entirely to his family.

Simon was astonished at the story. The parallel between his and Anne's marriage and his great-uncle and her great-aunt's was unnerving, and it seemed to cast a pall over his hopes. It was as though the tragic ending of Rebecca and Douglas's marriage did indeed destine their own to end with equal finality...the only difference being that this time the marriage would end from the fatal bullet of a divorce decree instead of a life lost on a battlefield.

He could read that finality in Anne's eyes, even before she spoke again. "Our families seem fated to have feuds and star-crossed lovers. You asked me to wait one more time...just a couple of months. But in the end, it wouldn't do a thing except delay the pain of our saying goodbye. I simply can't endure it any longer, Simon."

"How can you say that? Once everything is out in the open, we can begin a proper marriage and finally live together as we should."

"What about our fathers' reactions?" she challenged. "Even if the news doesn't bring on another heart attack for your father, the basic problem is still the same... our fathers hate each other. Because of their feud they ordered us not to see each other when we were teenagers, and as far as we can determine, nothing has changed to soften their feelings toward each other. What makes you think your father will accept me now, just because we're married? Or that my father will accept you?" Anne shook her head. "Simon, I'm tired of the whole thing. Just plain bone-weary tired. This problem has been dragging on now, not just for the past five years since we got married, but from the time we were in high school and first showed an interest in each other. I just can't wait in the background anymore. Even if you wanted to announce our marriage to the whole world right this minute, I'm convinced it would only stir up more problems because of our fathers' ill feelings. Well, I don't want to live that way, always tiptoeing around someone else's bristling hostilities. It's not fair to either of us to have to live that way, much less any children we might have."

"Anne, you don't mean all this," Simon pleaded. "You're disturbed right now, but things can still work out between us. Just have a little faith in the strength of our love."

"That's just it," she said sadly. "I don't have that sort of faith anymore. I love you, but I'm through. I'm truly sorry, but you have a right to be told...I'm going to get my divorce. Goodbye, Simon. Good luck with your life."

He wanted to argue with her, to convince her that her doubts were unjustified, but the words wouldn't come. Simon felt a cold tremor ripple through him. Anne really meant it, he realized. This time she was determined to go through with the divorce.

When he left her apartment building and walked along the street through the icy rain, Simon was scarcely even aware of the miserable, penetrating cold. He was aware of one single thing.

He had just lost the only woman he had ever loved.

Chapter Thirteen

Simon was utterly bereft. He didn't understand why, but losing Anne this time seemed far worse than the first time they'd separated. They'd been younger then, hot-headed and angry. This time there was no anger—only sorrow and emptiness.

He wondered when the terrible feeling would go away.

It had been two weeks since he'd visited Anne at her apartment, and he felt no better now than he had that night she'd said goodbye with such implacable finality. It was as though he were suffering from a virus that had laid him low with fever and aches and pains, and which refused to go away.

He sat at his desk at the hotel. It had been a hectic morning. Only the past forty-five minutes or so had been conducive to clear thought and productive work, and Simon had plunged into his paperwork with zeal. He detested work piling up and waiting on him, and since he ran two businesses that were thirty miles apart, there was always work waiting for him. He did his best to stay on top of each day's demands and clear the desk completely at one location before moving on to the other. Only now, when he was finishing up with the last tasks that absolutely had to be dealt with at the hotel this morning, the thought of Anne had suddenly intruded.

It was the young honeymooners, Mr. and Mrs. Glynne, who had first injected the thought of Anne into Simon's busy morning, but out of necessity he'd had to thrust the thought aside while he dealt with immediate problems.

Last evening in the dining room, the newlywed couple had been caught up in such floating-on-a-cloud, supreme happiness and were so blissfully wrapped up in each other, that they'd been oblivious to everyone else in the room, including their persevering waiter. Later in the kitchen Simon had overheard the man saying he'd had to ask every question of the couple at least three times before they even heard him.

But this morning it was quite apparent that the couple had had a lover's spat. Their long faces at breakfast told the story even before they went their separate ways for the morning . . . she to the hotel gym to join the aerobics class, he to take a solitary hike up the hillside.

Simon glanced at his watch. A quarter to twelve. He'd better finish dictating the last letter that needed a reply, and then a quick memo to the staff and be on his way.

Ten minutes later he was finished. He took his jacket from the coatrack by the door, shrugged into it and left the office.

"Are you leaving for the day, Mr. Tarrant?" Evelyn asked.

Simon nodded. "Yes. I'm meeting my father for lunch. I hope we're finished with crises here for the day, but I'll be at the *Sentinel* this afternoon if you need me."

"I hope we won't be needing you," Evelyn declared in a frazzled voice.

It had been a trying morning for everyone.

"I hope so, too," Simon replied. "There are a few letters and memos on the Dictaphone. Oh, and if that linen supplier calls back, tell him I'm sorry I wasn't able to talk to him today, but to try me again tomorrow morning." With a casual wave, he went out the door.

Simon took the private exit door near the executive parking area and headed toward his car. The day was cold and overcast and Simon's warm breath made steam on the air. A few snowflakes sprinkled his head and shoulders before he reached his car.

He appreciated the peace and quiet of the half-hour drive back to town. It had been the sort of morning to try a man's sanity.

The rural area between the resort hotel and Mount Evergreen was nestled in a wooded valley, and Simon never tired of it. In the far distance the mountains were blue-gray, punctuated by deep forest evergreen trees frosted with a powdered sugar dusting of snow. The road twisted and turned through stands of birch, a pine grove, and past a few isolated farms. As the car approached a narrow bridge that spanned a tumbling trout stream, Simon was reminded that he hadn't been fishing in ages. Maybe by springtime his father would be strong enough to go, and they could get in a little fly-fishing.

By the time Simon reached Mount Evergreen, he was feeling more relaxed. He hadn't realized how tense the events of the morning had made him until his knotted muscles finally untied themselves.

With only two and a half weeks remaining until Christmas, the town's main street had been transformed into a holiday fantasy land, with garlands and bells and trees with twinkling lights. A hearty, red-velvet-suited Santa Claus stood just outside his Candy Cane House in front of Ned's Five and Dime. As Simon drove past, Santa bent over to shake hands with a young admirer while the child's parents beamed.

Simon's throat tightened. It was beginning to look as though he would never be privileged with the simple pleasure of taking his own child to visit Santa, nor to experience any other of the myriad memorable moments in the life of a loving parent. He wanted a family of his own in the worst way—but he knew with deep inner certainty that no one would do for the mother of his children except Anne. And since she was out of his life, he was destined to remain childless.

He passed the *Sentinel*'s office and drove on down the street, struggling to throw off the less than ebullient mood his morning, and also his thoughts of Anne, had cast over him. His father was an invalid who'd been fighting his own depression of late, and he certainly didn't need an additional dose from Simon.

Lunch with Joseph turned out to be exactly what Simon needed. His father was recovering nicely, and because he was feeling better today than he had at any time since his heart attack, he was also in a more congenial mood.

They discussed business. At the best of times, it was a subject both men enjoyed. At the worst of times, such as today, his father was a good sounding board for Simon.

Joseph had nothing to do with running either the hotel or the newspaper anymore, but he liked to hear about what was going on, and Simon liked discussing his business problems and decisions with his father. Sometimes Joseph made shrewd suggestions that helped Simon get back on track when he wasn't quite sure about how to deal with a particular situation, but other times he rejected his father's advice in favor of a different approach. But no matter how Simon worked out his day-to-day business problems, father and son both enjoyed discussing them, and until today, Joseph hadn't felt well enough to inquire.

He had picked a heck of a day to ask whether Simon could use a sympathetic ear.

"This morning we had a fire in the kitchen and one of our desk clerks was caught stealing money from another clerk's handbag. Also, one of our hotel guests rear-ended another guest's car in the parking garage. Oh, and the agent of the entertainer who was booked for this weekend called up to say his client is ill and won't be able to fulfill his engagement contract. And I haven't even set foot in the *Sentinel* yet!"

Joseph chuckled. "I'm glad to hear everything's running so smooth and trouble-free," he teased. The slight smile on his lips disappeared. "How bad was the fire?"

They spent the remainder of the meal discussing the various incidents that had taken place and how Simon had handled them, or intended to. As his father nodded approvingly, Simon reflected that they were very much alike in many ways. Like Joseph, Simon enjoyed a challenge, despite his grumbling today when things had become a little overwhelming. Whenever problems beset Simon, he never entertained the notion of defeat. Instead, he always set about seeking an immediate solution, and became all the more determined to ultimately triumph.

It was that dogged, hang-on-at-all-costs persistence that had made his father a success; it was that tough determination, Simon was convinced, that had brought Joseph through the traumatic physical ordeal of the heart attack and subsequent surgery. Simon felt a strong surge of affection for his father. Joseph Tarrant was a fighter.

And so was his son.

As he remembered that truth, it was as though a light illumined Simon's mind. He'd been doing the very thing over the matter of Anne that would never have occurred to him if it had concerned a business problem. He'd been accepting defeat as a *fait accompli*.

Now he realized that he had to go at solving his problem from a different angle. Anne had said goodbye. But goodbye didn't have to mean goodbye—not if he refused to accept it! All he had to do was find a way—a fresh and successful way—to convince her that, despite her objections, they did indeed belong together.

The real problem was not their feelings for each other, but the hostility between their fathers.

But how to eliminate that? Since Simon didn't even know the reason for the quarrel between the two men, how could he possibly hazard a guess whether they would accept each other's children into their own families? Yet without such acceptance, there *was* no hope for him and Anne.

Then there was still the touchy issue of his father's health. Simon couldn't help worrying about the possible impact on Joseph's heart when he learned about his son's marriage to the daughter of his old adversary. Simon loved Anne dearly, but not at the expense of his father's life.

There had to be a way around the problem . . . but how?

Anne stood at her tenth-floor hotel window, gazing out at the lights of Houston. Her room was in deep darkness, for it was well past two a.m., and yet she had been unable to fall asleep.

She had arrived in Houston three days ago to speak at a seminar on professional photography. She had met some very nice people in the interim, and the seminar groups had been eager to learn and flatteringly attentive in her workshops.

She had met a very attractive man from Dallas who was also there conducting a workshop, and the two of them had hit it off immediately. Naturally they had photography in common, but they had hit it off on other counts as well. By the second night, Bill had invited her to go out with him, but Anne had turned him down, knowing all the while that she was being a fool for rejecting his offer.

She still thought so. Wasn't she as free as a bird, except for the formality of a signature on a legal document stating that it was so? Still, she couldn't bring herself to accept a date with another man.

It was ridiculous, actually. She'd had no such qualms during the five years that she and Simon had been separated, so why a little technicality like not being legally divorced bothered her now and kept her from going out with a very eligible and attractive man, she didn't know.

Anyway, what could have happened had she gone out with him? A serious relationship with Bill could scarcely have evolved during a single evening. Tomorrow morning—or rather, she corrected herself, later *this* morning—she would be returning to New York, so all she had actually accomplished was to deny herself a pleasant evening.

Anne turned her back on the twinkling, colorful lights below her window and padded across the darkened room and crawled back into bed. She had to try to get some sleep. In three more hours, it would be time to dress and get to the airport for her flight.

But unhappily, she remained awake, poignantly remembering the last time she'd been in a hotel room—that wonderful night in Denver when Simon had arrived unexpectedly. They had spent a glorious evening together of love and passion, expectancy and hope.

But the memory was only ashes now…ashes on the cold hearth of her heart. Anne flipped over, pounded the pillow, tucked it up beneath her chin and ordered herself sternly to stop thinking of Simon immediately. She *had* to get some sleep.

In desperation, she tried the old standby of counting sheep. One...two...t...h...r...e...e...

Simon ordered a beer and opened the menu, but his eyes were unseeing as he stared at the neat columns of words. He was tense with anxiety about what he was going to do and what reaction he might get. But he had to do something. It was essential, and this was the only way he knew to go about it.

He had driven down to New York this morning, after arranging this meeting by telephone. Now he glanced at his watch. It was almost one o'clock. Still a bit early. He could only hope that he wasn't going to be stood up.

Peeking above the menu, Simon's blue eyes kept watch on the restaurant's entrance. Each time the door swung open he surveyed the newcomer, but each time he was disappointed when it was not the person he was expecting.

The waitress brought Simon's beer. He took a sip, then impatiently drummed his fingers on the table. His gaze returned swiftly to the entrance as the door opened once more.

A distinguished-looking man wearing a conservative gray business suit walked into the restaurant. He had neat silver hair and a strong, intelligent face. He paused to speak to the hostess who smiled and nodded and turned to lead him across the restaurant.

Simon rose and extended his hand to the other man. "Thank you for coming, Mr. Lancaster," he greeted. "I really appreciate this."

Robert Lancaster shook hands with him. "I must confess you've captured my interest. Last month you came to see me at my office, demanding to know where my daughter was, and now, out of the blue you call and invite me to lunch. What's all this about, Simon?"

"Have a seat, sir," Simon invited. "Can I order you a drink from the bar?"

"I'll have a beer, the same as you," Robert said agreeably as he sat down.

"Fine." Simon beckoned the waitress and ordered Robert's beer. When they were seated across from each other, Simon placed his hands on the table and laced his fingers together, trying to determine how best to begin.

"How is Joe?" Robert asked before Simon could speak again. "Anne told me he'd had a heart attack and then surgery."

"He's doing very well," Simon reported. "His recovery has been remarkable."

"Then the doctors consider the surgery a success?"

Simon nodded. "They've told him that if he takes care of himself, he can possibly live to a ripe old age."

"I'm glad to hear that," Robert responded. "I've been concerned about him."

There had been a note of unmistakable sincerity in Robert's voice, and this heartened as well as surprised Simon. "Have you, sir? I was under the impression that you hated my father."

Robert gave a tiny shrug. "I've hated Joe for many a year now. But you know something, son? While love increases with time, hate wears thin the older you get . . . at least if you've got a smidgen of sense, it does. You just don't have the energy to expend on it anymore."

"That's as good a reason as any other to stop hating someone, I suppose," Simon chuckled.

Robert's beer arrived. He raised the mug toward Simon, and Simon lifted his as well. Their mugs clinked, and Robert toasted, "To Joe's good health."

They drank, and then Robert settled back in his chair, looked Simon straight in the eyes and demanded, "All right, son, now what's on your mind?"

"You and my father, sir," Simon replied without prevarication. "I need to know what happened between you that ended your lifelong friendship."

Robert scowled and took a long time answering. "That's between the two of us and no one else," he said gruffly.

"That's where you're wrong, sir," Simon said. "Your quarrel affects other people's lives, as well."

"Nonsense!" Robert snapped impatiently. "It's nobody's business but our own!"

"Maybe so," Simon conceded. "All the same, I need to know. It's vitally important to me, Mr. Lancaster."

"Why?" Robert asked in a cold, forbidding voice.

Undeterred, Simon plowed on. He had to get to the bottom of this matter, and Robert Lancaster was the only person who could help him.

"Because the fact is that your rift with my father is wrecking my life. And Anne's."

Robert's thick eyebrows rose quizzically and the expression in his dark eyes was penetrating. "All right, Simon," he said at last. "You've succeeded in gaining my undivided attention. Now you're damn well going to have to explain that statement if you have any hope at all of getting me to tell you something I've never discussed with another living soul except your father."

Simon nodded. "It's like this," he began.

Chapter Fourteen

She ought to feel hopeful and happy. After all, Darryl Miller had found a potential buyer for Lancaster House. But as Anne put out cookies on a plate while the coffee brewed, she was only conscious of a heavy depression.

She was at the playhouse. She had dressed simply in an autumn gold woolen dress accented with a wide brown belt. Her rich brown hair fell in sleek waves around her head and shoulders, and the small amount of makeup she wore gave a soft apricot glow to her cheeks and lips.

Anne's gaze traveled around the room, flitting from the furnishings to Aunt Rebecca's watercolor paintings on the wall to the crammed bookshelves, and suddenly her wide, dark eyes filled with tears. The playhouse had always meant so much to Aunt Rebecca as well as to herself. If the house was sold, Anne would never again have the privilege of visiting this familiar and comforting room, and the thought weighed heavily upon her emotions.

It was a cold December evening...the night before Christmas Eve, and Anne appreciated the warmth emanating from the radiator. Comforting as the heat was, though, it would have been warmer inside the house. There she could also have built a fire in the fireplace. But Mr. Miller had been most emphatic when he'd telephoned...their meeting should take place inside the playhouse.

The request had been made by the potential buyer. It seemed he was as taken with the playhouse as he was with the main house. He wanted to meet with Anne to learn about the house's history, and he'd asked for the meeting to take place here in the playhouse.

Anne wished this meeting was already over. She wished Christmas itself was over, so that she could hurry back to the protective, anonymous covering of the city. Here in Mount Evergreen, she felt vulnerable and exposed. Simon might see her or find out somehow that she was here. She had a dreadful feeling that if she was confronted by him, she would fall apart at the seams and beg him to take her back, no matter what.

She couldn't permit that to happen, of course. At all costs, she had to stay clear of Simon while she was here, which shouldn't be an impossible feat. She simply wouldn't leave Lancaster House until it was time to return to the city. That way there would be absolutely no risk of accidentally bumping into him.

She hoped.

Robert had compounded her anxiety about coming to Mount Evergreen by dreaming up the idea that as long as Anne had to be at Lancaster House so close to Christmas anyway, they should spend the holiday here rather than in the city. Accordingly Anne's father would be arriving tomorrow afternoon and they would spend Christmas Day together here in the house where Robert had grown up and where Anne had spent so many happy holidays and school vacations. Despite her nervousness about spending even as little as a single hour in such proximity to Simon, Anne supposed she owed her father one last Christmas at Lancaster House, if that was what he wanted.

She grabbed a tissue and dabbed at her eyes. It wouldn't do for her visitors to find her reduced to tears. With wistful fondness Anne gazed around the room once more. She had so many memories; there'd been so many happy and sad times here. The playhouse walls had chronicled the lives of two Lancaster girls of two different generations. Anne had to admit she would miss this place. Still, making a complete break from the past was surely for the best.

Yes, she hoped this man who was coming tonight would buy the house.

She began setting out cups and saucers and wished her father was here. She knew a good bit of Lancaster House's history, but not as much as Robert did. She'd tried to get him to come with her to Mount Evergreen tonight and meet with the history-loving potential buyer himself, but he had important business at the office Christmas Eve morning that demanded his personal attention. He couldn't break away sooner.

A knock fell on the door. Darryl Miller and his client were here. Anne set down the cup she held, smoothed back her hair and went toward the door.

When she saw who was standing there, Anne was so astonished she could say nothing.

The man on the doorstep gave her a courtly nod. His grayish hair was combed into a wave at one side of his head while ice-blue eyes gazed penetratingly at her.

"Good evening, my dear. May I come in?" he inquired politely.

Numbly Anne bobbed her head. "Mr. Tarrant," she murmured faintly. "This is a surprise," she added in a masterful understatement. "Er... is there something I can do for you?"

Joseph Tarrant came slowly into the room, leaning heavily on a cane. As Anne closed the door behind him, he answered her question. "Yes, please," he replied politely. "I could do with some of that coffee I smell. It's a fiercely cold night out there."

He wore a heavy coat over his clothes, and now that he was inside the room, he unwound the woolen scarf from around his neck.

"Of course." Totally confused by this unexpected turn of events, Anne did as she was asked and poured coffee for Simon's father.

When she turned to hand the cup to him, she saw that he had shed his overcoat, revealing a tweed jacket and wood-brown slacks. He was surveying the room with a slow, deliberate gaze.

"Do you mind if I sit down?" he asked when his gaze returned to Anne's face. "Unfortunately I'm not as strong as I would like to be."

"Please do," Anne replied hastily.

Joseph settled himself comfortably on the sofa and when he accepted the coffee cup from Anne, his eyes took on a distinct twinkle. "I suppose you're wondering what I'm doing here."

Anne nodded. "Well... yes, sir, I am."

Joseph gave a low chuckle. "I'm the potential buyer you're expecting," he explained.

"You!" she exclaimed in disbelief. "But... but why would you want Lancaster House? And anyway, where is Mr. Miller?"

"Darryl won't be coming tonight," Joseph surprised her by replying. "I'm afraid the real estate meeting was simply a ruse to get you here. I'm not in the least interested in buying Lancaster House." He lifted the coffee cup to his lips.

Anne stared at him. "I don't understand..."

Joseph smiled. "Pour yourself a cup of this delicious coffee and come sit here beside me, Anne. You and I need to have a little talk."

Warily Anne did as she was told, still totally mystified. Did Joseph know about her and Simon? It seemed unlikely that after all these years, Simon had finally gone to his father and told him about their marriage, especially since she was proceeding with the divorce. But what else could she and Joseph Tarrant possibly have to discuss?

"Are you here to talk about Simon?"

"Simon?" Joseph shook his head. "Not at all. I came here to talk about history."

"The history of Lancaster House." Anne nodded. "But... if you're not interested in buying the house, why are you interested in discussing its history?"

"I'm not," Joseph replied. "I'm interested in discussing *my* history, and I promise to try not to bore you too much."

"*Your* history?" Anne stared at him with blank astonishment.

"I believe I owe you an explanation," Joseph said. "I owe it to you because you're Bob's daughter and because I loved your mother very much."

Anne caught her breath. "You were in love with my mother?"

Joseph shook his head and stretched out his arm, covering her hand with his. "No, my dear," he corrected gently. "I loved her, but I wasn't in love with her. There's a vast difference."

Anne looked down at his hand covering hers. "I see."

"I doubt that you do, but I'll try to make it clear for you." Joseph was suddenly very serious. His gaze shifted from Anne's face to the wall on the opposite side of the room. There was a faraway quality to his voice, and on his face was an expression that said his thoughts were a million miles . . . or almost fifty years . . . away.

"When we were kids, I *was* in love with Lorrie. Bob and I both were. There was always a rivalry between us over her and she played both of us like fish dangling on a line. One week he was in favor and the next week, it was me. But there was never a doubt that one of us would grow up to marry her. The only question was which one of us would she choose in the end."

"I understood that you and my father were best friends," Anne said. "If you were rivals for my mother's affections, didn't that put a wedge between you?"

Joseph smiled reminiscently. "Bob and I were best friends, and competing for Lorrie was all part of the fun. She attended the homecoming dance with me, the prom with Bob, things like that." He paused, as though marshaling his thoughts.

"What was my mother like as a girl?" Anne asked hoarsely.

Joseph's face softened. "Lorrie was beautiful . . . a spirited minx who loved to tease. Sometimes she was so flighty it was like trying to grab hold of a cloud whenever she was around, and she had the sweetest sounding laughter in all the world." Joseph's hand tightened over Anne's. "You asked, and it's only fair that you know the whole truth about your mother, not just the good things."

Anne steeled herself, somehow knowing that she wasn't going to enjoy this story. There would be no happily-ever-after ending.

"Lorrie could also be selfish and manipulative and very hard-hearted when she didn't get her way. She was also very immature. Lorrie was . . ." Joseph hesitated for a moment before going on, "Lorrie was constitutionally unsuited to handle adult responsibilities once she grew up. However, I'm getting a bit ahead of myself.

"When Bob and I went off to college, Lorrie stayed behind in Mount Evergreen. Whenever we made visits home, it became more and more apparent that Bob was her choice rather than me.

"By then, however, it didn't matter to me anymore. I still loved Lorrie as an old and dear friend, but by then I'd met Betsy, my future wife, at college. It's important that I make all this quite clear to you, Anne, so let there be no mistake about your understanding this ... I had once been in love with your mother, but by the time I got married, I was very much in love with my wife, and only my wife, even though I had the deepest affection for your mother until the day she died."

"I understand," Anne murmured.

"Good." He squeezed her hand. "After we finished college, Bob and I borrowed some money from the bank and went into partnership and bought the *Sentinel.* We got married within three months of each other. For a few years everything moved along smoothly. As well as being business partners, Bob and I continued to be close friends. Lorrie and Betsy became good friends, as well, and the four of us often spent time together socially." Joseph squeezed Anne's hand once more. "Now comes the hard part," he added.

Anne tensed and waited silently. She understood that Joseph Tarrant had come here tonight for the express purpose of telling her what had caused the bitter enmity between him and her father all those years ago, and that her mother had played a major role in whatever had occurred.

"When you came along, my dear, the realities of being a wife and mother were just too overwhelming for Lorrie. She simply couldn't cope." As Anne tensed again at the import of the words, Joseph patted her hand as one would a small child who's been hurt. "You mustn't take what I'm about to tell you personally, Anne," he said stoutly. "Lorrie really couldn't help herself—she wasn't like you and your father, strong and self-reliant. She was weak and . . . well, she was weak. You must forgive her for that."

"Forgive her for what?" Anne asked huskily.

"For leaving you and your father." When Anne started, Joseph held on to her hand more tightly than ever. "I wouldn't tell you all this if you didn't need to know the truth about your father and me. You see, Lorrie grew unhappy at the restrictive, confined life of a young mother. She blamed her unhappiness on Bob, and she came to me and told me she'd made a mistake, that it was me she loved and wanted. I didn't play along, and I thought that was the end of the matter, but a few weeks later she called me and told me she was leaving Bob and moving to the city where there were bright lights, parties and fun. You see, Lorrie wanted to be eternally young, carefree and popular, a flirt like she'd been during high school. But there was Bob and you, a year-and-a-half-old baby, to consider."

Joseph fell silent, and Anne waited for him to continue, but when the silence stretched and still he said nothing, she looked up at him. "What happened, Mr. Tarrant? I know my mother died in a car crash, but that's all I know."

He sighed heavily. "It's difficult to talk about, even all these years later. Particularly to you."

"Please," Anne prompted. "I want to know."

Joseph nodded. "By that time I had inherited the Tarrant Inn Resort Hotel from my father, you know, so although I was in business with your father at the *Sentinel,* I managed the hotel alone. Anyway, Lorrie phoned me there one afternoon. I remember it as clearly as though it happened only yesterday. It was late on a Wednesday afternoon in April, and it had been raining all day.

"Lorrie was crying and she said she needed to see me. She said she was going to leave Bob. They'd had a terrible argument that morning and she insisted she was leaving him immediately. I invited her to drive down to the hotel to have dinner with me and discuss the matter. I thought I could talk her out of it." Joseph paused and shook his head sadly.

"But I couldn't dissuade her," he went on after a long time. "Lorrie was really serious about leaving. She'd left Bob a note telling him so. When she arrived at the hotel, she was alone, without you. She'd left you in Miss Rebecca's care, without saying where she was going. She told me that you'd be much better off with Bob and his aunt than with her. I begged her to go back home to Bob and you, but she wouldn't listen to me. She was determined to drive herself to New York that very night. I tried to talk her out of driving in such bad weather. I offered to book her a room at the hotel for the night, but she refused." Joseph stopped and sighed heavily. "She just wouldn't listen to me," he added again in a sad voice.

"And the rest," Anne murmured, "as they say... is history."

Joseph nodded. "Yes. She was driving fast and recklessly and the car skidded off the road only five miles from the hotel. They said she died instantly."

They both fell silent. Anne was cut to the quick to learn her mother had walked out on her and her father. It would take time to deal with this wound to her heart, and yet, somehow she wasn't terribly surprised by the news, either. All her life, whenever she'd asked others to tell her about her mother, she'd sensed a reserve in them. She'd been conscious of the fact that she'd never received a straight answer about what her mother had really been like. Until tonight. Painful though it was to hear, Anne had no doubt whatsoever that what Joseph Tarrant had just told her was the absolute, unvarnished truth.

"My father blamed you for my mother's death, I suppose," Anne said at last.

"Indirectly," Joseph answered. "He'd already read her note saying she was leaving him when he got the news about the accident. When he heard where it had occurred, he knew there was only one place she'd been coming from so far out in the countryside...my hotel. What Bob really blamed me for was something I hadn't done. He believed I was having an affair with Lorrie."

Anne gasped. "You...and my mother...?" she whispered hoarsely. She didn't want to believe it! Oh, she didn't want to believe it. "But you said earlier..."

There was a rattle at the door. Anne broke off and swung her head around toward the sound. The door opened, and to her amazement, her own father stepped into the room.

"'Evening, Anne," Robert Lancaster said. "Have you been having an interesting conversation with Joe here?" He nodded briefly toward the other man.

Anne got to her feet, filled with trepidation. These two men despised each other. What if an ugly quarrel broke out between them?

"Dad!" she exclaimed breathlessly. "I wasn't expecting you until tomorrow evening. What are you doing here tonight?"

"The same thing Joe is doing here," Robert astonished her by saying. "I came to talk to you." He began to unbutton his coat, adding, "That coffee smells awfully good. Mind pouring me a cup, honey?"

Anne hesitated a moment, casting a suspicious glance from her father's face to Joseph Tarrant, then back to her father again. It was just beginning to dawn on her that this entire evening had been planned out between the two former friends.

At the look on her face, both men chuckled. "Kind of taken your breath away, haven't we?" Robert asked rhetorically. He waved a hand toward the coffeepot and reminded her, "Coffee, please?"

Numbly Anne poured the coffee and carried it to her father. Mechanically she refilled her own and Joseph Tarrant's cup.

"Extra cold tonight," Robert said conversationally to Tarrant.

Simon's father nodded. "Reminds me of that night we were driving back from college in my old car. It—"

"Car? You dignify that old junk heap with the title 'car'?" interjected Robert with a grin. "Lord, how many miles did we end up hiking that night after it broke down?"

"Ten, at least," Joseph chuckled. He leveled a grin at Anne. "Cold as it was, it felt like a hundred miles. But we survived. We were pretty tough back then. We could take a little hardship and think nothing of it." He shook his head. "I'd sure hate to think I had to endure that tonight, though."

Robert laughed and mused, "Funny how the older you get, the more important your comfort becomes."

"Isn't that the truth?" seconded Joseph.

Anne's suspicions had been correct. The pair had collaborated in setting her up to come here this evening. But why?

"Okay," she said dryly, thoroughly exasperated now. "What's going on here? You guys are supposed to hate each other, yet here you are chatting away about old times as though you're the best of friends!"

Robert set down his cup and went to Anne. He put his hand on her shoulder and squeezed it. "You're right. We just wanted to give you a bit of a hard time." He paused, then added seriously, "I heard Joe tell you I accused him of having an affair with your mother. It's true... I did. I believed it, and so of course, I hated him for it. It was easier to believe Lorrie had left me—and you—for the other man she'd always loved than to believe she'd just left us without a real reason. And she did run to him. I had to blame her death on someone, and Joe was that someone. Over and over he tried to tell me it wasn't true, but I was too angry and hurt and grief-stricken to listen to him.''

"And I was angry, too," Joseph added. "I was devastated that Lorrie was dead, and I blamed Bob. I felt that he must've been a rotten husband to her, that he'd driven her away—that if he'd treated her better, she would never have left him and she wouldn't have died. And I was outraged that Bob would believe the worst of me, his best friend, that he could think for a single moment that I would have an affair with his wife!''

"It was an easy assumption to make, you see," Robert added. "Once when we'd been quarreling, Lorrie told me she loved Joe, not me, so when I realized she'd gone to him at his hotel the night she died, naturally I believed she'd gone there to be with him romantically. No matter what Joe said to the contrary, I couldn't get past that picture in my mind.''

"What both of us had forgotten, or didn't want to deal with, was the truth about Lorrie herself," Joseph explained. "She'd always lied whenever it suited her, and she'd always been manipulative, playing one of us off the other. That's what she'd been doing again, telling Bob she was in love with me, telling me how awful he was treating her. She was still trying to make us jealous of each other, or to thrust a wedge between us, and in the grief we shared over her death, we didn't stop to consider that fact. We were too busy hurling accusations at each other.''

"The upshot of the whole thing," Robert said, "was that our friendship and business partnership couldn't survive. I sold Joe my half interest in the *Sentinel* and took you with me to New York where we could start a new life.''

"Why are you telling me all this now...after all these years?" Anne asked huskily.

"It's not to hurt you with the truth about your mother, honey," Robert said softly. "It's precisely because we didn't want you hurt that none of us ever told you the truth about Lorrie. I didn't want you to have a bad image of her."

"We're telling you now," Joseph said, "because you need to know. Because of our bitterness toward each other, neither Bob nor I encouraged our children to be close. But it happened in spite of us...the friendship between you and Caroline when you made visits to Mount Evergreen. Even though I would've liked to, I couldn't bring myself to put a stop to my daughter's friendship with you."

"But then came your interest in Simon when you were teenagers," Robert said. "That was a different matter entirely, and because of our hostility toward each other, both Joe and I just naturally forbade you to date each other."

Joseph nodded. "It never occurred to either of us that you'd go behind our backs to see each other. Much less that you would secretly marry."

Anne caught her breath. "How did you find out?" she asked quietly.

"Simon came to visit me. He told me," her father surprised her by saying. "He insisted upon knowing the truth about what Joe and I had quarreled about all those years ago. He wanted to tell Joe about your marriage, but he was concerned about whether Joe's heart could take the news."

"Bob realized then how our anger over the years had hurt the two of you, all without our knowledge," Joseph explained. "So after Simon's visit, Bob came to see me. You can imagine my astonishment when my housekeeper showed him into my living room."

"Did the sparks fly?" Anne asked with the beginnings of a smile.

"They might have," her father conceded, "but I'd had time through the years, as had Joe, to mellow and reflect . . . and to remember Lorrie as she'd *really* been, instead of seeing her with rose-colored glasses.

"Joe had always been straight with me all our lives," he continued. "He'd never lied to me about anything else, even when we were teenagers and the two of us were openly competing for Lorrie, so I had to reconsider the validity of his oath that he hadn't had an affair with her."

"Suffice it to say," Joseph added, "that after Bob told me about your marriage to my son, we resolved to heal our old wounds . . . for your sake, certainly, but also for our own."

Anne shook her head. "I'm glad," she said simply. "But for your sake, not mine. It's too late for Simon and me . . . years too late. Perhaps he didn't tell you, Dad, but I've filed for a divorce."

Robert nodded. "He mentioned it."

"Not that it means anything until you've signed the final papers," Joseph pointed out. "Which, of course, we're hoping to persuade you not to do."

"Hoping?" Anne stared at Joseph. "You mean you're *glad* we're married?"

Joseph didn't get the chance to answer her question. Another knock came at the door.

"My goodness," Anne murmured as she got to her feet. "The playhouse is like Grand Central Station tonight."

It was Simon. Perhaps after this surprising evening, Anne shouldn't have been taken aback to see him, yet she was. And clearly he was as astonished to see her as she was to see him.

"Anne!" he exclaimed. "What are you doing here?"

"Me?" she gasped. "What're *you* doing here?"

Robert spoke up. "I left a message with Simon's secretary asking him to meet me here tonight. Come on inside and get out of the cold, son."

Simon stepped inside the room and closed the door behind him. But his eyes never left Anne's face. She'd gone pale at the sight of him, but she was as beautiful as ever. Tonight her brown eyes were enormous as she gazed up at him, and her pink lips quivered slightly, betraying an underlying vulnerability. He had to restrain himself from reaching for her, from pulling her into his arms. But because they weren't alone, he had to control his urge.

Slowly he turned toward Anne's father, intending to politely acknowledge him. He was thoroughly confused when he saw not only Robert Lancaster, but also his own father comfortably seated on the sofa.

"Dad!" In a deeper voice, he demanded, "What's going on here?"

Joseph didn't reply at once. He set aside his cup and struggled to his feet. "Anne can fill you in on all the details," he told Simon as he began to shrug into his overcoat. "The important thing is that you're here now, and Bob and I can leave."

"What are you talking about?" Simon asked in exasperation.

"Bob and I've buried the hatchet," Joseph replied in an easy, conversational tone. "And we think it's time you and your wife do the same." Joseph Tarrant went to Anne, kissed her cheek and murmured, "Please, out of the goodness of your heart, take my son back again. He's been so moody and unpleasant recently, nobody can stand being in his company." Then he moved purposefully toward the door.

Robert, who had also pulled on his overcoat, followed, but he paused at the door and turned back to them, saying, "In the unlikely event the two of you want to see us again this evening, we'll be at Joe's house sharing a drink and rehashing old times.''

But Simon and Anne had scarcely heard him. The sound of the door closing escaped them, too, for they were too absorbed in each other to notice anything else.

Tonight it was beyond either of them to conceal the true state of their feelings. They gazed at each other with longing and love openly blazing in their eyes.

Simon stepped toward Anne, closing the gap between them. Without hesitation, she flung her arms around his neck. Their lips met and the emotional impact of the searing kiss left them both unsteady.

Simon's hands moved up to cup Anne's face. "It's obvious that I was lured here tonight under false pretenses," he murmured. The tiniest quirk of an endearing grin flitted across his lips, mesmerizing Anne.

"That makes two of us," she answered as her forefinger, of its own volition, moved to trace the curve of his lips.

Simon raised his eyebrows. "You mean you're not part of this setup?" he asked in surprise. "But . . . Dad said you could explain everything."

Anne laughed softly. "The truth is I didn't know a thing myself until a half hour ago. Your father tricked me into coming by having Mr. Miller call me and say a potential buyer for the house wanted to meet me. What bait did they use on you?"

"A couple of days ago I went to see your father," Simon admitted. "Anne, I told him about our marriage. I also asked him to tell me what had happened between him and Dad so I could judge whether I could chance telling Dad about you and me. I was desperate to win you back, and I knew the only hope I had was to get the truth out in the open. Your father still wouldn't tell me what their quarrel had been about, and he cautioned me not to talk to

Dad, but plainly he knows about our marriage now. Did your father tell Dad about us himself?''

"Yes. And your father came here tonight to tell me what had happened between them all those years ago," Anne acknowledged. "It involved my mother," she ended sadly.

"Want to tell me about it?" Simon asked gently. He sensed that whatever it was, it was painful for Anne.

She gave her head a brisk shake. "Later,' she answered huskily.

Simon gazed at her questioningly for a long moment, concerned about the unhappiness that had come over her when she'd mentioned her mother. Then he grinned and shaking his head, said, "Obviously the news of our marriage did indeed affect Dad's health," he stated. "It's been years since I've seen him as pleased with himself as he was tonight."

Anne giggled. "Come to think of it, *my* dad seemed to be feeling awfully good himself."

Simon grinned. "Yes. They were both smug and gloating over having managed to get us both here."

"And they were in a mighty big hurry to leave once you arrived," Anne laughed. "I suppose they figured if there were going to be any fireworks, they wanted to be safely away before the sparks started to fly."

"I can think of some fireworks I'd like to start," Simon confided with a sudden twinkle to his eye. His hands slid slowly down her arms. "But they're not the kind that come from fighting." He gave Anne an assessing look.

"So who's fighting?" Anne retorted.

Simon wrapped his arms around her then, in a bear hug. He lifted her from her feet and swung her around. They collapsed onto the sofa in a tangled heap of arms and legs.

"Do you know," Simon murmured as he stroked her hair, "it was right here in this room where you first said you loved me."

"I know." Anne's voice was soft and unsteady.

"Tell me again."

"I love you, Simon."

Simon sighed heavily. "Now tell me you forgive me for keeping quiet about us from the beginning. I guess I was a coward, but you've got to believe me, Anne, when I say it wasn't because I was ashamed of our marriage, or because I didn't want to live openly with you, or..."

"Hush, darling." Anne placed her fingers to his lips, then followed up the action by leaning forward to kiss him lightly. "I know it was never cowardice," she assured him. "Unless loving your father enough to be concerned about his health and welfare is the new definition of a coward. No, Simon, there's nothing to forgive. Our love was just caught up in bad timing, and I'm afraid I wasn't the most patient and understanding of souls. All I did was compound all your other problems, and I'm sorry for that. I never set out to hurt you anymore than you did me."

"But it happened all the same," Simon said huskily. "The hurting. On both sides. Anne..." he added urgently, "you've got to drop your divorce suit immediately."

"I will," she replied agreeably as his fingers moved down to lightly graze her throat and chin.

"Tomorrow," he stated flatly. "First thing tomorrow."

Anne shook her head. "It'll have to be the first thing after Christmas. Tomorrow's Christmas Eve, remember? I have a feeling the attorney may have other things on his mind tomorrow, and I know I certainly will."

"Yes?" Simon snuggled his cheek next to hers. "Like what?"

"Umm," she murmured. "Like shopping for some last-minute gifts for the two Tarrant men who are now in my life to stay. Like putting up a Christmas tree in Aunt Rebecca's parlor and buying food for Christmas dinner, and..."

"Mrs. Potter, Dad's housekeeper, is making Christmas dinner, so you don't need to worry about that part," Simon said. "As for the Christmas shopping, come to think of it, I've got some of my own to do. Maybe something glittery that'll go with that plain gold wedding band I gave you so long ago." Wistfully he added, "Or did you throw it away?"

"It's in my purse," she admitted. "I've always kept it with me."

"Even when you hated me?" he asked thickly.

"Even when I *tried* to hate you," she corrected gently. "It just never worked."

"I tried, too," he confessed. "It didn't work for me, either. I guess it means we're two pretty hopeless cases."

"I'd say that's a safe bet," Anne said with a sigh. Her arms wound around Simon's neck and his lips came closer to hers.

"I love you, Anne," Simon whispered. "I love you with all my heart." Sparkles suddenly danced like blue fire in his eyes. "Know what?" he asked whimsically. "I can almost sense the approval of our poor star-crossed ancestors."

"Douglas and Rebecca," Anne mused. She nodded and added, "So can I. I think they're happy for us. And...who knows? Perhaps they're happy together at last themselves."

"Let's hope so." Simon said. "Meantime..."

"Meantime?" Anne prompted when he broke off.

"Meantime, we've got tonight." Simon's embrace tightened around her and his voice grew thick with emotion. "And tomorrow night and the next, and the one after that. For all the rest of the days and nights of my life," he promised solemnly.

Anne was so touched by his words that she couldn't speak. The words stuck in her aching throat as tears misted her eyes. She tried to smile, and gave up the attempt, burying her face against his neck.

"Hey," Simon chided gently as his fingers slid through her hair. "I thought this was a happy evening."

"It is!" she maintained stoutly as she quickly wiped her eyes and gave him a dazzling smile. "Oh, Simon, it is!"

Simon smiled back and then stood up and extended his hand to her. "Come on, wife of mine. Let's go back to the house. It's past bedtime."

"Why, whatever do you mean?" Anne chuckled. "It's not even eight o'clock yet."

"Exactly my point," he said with a teasing gleam in his eyes. "We've got the whole long evening ahead of us."

Hand in hand, they strolled across the dark lawn. The cold air was biting, but they scarcely felt it, warmed as they were by their love.

Ahead loomed the black silhouetted shape of Lancaster House.

Ahead lay their future.

Epilogue

The March air was sharp and chilling, but the sky was cloudless and deep blue. It promised to be an exceptionally fine day.

Joe Tarrant sat rocking contentedly on the front porch swing at Lancaster House. His hands were warmed by the coffee mug he held. The steam curled and slithered upward, then vanished as it entered the current of fresh morning air.

The maple tree in the yard was putting on new leaves and the grass was trying to green. Near the driveway a bank of crocuses was starting to bloom. Joe watched a squirrel scamper from one tree branch to another as the front door of the house squeaked open. From the interior came the cry of a baby, quickly hushed. No doubt the infant was being comforted by its mother and father.

Robert Lancaster came out of the house, carrying a mug of coffee for himself. He walked toward Joe and joined him on the porch swing.

"Well?" Joe asked.

"Well, what?" Robert retorted.

"Are they the most beautiful babies you ever saw in your life, or what?"

Robert grinned, and it seemed to spread from ear to ear. "If you're ready to pick a fight, Cotton, you'll have to find someone else. I agree that they're the most wonderful babies ever born. Bound to be highly intelligent, too. After all, I *am* their grandfather!"

"Humph. You're not getting away with that boast, Bucky, my old friend! It's *my* genius they've inherited! All they probably got from you is some doggone contrariness!"

Both men chuckled as they continued to bicker amiably.

The twins, a girl and a boy, had been born a week ago in a hospital in Albany. Only two days ago their father had brought them and their mother home to Mount Evergreen. Robert had driven up from New York early this morning and this was his first opportunity to meet the newborns.

Simon and Anne had named the twins Rebecca and Douglas Tarrant, a rather fitting tribute to the two members of their families who had never been able to acknowledge their love to the world. Now, bearing their names and living in Lancaster House in Mount Evergreen, the children would help ensure that the memories of the first Rebecca and Douglas would live on.

"I never thought Anne would be content to put her career on hold for any reason, especially to live in a small town and be a full-time wife and mother," Robert said. "But she seems to be thriving in her new life."

"Unlike her mother," Joe said softly.

Robert nodded. "Yes. She's completely the opposite of her mother." He sighed heavily.

"Poor Lorrie," Joe murmured. "She seemed to need so much love, but she didn't know how to give it. Anne, on the other hand, has a remarkable gift for giving love. I've never seen Simon so happy. I only regret that my stubbornness caused them so much pain for so long."

"Mine, too," Robert admitted quietly, accepting his share of the blame.

"I'm glad we're friends again," Joe said after a moment.

Robert looked at him. "So am I. I missed you during all those years, Cotton." The two men fell silent for a time, the companionable silence that can only exist between very old, very close friends. Robert sipped at his coffee, then observed idly, "It's shaping up to be a nice day."

"Yep," Joe replied. "A good day for trout fishing."

"So it is. So it is."

They turned toward each other spontaneously. "It's been a long, long time since we went fishing together," Robert said, sounding wistful.

Joe nodded. "Too long," he answered.

"You up to it?" Robert asked, indicating Joe's cane, which was propped against the wall near the swing. "You up to walking down to our favorite spot?"

Joe grinned. "I'm not only up to it, you're going to have to work hard to keep up with me." He reached for his cane. "Time's wasting. Let's get going."

"I'll have to see if Simon has some gear I can borrow. I wasn't planning on going fishing today and I didn't bring any of mine from home."

"Don't worry, Bucky. I've got enough fishing gear at the house for both of us. Had Mrs. Potter make up a room for you, too, just in case you want to stay overnight at my place."

"I'll take you up on the offer," Robert said. "I know Anne and Simon won't mind if I spend the night here with them, but I've got a sneaking suspicion they'd just as soon be left alone together for the time being. They need time to get used to being a real family now."

Joe stood up, leaning heavily on his cane. "Let's go inside and tell the kids where we're going."

Robert got up, too, and he laughed as they headed for the door. "Just think, Joe...one of these days, we'll be able to take our grandchildren to our fishing spot."

Joe grinned. "Now that's a pleasant contemplation, if I ever heard one."

Robert opened the door and they went inside. The two old friends would pay one last visit to their newborn grandchildren before going off to spend the remainder of a perfect fishing day together.

* * * * *

presents

SONNY'S GIRLS

by Emilie Richards, Celeste Hamilton and Erica Spindler

They had been Sonny's girls, irresistibly drawn to the charismatic high school football hero. Ten years later, none could forget the night that changed their lives forever.

In July—
ALL THOSE YEARS AGO by Emilie Richards (SSE #684)
Meredith Robbins had left town in shame. Could she ever banish the past and reach for love again?

In August—
DON'T LOOK BACK by Celeste Hamilton (SSE #690)
Cyndi Saint was Sonny's steady. Ten years later, she remembered only his hurtful parting words....

In September—
LONGER THAN... by Erica Spindler (SSE #696)
Bubbly Jennifer Joyce was everybody's friend. But nobody knew the secret longings she felt for bad boy Ryder Hayes....

SILHOUETTE·INTIMATE·MOMENTS®

IT'S TIME TO MEET
THE MARSHALLS!

In 1986, bestselling author Kristin James wrote A VERY SPECIAL FAVOR for the Silhouette Intimate Moments line. Hero Adam Marshall quickly became a reader favorite, and ever since then, readers have been asking for the stories of his two brothers, Tag and James. At last your prayers have been answered!

In August, look for THE LETTER OF THE LAW (IM #393), James Marshall's story. If you missed youngest brother Tag's story, SALT OF THE EARTH (IM #385), you can order it by following the directions below. And, as our very special favor to you, we'll be reprinting A VERY SPECIAL FAVOR this September. Look for it in special displays wherever you buy books.

Silhouette Books ®

Take 4 bestselling love stories FREE

Plus get a FREE surprise gift!

Special Limited-time Offer

Mail to
Silhouette Reader Service™
3010 Walden Avenue
P.O. Box 1867
Buffalo, N.Y. 14269-1867

YES! Please send me 4 free Silhouette Special Edition™ novels and my free surprise gift. Then send me 6 brand-new novels every month, which I will receive months before they appear in bookstores. Bill me at the low price of $2.92 each—a savings of 33¢ apiece off cover prices. There are no shipping, handling or other hidden costs. I understand that accepting the books and gift places me under no obligation ever to buy any books. I can always return a shipment and cancel at any time. Even if I never buy another book from Silhouette, the 4 free books and the surprise gift are mine to keep forever.

235 BPA AC7Q

Name	(PLEASE PRINT)	
Address		Apt. No.
City	State	Zip

This offer is limited to one order per household and not valid to present Silhouette Special Edition® subscribers. Terms and prices are subject to change. Sales tax applicable in N.Y.

SPED-BPA2DR

© 1990 Harlequin Enterprises Limited

Coming Soon

Fashion A Whole New You.
Win a sensual adventurous
trip for two to Hawaii via
American Airlines®, a
brand-new Ford Explorer
4 × 4 and a $2,000
Fashion Allowance.

Plus, special free gifts* are yours to
Fashion A Whole New You.

From September through November, you can take part in
this exciting opportunity from Silhouette.

Watch for details in September.

* with proofs-of-purchase, plus postage and handling

Silhouette Books™

SLFW-TS